IN a strongly barred enclosure a gorilla was standing erect. Its powerful long arms dangled to its knees, and the swelling muscular black torso looked about to burst through its skin. The gorilla's head turned to look at her. The skull revealed familiar heavy frontal brows and small black, staring eyes. But the thickened blue-black lips had an oddly human contour, and the facial skin seemed different in texture and color from an anthropoid ape. The forehead was smooth, and in the cheeks she saw lines that might have appeared in a human face.

The beast bellowed while its eyes glared at Mary with a wild, murderous rage. And then she had an auditory hallucination. For the thundering roar took on a kind of meaning.

"KONRA-A-ADDDD!"

The Sendai

A NOVEL BY

William Woolfolk

FAWCETT POPULAR LIBRARY • NEW YORK

THE SENDAI

Published by Fawcett Popular Library, a unit of CBS Publications, the Consumer Publishing Division of CBS Inc.

ISBN: 0-445-04628-7

Printed in the United States of America

First Fawcett Popular Library printing: January 1981

10 9 8 7 6 5 4 3 2 1

For Reginald Rose
fine writer, unerring critic, steadfast friend.

My grateful thanks go to the following, who did not allow me to take liberties with the scientific and medical data on which this fictional narrative is based.

James K. Reynhout, Ph.D., Assistant Professor,
    Department of Biological Sciences
    Oakland University, Rochester, Michigan.

Richard L. Cross, Ph.D., Associate Professor,
    Department of Biochemistry
    Upstate Medical Center, Syracuse, New York.

John T. Galdamez, M.D., Lieutenant Commander,
    United States Public Health Service

And, of course, to my wife and collaborator, Joanna Woolfolk, whose contribution to my work, as to my life, is beyond measure.

Chapter

1

On the drive home, Tom Pollard tried not to look at Jane or at the baby wrapped in a blanket on her lap. She cooed to the baby as she fed him from a bottle. Tom was grateful she had decided on bottle feeding. The thought of that small brutish face pressed against his wife's breast was repellent.

The spring foliage was particularly beautiful on this May morning. As the Chrysler New Yorker glided through the sun-and-leaf-dappled streets of Portchester, Tom concentrated on not listening to his infant son smacking and sucking greedily on the bottle.

He was remembering a spring day one year ago.

"That way of having a baby doesn't seem natural to me," he had told their doctor.

The doctor replied, "We have always manipulated nature, you know. You do that even when you plant a garden. I don't think there is anything completely natural once human beings get involved."

Tom said, "It's almost as though she'd be having a baby by another man."

"It's not an unproven technique," the doctor said. "Approximately two hundred children are around today who owe their existence to in vitro fertilization."

"I realize that. It's just . . ." Tom glanced helplessly at Jane seated beside him in the doctor's private office. She did not return his glance. She stared straight ahead, her hands tightly clasped in her lap. "Babies made in a test tube," Tom said. "You don't call that unnatural?"

Jane said, "No one has to know how the birth took place, do they, Doctor?"

"No. And the child will be yours—both of you will be its parents."

"Is it safe?" Tom asked.

"As safe as regular childbirth. The Karyll Clinic, here in Westchester, has an ongoing program."

A week later they applied to the Karyll Clinic and were told they would have to undergo tests before being accepted for the "treatment." Genetic disorders such as Tay-Sachs disease, diabetes and congenital heart problems had to be ruled out. After their physical examinations, they were screened by a psychoanalyst, who probed their feelings: Do you become angry at relatives and friends who keep asking when you are going to have a baby? The analyst was very interested in the fact that they had adopted a Vietnamese orphan who had needed facial and bone surgery as the result of injuries suffered during a bombing in her village.

"Do you consider Lee Thi a real member of your family?"

"Of course," Tom said.

"We love her very much," Jane added.

Lee Thi was thirteen, and they had adopted her when she was seven.

"Is she well adjusted?" the analyst asked.

Jane laughed. "Typically American. All she does is watch television."

"Will she accept another baby in your home?"

"We've prepared her for that," Tom said. "She knows we've always wanted a big family. We've told her we'll love her just as much."

The analyst jotted down a note: *High level of nurture capacity*.

Their next interview was with Dr. Peter Bradford, Chief of the Department of Neonatology and the world-renowned doctor who ran the Karyll Clinic. He was a large-bodied, fifty-year-old man, with a triangular white face and large liquid gray eyes.

"Are you worried about the in vitro method of conception?" he asked.

"My husband is more than I am," Jane said. "I'm more worried about the possibility of failure, because I want a baby so much."

Dr. Bradford said with sympathy, "I realize that this is not your first choice as to how to have a baby. But you are choosing it together. What we are all trying to do is help nature."

Jane said, "We understand that, Doctor. And we're both very eager to go ahead with it."

Their application was approved, and the next week Jane began the "treatment." She was given hormones to stimulate the maturation of eggs in her ovary. Dr. Gaby Latolier, in charge of her case, was Chief of the Ob-Gyn Department at the Karyll Clinic. Dr. Latolier explained in advance exactly what she was going to do. She told Jane that a tiny incision would be made on the rim of her navel, which would leave no visible scar. Then her abdomen would be inflated with carbon dioxide gas to provide an unobstructed view and reduce the chance of injury to any body organ. Through the incision Dr. Latolier would insert a laparascope, an optical system that would give her a direct view of the ovary. A needle would then be inserted into the ovary to draw out the eggs. The entire operation would take less than twenty minutes.

Then, using Tom's sperm, which he would provide by masturbation, the fertilization would be accomplished. After they had a fertilized egg, it would be transferred to a dish of blood serum and sustaining nutrients and allowed to incubate there until it began to divide. In about four days the fertilized egg would divide into a cluster of cells.

"We call this a blastocyst," Dr. Latolier told Jane. "It's the nucleus of the embryo. You'll be given further hormone treatment to prepare your uterine lining. Then I'll perform another minor operation, much like the first one, to place the blastocyst in your uterus. It will attach itself to the wall, and normal embryo development will begin. In nine months, if all goes as we expect, you will have a perfectly normal healthy baby."

In nine months they had a little monster with coarse brown hair that covered its entire body and a small hump between its shoulder blades. The forehead was steeply slanting, and the jaw protruded. Long, hairy fingers had very pronounced knuckles.

Gaby Latolier was distressed. "There was no indication of abnormality in the six-day test after the fertilized egg was implanted in your uterus," she told the Pollards. "The pregnancy seemed to be developing in a completely normal way. We simply don't know where it went wrong. It might be some unknown mutagen."

"Mutagen?" Tom asked numbly.

"A chemical or physical agent capable of penetrating cells and damaging DNA molecules. There are more than two thousand such mutagens in the environment today capable of causing birth defects."

"I blame myself for causing this baby to be born," Tom said.

Jane said, "That's not fair," and caught herself upon the verge of tears.

Dr. Latolier said, "All I can tell you is that what happened has nothing to do with the way in which the baby was conceived."

Tom's guilt was too personal and deep to be reached by such arguments. "What are we to do? We can't look after a baby like this." He was unnerved whenever he looked at his son's hairy little body, its sloping forehead and prognathous jaw.

"I can," Jane said.

Dr. Latolier said, "We can't allow you to take the baby home. It belongs here in the hospital where we can look after it properly."

"I'm the mother. I know how to look after my own baby."

"I don't think you appreciate all the risks and problems," Dr. Latolier insisted. "You must leave the baby with us for further observation. We will give it the best possible care. There will be no charge for hospitalization or treatment."

"I'm sorry. I can't do that."

"You can visit him whenever you wish. Perhaps eventually you can take him home, but at this stage it would be irresponsible. You can't look after him properly."

"You and your science have done everything you can," Jane replied, her mouth set in a thin line of determination. "I'll take charge of my son from now on."

All she would promise was to bring the infant back to the hospital once a week so the doctors could check on his condition.

The first night, Jane put the baby to bed in the nursery room. Tom's anxieties kept him from going in. He wanted to, but could not. The range of normality was very wide, but this strange mutant-child was beyond the bearable limit.

He was a large infant, always ravenously hungry. Every two hours the baby needed another feeding. His tongue was a square thickness that was always panting for food, like a starving animal. Despite his size and appetite, however, the infant appeared docile. He lay quietly in the crib, staring with almost blank eyes.

Every weekday morning, Tom left for work without a glance into the nursery. The baby was Jane's responsibility. She kept him home all day. When he was three weeks old she dressed him in denim overalls and a long-sleeved T-shirt—sized for a six-month-old infant—and took him out in a carriage, defying the pitying looks of neighbors. One mother, who herself had a mongoloid child in an institution, took one look at him in the carriage and burst into tears and ran away. After that, Jane did not take him out again.

At the bank, Tom discouraged inquiries by letting it be known that the baby was retarded. The pity of his coworkers was expressed in silence. Friends, too, were never asked to see the infant. Relatives were a different problem. Jane's father gave the coldest appraisal: "You can't try to care for a baby like that. He belongs somewhere where they have people trained for that sort of thing." Jane's mother agreed, and that began a long quarrel.

One weekend, Tom's brother and wife drove down to see the baby. They intended to stay the weekend in Portchester but left the next morning. Only Robert, Jane's older brother, showed up at Christmas with presents for both Lee Thi and the baby. Robert was a lawyer. He advised them to sue the Karyll Clinic, despite the fact that they had signed a waiver.

"It wasn't informed consent. If enough malpractice suits are filed, maybe these damn doctors will stop their crazy experiments."

"I don't believe it's the doctors' fault," Jane told him.

"Well, it's *somebody's*. If you don't sue, maybe your son will at some future time. For wrongful life."

The next day Robert left, with some lame excuse about having to get home because his wife had the flu.

When Jane brought the baby in for his regular weekly examinations at the Karyll Clinic, she rarely reported to Tom on the result. And she never asked him for help. Lee Thi helped her with the baby.

One evening, when the baby (Tom never thought of him as having a name) was eleven months old, Tom accepted an invitation from their neighbors George and Grace Leary. He and Jane used to play bridge there almost every week, but that had changed along with everything else in their lives. George Leary called because another couple had canceled.

"We can't go," Jane said. "We can't leave Lee Thi alone with the baby. She's forgetful. She'll promise to do something and then she won't. You know how she is."

"She's fourteen, and as capable of looking after him as you are. He's not exactly a newborn infant. Good God, he weighs nearly fifty pounds."

"If there's a problem . . ."

"All she has to do is call us."

Jane left specific instructions for Lee Thi. She gave the baby a bottle and told her when to feed him again. But at the Learys' home that evening she was nervous and preoccupied and played bridge badly, and she did not join in the general conversation.

At a few minutes before eleven o'clock, the telephone rang.

The call was from Lee Thi.

Jane went to the telephone and spoke in a guarded whisper. Then she went directly to the closet for her coat.

"She wants us to come right away. Something's wrong."

She put her coat on and went out the door, leaving Tom to mumble an apology and hurry after.

The drive was only half a mile, but Jane sat forward in her seat, staring through the windshield, urging the car on. When Tom stopped the car in their driveway she jumped out and ran to the front door.

Lee Thi opened the door. "He's gone!"

"What?"

The door to the nursery was partly open. In the light that shone from the hallway, blue elephants, monkeys and giraffes gamboled playfully on the wallpaper. The dim nightlight revealed the crib.

"Look!" Jane said.

Several bars of the crib were broken, making a passage large enough to crawl through. The wooden edges were jagged, splintered white against the dark, smooth unbroken portion.

Jane said, "I told you Lee Thi couldn't handle him alone." She stated the fact calmly, without accusation. It was as if she were correcting a student who had given the wrong answer in a classroom.

Tom examined the jagged edges. "No eleven-month-old infant could have done this." He asked Lee Thi, "Who else has been here?"

"N-no one."

"You didn't hear anything?"

"I swear!"

Jane's palm cut across Lee Thi's face with a sharp splatting sound.

Tom was shocked. He had never seen her strike Lee Thi before.

"He was hungry because he missed his ten o'clock feeding," Jane said. "So he began shaking the bars and broke them. She was watching television and didn't hear him."

Lee Thi began to weep.

Tom said, "It couldn't happen that way. No baby that age could break out of a crib."

"Let's search the house," Jane said. "He's probably hiding somewhere."

When they returned to the living room, having searched the house, Jane called the police. In a chair near the corner, red-eyed, Lee Thi snuffled.

Jane hung up on her call to the police and began to call their neighbors, making an admirable effort not to sound alarmed. "This is Jane Pollard. Oh, yes, I'm fine.

I'm sorry to call at this hour, but you haven't seen our baby, have you? He doesn't seem to be in his room. We thought he might have gotten outside somehow . . . I know that sounds unlikely. I'll explain later." She was making her fourth call when the police arrived: two policemen, both young, one short and stocky, the other tall and slender.

"Let's have another look around the house," the short policeman said. "Kidnappers usually leave a note."

A window was half open. The tall, slender policeman lifted the window further and put his head out. "Look, there's something. On the ground near the drainpipe. Looks like a piece of paper."

They ran outside. What appeared to be a piece of paper was a tiny bit of cloth. The short policeman picked it up, fingering it.

"Cotton." He looked apologetically at Tom and Jane. "Might have been from a baby's diaper."

They searched the backyard in earnest, flashlights probing the dark. They found a questionable trail in the grass leading to the fence. The neighboring house was dark.

"I tried phoning them," Jane said. "They aren't home."

They climbed over the fence.

"They have a dog," Tom said. "Be careful." He was surprised that the fierce little terrier did not bark.

Then he heard a muffled exclamation.

"What is it?" he called.

The short policeman held his flashlight steady, and his tall partner mingled his beam with it. They all saw what was in the backyard, just a few feet from the fence.

The baby was holding the terrier in a crook of his elbow. The terrier's head was twisted to one side by a grip that had broken its neck. In death, the terrier had not loosened its own hold. Its sharp teeth were fastened on the baby's throat.

Jane's shoulders were shaking, then a moaning sound came from her. She did not open her lips, but the moaning kept increasing, becoming shriller. Tom put his arm around her. She kept looking at the dead bodies on the ground, and finally she began to scream.

Chapter

2

On a cold afternoon in December, Delaney and a plump redheaded woman drove in a rented Ford Fairmont through the Ozark mountains in northwestern Arkansas. There was little traffic. The desolate highway connected a town of almost no importance with a town of lesser rank. Along both sides of the highway, the bordering line of bare, gaunt trees occasionally opened into a small clearing in which there was a general store with a gas pump in front. The stores were closed, windows boarded over; the gas pumps were dry.

Delaney was a big man, with a solidly boned face, powerful long arms and sloping shoulders. He was forty years old. The only sign of his advancing age was a slight paunch.

Estelle, the plump redheaded woman with him, was thirty-two, reasonably attractive, with a freckled round face. Her skirt did not quite cover fleshy knees.

They had not spoken for the past seventy miles. After a few futile attempts at conversation, Estelle gave up and turned on the radio. Now she was listening to country western music.

"How are we going to find 'em when we get to this godforsaken place?" she asked suddenly.

"I'll take care of that."

She lapsed back into her country western music. The radio was a lot better company than Delaney.

Delaney checked the odometer. He was a dozen miles from his destination, and knew there should be a turnoff a few miles ahead. This was moonshiner country, populated by sparse settlements of a hard-grained, solitary and unconfiding people. With the decline of moonshining they had gone back to farming mostly, scrabbling a living out of these grudging hills.

He found the turnoff, then drove seven miles farther to a United States post office substation at Ozark Junction Crossing. The town consisted of a few dozen small frame houses, a general store and gas station, and a diner. He parked the Ford Fairmont alongside the post office building, on the side that had only one high window.

"Be right back," he told Estelle. He removed a triangular green package from the trunk of the car and brought it into the post office.

"Parcel post?" the clerk asked, weighing it.

"First class. It has to be delivered tomorrow morning."

He drove out of Ozark Junction Crossing along the route that led to Missoula, a town that most maps had forgotten. He found the spot he wanted, a towpath along a canal that passed under a small wooden bridge. He drove down almost to the brink of the canal. The Fairmont was out of sight of the road, but to make sure Delaney picked up loose twigs, stripped some branches and piled both onto the car roof until the camouflage passed inspection.

"Would you mind telling me what's going on?" Estelle was standing beside the car, watching.

"We're spending the night here. I've got blankets, and a hamper of food and drink in the trunk. Make yourself at home."

"You sure know how to take a girl on a date." Her glance was appraising.

"This is business," Delaney said.

She slept curled up on the back seat under a blanket. Delaney was awake with the first light of dawn. He stretched, yawned, got out of the car and peed into the canal. The morning was fresh and cool, not as cold as during the night. Estelle's complaints about the cold had become so bitter he had turned on the car engine in order to use the car's heater. He was sure she would not have objected if he chose another method to keep her warm. But Delaney never mixed pleasure with business.

Half an hour later the first car sped by, going at least seventy-five miles an hour. He opened the food hamper and took out fresh oranges and peeled them with a knife. Another car raced by at high speed. Delaney shook Estelle's shoulder. She stirred restlessly. A few minutes later he heard the approach of another car engine. He handed her a peeled orange and put a finger to his lips. Then he took up a watching position in the shelter of the bridge. A mail truck rumbled past at a sedate thirty miles an hour.

Delaney returned to the car and brushed off the leaves and twigs from the roof. As soon as Estelle got in the car he started the engine and drove back onto the highway. He drove at forty miles an hour until he glimpsed the mail truck up ahead, then slowed to keep the truck at a distance. Each time the mail truck stopped Delaney waited.

An hour later, after several stops along the highway, he passed a sign beside the road: *Missoula, Founded 1760, Population 764*. The mail truck left the paved highway and traveled dusty, bumpy roads. Delaney followed at a distance; he did not want his car to be visible in the mail truck's rearview mirror.

Finally the mail truck stopped at a farmhouse, with a barn, and a black Ford of ancient vintage parked in front. The postman carried a triangular-shaped green package to the front door of the house, where he delivered it to what appeared to be an older woman. By then, Delaney had turned the Fairmont around and was heading rapidly in the other direction. He left Estelle in the car safely out of sight in a belt of woodland a quarter-mile away. He went back to the farmhouse on foot.

There were scattered clouds in the sky, and a shrunken sun stared wanly. Delaney settled down behind a small hummock of yellow withered grass frosted with last night's cold. Through binoculars he studied the farmhouse. The ramshackle frame building had no telephone line, no utilities, no TV antenna. A small outhouse in back. A large shed. A much larger barn, faded to a dingy, pale, flaking orange color. The front yard was grassless dirt, over which a few disconsolate hens wandered about in search of provender. A not-quite-perpendicular brick chimney poured forth brown-dark smoke.

Beyond the farmhouse was open land, now lightly sprinkled with snow.

During the next two hours a lean man in overalls left by the back door to visit the outhouse. Then, in order, Delaney saw a young woman in her teens with brown hair and a softly round figure, a straw-haired slightly older young woman, a young boy of about fourteen with uncombed hair wearing overalls.

A few minutes before noon a troop emerged from the front door: the older man, the brown-haired younger woman, the teen-aged boy, followed by a spotted, tongue-hanging dog of motley parentage. All climbed into the vintage black Ford. Heaving and wheezing, the car got underway.

As soon as the Ford jounced out of sight on the road, Delaney sprinted rapidly to where Estelle was waiting in the Fairmont.

She looked at him bitterly. "What the hell have you been doing?"

"Scouting." Delaney got in. The engine was slow responding because she had run down the battery a little listening to the radio. He pulled out of the woodsy hideaway and drove to the farmhouse. He parked fifty feet down the road.

"I'll handle whoever's inside," he told Estelle. "You get the kid."

They walked toward the farmhouse. Estelle followed him to the front door. He tried the door. It was unlocked.

As he stepped in he heard someone stumble toward him from another room.

A slightly querulous "Who is it?" in an old woman's voice.

"Census taker," Delaney answered. He motioned to Estelle to go ahead.

A moment later a thin, angular old woman appeared. She wore a nondescript shapeless dress of a faded design. When she saw Delaney she paused, one hand partly in front of her, as if it were an antenna searching out his exact location. Her eyesight must be very poor, Delaney thought. All to the good.

"What'd you say?" she asked.

"I'm a census taker," Delaney repeated. He was not sure the old woman had seen Estelle. By now Estelle was in the narrow hallway. She was going to search the back rooms.

"If you're tryin' to sell somethin', we don't need any."

The old woman had a faint moustache, and her eyes were wide and glazed. Her skin was wrinkled heavily on her face and neck. Her gnarled veined feet were bare in sandals.

"I'm not a salesman," Delaney said politely. "I'm with the federal government. The census." He removed his wallet and opened it to show the photograph on his driver's license. "My identification."

She peered at it for a moment, looked up at him with a quizzical expression. "You kin talk to my niece Debbie."

"I need to know how many people live here," Delaney said. "It's just routine."

"I'm not good at answerin' questions," she said, adding, "I'm sixty-one."

She looked twenty years older.

"I'll start with you," Delaney said genially. He took a notebook and a ballpoint pen from his coat pocket. "You just told me your age. Now I need your full name and . . ."

"Who is it, Hennie?" a voice called from upstairs.

"A man from the guvment."

Estelle was coming back down the hallway, carrying the baby wrapped in a blanket. Delaney indicated with a quick nod that she should go out the back door.

But the straw-haired young woman appeared suddenly in the hallway. She was barefoot, wearing only a light cottony shift and nothing underneath. Her hair was damp.

Her glance went to Estelle holding the blanket.

"What the *hail* you doin' with my kid?" Her tone was shrill. "Hennie, these ain't guvment people!"

She flung herself at Estelle, flailing, screaming at the top of her lungs. Delaney reached her in one long stride. She whirled at him, trying to scratch and claw. Delaney took her head between both hands and pressed. Her eyes darted wildly. He shifted his hold so the palm of his right hand was below the angle of her jaw. His hands made a powerful twisting motion. There was a sharp crack as her neck broke. She went down so quickly she might have been pushed down.

Delaney said to Estelle, "Take the baby to the car."

She hurried out.

From the back door to the house, Delaney paused to look thoughtfully after the old woman now running across the frost-stubbled open field, holding up her skirt. She was surprisingly agile for her age. She ran blindly, without any purpose except escape. He could easily catch up with her and kill her too. But if he let her go, she could not give anyone a clear description of him. Any description she gave would be more likely to confuse. If she repeated the story about a census taker for the federal government, that might confuse people more.

Let her go.

He got into the car beside Estelle. She was holding the baby and humming to it. A corner of the blanket was turned up, so he could not see the baby's face. He was not curious about it. His job had been to get the baby and bring it back, and that was what he would do. *No unnecessary force* was the only other instruction. In his mind he had not disobeyed. The young woman had fought like a wildcat. If he had merely knocked her unconscious, she would have recovered to give too good a description. No sense taking chances. Kidnapping was a capital crime.

Ordinarily, Delaney would have preferred to work alone. But he was told Estelle was needed to look after the baby. This was a very important infant. Why the infant son of a dirt poor farmer in Missoula was so important was none of his business, and he was not curious about that either.

They drove two miles without exchanging a word, and the baby in the blanket did not utter a single cry. Estelle began to rock the baby a little, crooning. She had turned back the corner of the blanket, and he saw a small, hairy face with blank, solemn eyes.

"He's a good baby," Estelle said. "Ugly as sin, but he's got a real sweet disposition."

Chapter

3

As the train entered a cavern below Pennsylvania Station, Mary Oliver glanced out the window. The interior of the train was reflected in the window, and the tweedy young man across the way was looking at her again. For the past hour, since the train left Philadelphia, she had been aware of him. It was rather sweet, really. That was one way of identifying a nice man: He did not know how to start a conversation with a strange young woman. And she was not in a mood to encourage him. Not now.

Mary was twenty-five years old, very pretty, stylishly dressed. She had short light-brown hair, dark-brown eyes and a clear skin with a healthy color. She gave the appearance of being alert, intelligent and self-reliant—and the appearance was not deceiving. Her employer at the Chilwind Air Conditioning Company, where she was employed as a structural engineer, would have been glad to endorse that assessment. However, at the moment she felt drab, colorless, not at all bright and totally incapable of knowing what was good for her.

The train stopped. As Mary stood up to get her suitcase from the overhead rack, the young man appeared beside her. He pulled her bag down in a single motion.

She gave him a brief, nonencouraging smile. "Thank you."

"I noticed you put it there when you came in."

She maintained the smile at its forty-watt level, picked up her suitcase and left the car. The young man was trying to get his own blue totebag down from the rack.

Before she reached the ramp leading upward from the train level, he appeared abreast of her, the blue totebag in his left hand.

"Can I help you with that?" he asked, indicating her suitcase.

She quickened her step. "Someone is meeting me." She waved to Harry Conklin standing at the bottom of the ramp. Harry waved back. The young man muttered an embarrassed apology and moved away. Paths cross only when they are destined to cross.

Harry Conklin took her suitcase and gave her a peck on the cheek, a brother-in-law's salutation. He was a tall, soft-faced man in his late thirties.

"How's Emily?" she asked.

"Oh, she's fine!"

Instant upbeat response. The instinct of the born salesman. They climbed the ramp to the main level of the station with its long row of lighted ticket-seller booths and up and down escalators.

"My car is parked a few blocks from here. Shall I get a taxi?"

"I like to walk."

They rode up the escalator and passed by a line of impatient people waiting for taxis.

"How is Emily?" Mary asked again. Often she could get a straight answer from Harry on a second try.

"A little nervous. You know how it is. At her age. Her first."

Emily was thirty-five, ten years older than Mary. Their parents had spaced the children exactly five years apart. Emily was born near the end of World War II, a few months before the final victory over Japan. Lorraine, the next oldest, arrived during the war in Korea. Mary was the first to arrive in peacetime. Adele, the youngest came along on the very day John F. Kennedy was elected President.

"What does the doctor say?"

"Better let Emily tell you about that."

Dinner with the Conklins was quiet past the point of dullness. Sensitive, shy, withdrawn, Emily sat like a female Buddha contemplating her swollen navel. In her eighth month of pregnancy, she had put on little weight except in her belly, which had grown to an enormous sphere.

After dinner, Harry announced that he had to see a prospect about a life insurance policy. He left at eight o'clock.

"Harry has to be away so much at night," Emily said sadly. "That's why I need someone to be with me. I'm afraid if anything happened while he was away . . ." Her voice trailed off.

"Nothing's wrong, is there?"

Vertical lines in Emily's cheeks deepened. "I didn't get pregnant the regular way."

"What do you mean?"

"The only way I can have a baby is like that woman in England."

"A test tube baby?"

"Dr. Gerson, my obstetrician, said there wasn't anything he could do to correct my problem. He recommended that I go to the Karyll Clinic. Harry didn't like the idea at first. But I wouldn't feel like a whole woman if I couldn't give him a child."

Mary winced inwardly. Her sister's life was guided by her treasured clichés.

"A lot of women seem to feel that way," she answered gently.

"Anyway, it's one reason I'm nervous. And I'm so grateful to you for coming to stay with me until the baby comes."

"You couldn't have picked a better time to invite me."

"Why?"

The warning twinge of pain was like coming back from the dentist and feeling the novocaine start to wear off.

"It has to do with a man I've been seeing."

"Do you like him?"

"Yes."

"Are you going to marry him?"

"Not necessarily. That's a big decision. And we still have some problems to work out."

"You can't afford to make a mistake. After all, marriage is for life."

Mary wondered if Emily had ever read the statistics on divorce, or whether she simply chose not to believe them.

On her twenty-fourth birthday Sam had given her

twenty-four long-stemmed red roses, taken her to an extravagant dinner and asked her to move to Washington, D.C. with him. She had said no because he was so confident that she would say yes. He hadn't seemed at all concerned that the move would mean starting all over again in her career.

Emily said, "Whatever you do, don't let him talk you into doing anything wrong. A man doesn't respect you afterward. My Harry was very happy that I was a virgin on our wedding night."

Emily's opinions had been formed in an earlier era, and Mary had little hope of reconciling their viewpoints. There were many topics they would have to avoid during their time together, waiting for Emily's baby to be born.

"How about playing Scrabble?" she asked. "That will pass the time until Harry gets home."

At ten o'clock they watched a local television news program. The one-year-old infant of a woman in Portchester had been killed by a neighbor's watchdog. That upset Emily, who asked Mary to turn off the television set. Her fingers tapped the chair arms. Her eyes wandered restlessly. She appeared to be having an anxiety attack. Mary sat in a chair near her and talked about anything she could think of. Emily was only half listening.

Suddenly Emily's arms tightened on the arms of the chair. "It's started."

"Try to be calm. Relax."

"It started during the news. I wasn't sure then. *Oh!*" Her face wrenched. "Now I'm sure."

"I'll call the doctor," Mary said.

There was a delay before the operator at the Karyll

Clinic finally put her through to the Department of Obstetrics and Gynecology. Mary asked for Dr. Latolier.

"Doctor Latolier speaking." The woman's voice had a faint trace of a French accent.

"I'm calling about my sister Emily Conklin. She started labor pains thirty minutes ago."

"Hold on." After a moment Dr. Latolier came back on the phone. "I'm sending an ambulance from a location near you. Try to keep her comfortable until the ambulance gets there."

"Yes, I will. Thank you, Doctor."

Mary helped Emily to the sofa, where she lay down. Mary put a pillow beneath her head.

"I'll be all right, won't I?" Emily asked faintly.

"There's nothing to be afraid of."

"God will punish me for what I'm doing. He won't let me have this baby."

"Shhh," Mary said. "Don't talk nonsense."

When the downstairs bell rang Mary answered it. A minute later she heard a knock on the door, and two white-coated men came in. They put a stretcher down beside the sofa where Emily lay, looking oddly small and thin except for her stomach bulking hugely. They helped her from the sofa to the stretcher.

"Can I go with her?" Mary asked.

"Sorry, miss. Can't take anybody but the patient. She'll be all right."

Mary accompanied her downstairs to the waiting ambulance. From the ambulance, Emily stretched out hands to her imploringly. "Don't leave me. *Please!*"

"I have to wait," Mary told her. Then, an inspiration: "I'll bring Harry soon."

The ambulance drove off, and Mary returned to the empty apartment. She lit a cigarette and settled down to wait for Harry.

At five o'clock in the morning the maternity ward at the Karyll Clinic was quiet. Breakfast and the first rounds of the morning were hours away. A porter pushed a floor polisher almost noiselessly along the hallway. He moved his polishing machine aside to make way for a hospital cot being wheeled quickly by a nurse. On the cot a young pretty woman was covered to the shoulders by a white sheet. Her belly was like a great pumpkin beneath the sheet.

Mary was in the waiting room, smoking a cigarette. An old movie starring George Sanders was playing on a nearby television set. The volume was turned very low. No one else was in the room. Melodrama continued on the small screen while a real life drama was taking place not many feet away. She lit another cigarette, her hand trembling. When Harry returned she put the cigarette out in an ashtray.

Harry gave her a quick meaningless mouth twitch that passed for a smile.

Mary asked, "How much longer do they think it will take?"

Harry sat in a chair beside the small plastic bench on which Mary was seated. "No one seems to know. They just keep telling me to be patient."

"How is she?"

"Having a hard time. She just lies there moaning. There's a big rubber strap holding a microphone on her stomach, and it's connected to a machine next to her.

The machine is drawing a picture of each contraction. I could see the lines on the graph."

"Can't the doctor give her some help?"

"Dr. Latolier says we have to expect a harder time because it's a first pregnancy and there's a complication. The baby will come out feet first and face up. She says that's a bad position." There were tears in his eyes. "I told the doctor, if there's any choice during the delivery, Emily comes first. We both want this baby very much, but ... well, if it comes to that, she's the one I want them to save."

"That isn't going to happen," Mary said. She reminded herself that the Karyll Clinic had the most modern facilities in the world, that medicine had learned many new ways of dealing with emergencies, that there were antibiotics against infection, blood transfusions against hemorrhage, new ways to control toxemia. Her cigarette burned down almost to her fingertips, and she quickly ground out the stub in the ashtray, vaguely aware that sparks burned her skin.

She got up and stared out the window of the waiting room. In the park below the air was not saturated with the smell of automobile exhausts, no buses whined and roared, no black bulging garbage bags lined the curbs. Squirrels scampered and birds flitted among the trees and sunlight sparkled on a pond. In this quiet, peaceful world it was inconceivable that anything bad would happen to her sister.

The door opened behind her and a plump redheaded nurse entered. Harry clearly expected the worst. But the nurse only brought a permission form for a Caesarean, which she asked Harry to sign.

"Is that what it's going to be—a Caesarean?" he asked while he signed.

"It may have to be. The baby's head is bigger than your wife's pelvic outlet. There isn't much dilation yet."

Harry handed her the form. "Remember, if there's any choice, I want you to save my wife."

"Your wife is in no danger," the nurse assured him briskly.

Dr. Roy Harrison, the anesthesiologist, stood ready beside his machines and cylinders. He was part of Dr. Latolier's "team," as was Estelle, the plump redheaded scrub nurse, and Janet, the pretty dark-haired circulating nurse. Gaby Latolier knew she could depend on each of them; they had been carefully chosen and instructed in their duties. There was no necessity to discuss any part of the procedure. Dr. Harrison would use caudal anesthesia to at least the tenth thoracic segment in order to allow for an ample abdominal wound and a uterine incision without pain to the patient. In the final crucial minutes before the baby was delivered, a few whiffs of nitrous oxide would put the patient completely under.

"I didn't know it was such a hard thing to have a baby," Emily murmured. Her voice was thick because the atropine made her tongue sticky. She was already partly detached from her surroundings, floating in space.

The delivery table was lit from above by two large movable lights. Estelle painted Emily's stomach with Betadine, and draped it with a plastic sterile skin barrier that adhered to the abdomen where the incision would be made. Layers of cloth were laid over this until only the area where the incision was to be made was visible. Dr. Harrison gave a final check to Emily's blood pressure.

Gaby Latolier took the scalpel and made the first cut, a horizontal line across the lower abdomen. The flesh wall was thinner in the lower region and not so interlaced with large blood-filled sinuses. Very carefully she traced the line over in the same channel and tied off blood vessels. With her gloved finger she separated flesh from muscle, while Estelle sponged the blood that oozed from the incision. The soiled sponge was discarded into a towel resting on a kick-bucket.

Dr. Latolier drew the abdominal incision apart by retractors until a portion of the uterus was exposed. She grasped the loose peritoneum with dissecting forceps, choosing a point below its firm attachment to the anterior wall of the uterus. Then she separated the peritoneum and upper posterior surface of the bladder from the uterine wall. This formed a short upper flap terminating where the peritoneum was firmly attached to the uterine body, and a longer lower flap consisting of the vesical peritoneum and the posterior surface of the bladder. As the bladder flap was separated from the uterus, she deflected it downward and made a neat incision in the wall of the uterus. Membranes ruptured. Amniotic fluid splashed out and was suctioned away.

Estelle kept wiping away blood and handing Dr. Latolier instruments as needed from the surgical cart. Dr. Harrison's eyes were fixed on Emily's face, studying every line and movement, his hand hovering near the gauges. Janet, the floating nurse, removed used sponges in a towel from the kick-bucket, and recovered the bucket with a fresh towel.

Part of the fetus's face now appeared within the cavity. At this point, Dr. Harrison gave Emily enough nitrous oxide to put her under completely. He nodded to Dr. Latolier, who put a finger into the baby's mouth, rotated it anteriorly and raised the chin above the upper edge of the wound. Putting her hand into the open womb, she got behind the baby's head. Estelle pushed on the stomach while Dr. Latolier eased her fingers in to pull out the baby. For a moment she and the baby protruding from Emily's body were suspended as though in a still photograph. Then, suddenly, almost completely freed of the mother, the baby was lying on sterile cloth. The umbilical cord was thick and shiny in the bright overhead light.

The baby's faint blue color was rapidly turning pink. Dr. Latolier pried open the baby's lips with her finger, took a small rubber tube from the nurse and placed it between the lips. The tube sucked out blood, fluid and amniotic debris from the throat.

Then the umbilical cord was cut. Flailing its arms, with a sound between a squeak and a croak, the infant took its first breath.

And with that breath, the tiny aquatic animal that had been afloat in a warm sea was transformed into a lung breather, capable of acquiring and using oxygen in a wholly new way. Never again during its life would its body functions change so abruptly. As a fetus, it was sustained by a complex system of detour blood vessels and a temporary valvelike opening between the right and left heart atria. Now, with the first gulp of air, an amazing transformation took place. The detour routes the blood had traveled were switched off. New routes switched on. Collapsed blood vessels in the lungs expanded and filled. The bypass duct that had diverted the flow of blood away from the lungs closed. The valvelike opening between the right and left atria fused shut. All the connections that tied the circulation system to the umbilical cord collapsed. Blood and air began to be pumped through the lungs.

Dr. Latolier held the baby up. "A fine healthy girl."

"Almost pretty," Estelle said.

"A little big for her age?" Dr. Harrison asked dryly.

"Perhaps a little," Dr. Latolier agreed.

Then they laughed inside their sterile hoods and masks.

In the waiting room, Harry said, "I don't know what I'll do if anything happens to her. I keep thinking of when we first met. At that resort. She was playing tennis. Did you know your sister was a good tennis player?"

Mary recognized Harry's need to keep talking.

She said, "I never saw her play. I know she used to go weekends to the public courts."

"She hasn't played in years. But in those days she was really good. I was attracted to her right from the beginning. There was something about her even then, something . . . different. She was the kind who would never fool around. We never did anything until after we were married." He added: "We've been married almost eleven years. God, where is that damn doctor?"

A few minutes later the door to the waiting room opened again. An attractive woman, wearing surgical greens and a cap, came in.

Harry tried to stand up, then settled back as though his legs were too weak to hold him. He said, "Dr. Latolier."

Dr. Latolier's expression was somber. "I'm afraid I have bad news."

Mary's emotions tangled and twisted, and all the strength seemed to drain out of her.

Harry stared up at the doctor. "My wife?"

"She's fine. It's the baby. We couldn't save it. We did everything we could."

Harry groaned and bent his head between his hands. Mary moved closer and put one arm around his shoulders.

"I'm so sorry," Dr. Latolier said. "Your wife is a lovely person. We are all terribly, terribly upset."

Chapter

4

Everything in Rudy Gerson's life, except giving up smoking, had come easily to him. He was not able to give up smoking until his twenty-sixth year, although he knew all the multiple physical ailments that tobacco made men heir to.

Rudy's father, Charles Gerson, was a renowned man of medicine, a towering medical pioneer who, when he failed, failed alone, and when he succeeded, succeeded for everyone. Rudy admired and loved him, respected and resented him. Admiration and respect were for obvious and excellent reasons; it was harder to love a father who considered him a small part of a life crowded with other achievements.

Outside of a penny-pinching frugality and transitory meaningless affairs with women, Charles Gerson had no human failings. He neither drank nor smoked nor cheated on his income tax. His incurably orderly mind could have found a pattern even in chaos, but that part of his character that had to do with such distractions as personal ambition, jealousy and anger had simply been omitted. He did not understand them, and so they did not exist in the vocabulary of his motives.

Shortly after his father's death, Rudy's mother reminisced about him to her son. She spoke of how they met and how she had known at once he was "someone very special." She had been prepared to take her place as a common soldier in the legion of his female admirers. Instead, he proposed marriage. Remembering that, she broke down and truly mourned. "I wish," she said, "he had been more of an ordinary man."

At times Rudy, too, had felt as if he were standing beside an immense pedestal and staring up at a remote stone figure at the top, tall and spare, rimless eyeglasses resting on a bony prominent nose, tantalizing and inaccessible.

From his fourteenth year it was clear that Rudy would become a doctor. As Charles Gerson's son, he was called on to carry out a great tradition. To do otherwise would mean that his father's life would end in a blind alley, with an ungrateful son.

The spring before his medical internship ended, Rudy accompanied his father to a meeting of a medical society at which his father was due to receive yet another well-merited honor. Twenty minutes from their destination a discussion began quietly, with his father telling him that Peter Bradford, a member of his staff for whom he had great admiration, had decided to branch off on his own. Bradford had been conducting certain important experiments, but was going to pursue an interest in neonatology and genetics.

"He'll leave a very big gap," Charles Gerson said. "I don't know many men who combine his boldness and imagination with a ruthless need to get things right. I don't see many of his kind in the new generation of scientists."

Rudy felt the obscure reproach—perhaps even an exhortation. He realized that the moment he had awaited, cruelly balanced between anticipation and impatience, had come. His father was actually inviting him to join him in his work.

"I don't think I could fill that gap," he said.

"If your record at school was disappointing, I believe it is due to the fact that you didn't apply yourself diligently. That's only natural at your age, and it will change when you begin doing work that interests you. At the moment you are like a rich soil in which nothing is growing."

"I don't have your kind of dedication."

"That will come, too. The deeper you get into anything, the more fascinated you are by it. It's what always happens."

Rudy did not believe that. No sense of mission thrilled in his blood. At times he feared he was trying to master a craft for which he had no talent. Like so many young men, he had been waiting around to find out what to do with his life. Now he had made his decision. But he put off announcing it because he knew what his father's attitude would be.

"I'm afraid it won't happen in my case." He was nervous now that the moment of reckoning had come. "I'm going into ob-gyn."

"That's ridiculous."

"I've already talked to Mother about it. She thinks it's a good idea."

"Your mother doesn't know anything about the medical profession. She'd be the last person I'd go to for advice in a matter as important as this."

His mother and father never really had much in

common. Charles Gerson's life began when he crossed the threshold to his laboratory, and her life stopped there. She came from a centuries-old Italian family with a proud heritage. A framed reproduction of their genealogy, *Patria E Familia,* hung on the wall in their living room. Charles Gerson was Jewish, raised in a crowded Brooklyn ghetto where one of his two brothers had died at fourteen from an overdose of drugs jammed down his throat by a street gang.

"I didn't go to Mother for advice," Rudy said. "I simply told her what I intended to do."

"An LMD," his father said. "Is that all you hope to make of your life?"

The mild contempt felt by his father for local medical doctors was well known to Rudy. To a man like his father the idea of having a son as an LMD was almost shameful. His son had to be an extension of himself, a part of his will.

"It's my life," Rudy said. "I won't be happy unless I do what I want to."

"No one wants to be ordinary," his father replied. "I won't let you throw yourself away like that. If you're going to succeed as a doctor, you must love medicine— you must be mad for it—it must be your whole life."

Charles Gerson commanded absolutely the small world in which he lived, and part of that world was his family. He had never listened to his wife, and saw no reason why he should listen to his son.

"I can't ride your obsession," Rudy said as calmly as he could.

"A man riding an obsession is at least going somewhere," his father answered.

The discussion that evening stopped a heartbeat short of a serious quarrel.

Three days later, Charles Gerson traveled to Haiti to test the new vaccine he had devised against a rare tropical disease. The government refused to provide subjects on whom to test the vaccine. To prove its efficacy Charles Gerson injected himself with the disease and then tried to cure it. His vaccine failed; and he died.

Rudy was twenty-six when his father died. That was the year Rudy gave up smoking. It had been a mark of rebellion, an assertion of identity. As Charles Gerson's son, he needed it. As Rudy Gerson, he did not.

Early on a Thursday afternoon Rudy was in his office, between Madison and Fifth Avenue on 85th Street, discussing with a small freckled man with eyeglasses and a worried-looking blonde whether they should consider natural childbirth.

The interoffice phone buzzed and Rudy picked it up.

"Emily Conklin," Mrs. Sherwin announced over the phone. "A one-thirty appointment."

"Send her into an examination room. I'll be ready in a moment." Rudy replaced the receiver and continued his conference.

"I'm just not sure I could go through with it," the blond woman said. "It's my husband who wants me to."

Her husband removed his eyeglasses and polished them. "I think it might be good for us to share the experience. A friend of mine's wife had a natural childbirth, and he says it's the only way. It helps to bring a couple closer together."

"There's something in that," Rudy agreed.

The blond wife looked more worried than ever. "We decided to leave the decision up to you, Doctor."

"It's the parents who must decide if they're the right type for natural childbirth. Why don't we see how it works out when the time comes? I believe in letting nature take its course—but only as long as it's heading in the right direction."

As they were leaving, the woman turned back for a moment to whisper, "Thank you."

When Rudy entered the examination room Emily Conklin was waiting for him, wearing the blue paper disposable wrapping. Another young woman was in the room with her.

Emily said, "Dr. Gerson, this is my sister Mary Oliver."

"Hello," he said. "We meet again."

"We do?"

He remembered her voice, pleasant, low pitched, a curious mix of midwestern twang and New England diction. "We shared a train from Philadelphia together."

Suddenly she smiled with recognition. "You tried to help with my luggage."

He nodded and turned to his patient. "How are you, Mrs. Conklin?"

"I just had to talk to you, Doctor. You can examine me later if you like."

He sat down and opened her file folder. "What's bothering you?" he asked, noticing the last date under her name. He had examined her a year ago for a fertility problem caused by uterine fibroids. No other anatomical defects or hormonal deficiencies. He had recommended her to the Karyll Clinic for an in vitro impregnation.

"Did you go to the Karyll Clinic?" he asked.

She nodded. "They gave me tests, Harry, too, and didn't find anything except for that problem with my oviducts. They said it wasn't important with the way they'd do it."

"That's true. What happened then?"

"Well, I got pregnant. I carried the baby for eight months and . . ." Emily began to cry. She squeezed her eyes shut and reached out a hand blindly. Her sister produced a paper tissue for her.

Rudy turned to her sister. "Perhaps you can tell me."

"She was in labor six hours and they finally did a Caesarean. She lost the baby."

"Lost it?"

"The umbilical cord got wrapped around its neck." She forced the words out, as if they were heavy with burdens of pain. "It was born dead."

Emily's head was bowed and she was still crying.

Rudy said, "When something like that happens, all the electronic helpers and skill in the world can't prevent it."

Mary said, "They didn't let her see the baby afterward. They said it was a . . . not normal . . . What my sister would really like to know, Doctor, is . . . *can* she have a normal baby?"

"I can only answer that after a thorough physical examination. Perhaps you'd better wait outside."

When Rudy finished with the physical exam, he asked Emily to dress and wait with her sister in his conference room. As he entered they were both seated in dark leather club chairs opposite his desk. He was struck again by what a good-looking young woman Mary Oliver was.

He said to Emily Conklin, "I've given you a thorough examination, and there's no reason you can't have a normal baby by the same process. I'd suggest you go back and try again—as soon as possible."

"I'm not sure I'd be willing to do that."

"Why not? It's perfectly safe."

"What happened may have something to do with how I got pregnant."

He recognized at once that there was no assurance he could give her that would allay her fears.

"Who was your doctor at the Karyll Clinic?" he asked.

"A woman. Dr. Latolier."

"She's chief of obstetrical surgery. You couldn't be in better hands. I can talk to her and find out what was wrong with your baby."

"Would you?"

"I'd want to check anyway, for my own records. Ask my secretary to give you another appointment in a few days. By then, I'll have the answer."

The next day, at the Park Hill Clinic, Rudy's last patient complained that she had pelvic pain when she menstruated. The pain was in the suprapubic region and the lower portion of the abdomen. Probably a uterine or ovarian tumor, Rudy thought. The pelvic pain could be due to distention within a hollow viscus and stretching of the capsule, or to a hemorrhage within the tumor because of changes in its blood supply. There was no way to know without a thorough examination and a probe in the uterus. He scheduled her for another appointment at the clinic.

In an empty consultation room he picked up a telephone, got an outside line and dialed the Karyll Clinic in Westchester. He made an appointment to see Dr. Gaby Latolier. Rudy could have discussed Emily Conklin's problem over the telephone with Dr. Latolier, but this was a rare opportunity for a first-hand look at the Karyll Clinic's advanced facilities.

Less than an hour later he turned off the Hutchinson Parkway in Westchester. Three immense buildings were set on the sprawling grounds of what had been the late Hector Karyll's estate. Order, consistency, grandeur. The sharp, clean lines of an architect's drawing combined with the solidity of structural form.

The Karyll Clinic was unique because all its facilities were devoted to problems involving human reproduction. There were maternity wards, neonatology departments, fertility clinics, a surgery center for pediatrics, an entire building set aside for genetics research, even a film studio where educational films were produced to bring doctors and medical schools up to date on the latest techniques and developments.

The physical plant was the embodiment of the vision of one of the world's great doctors. Peter Bradford's reputation as both a geneticist and a neonatologist had become legendary.

Rudy drove into the main parking lot of the Karyll Clinic and left his Porsche there. He entered the central hospital building, and at the information desk spoke to the woman on duty.

"I have an appointment with Dr. Latolier."

"Your name, please?"

"Dr. Gerson."

She pressed a button and glanced at a computer console. "Dr. Latolier is in surgery, but Dr. Bradford left word that he would like to see you. Do you know the way to his office?"

Dr. Peter Bradford's anteroom was furnished with a secretary's desk, two straight-backed chairs, a tall philodendron in a large pot in a corner. The floor was dark, polished linoleum.

A young secretary was listening to a man and woman in the anteroom.

The man sounded angry. "I don't care how busy he is. The name is Pollard. P-o-l-l-a-r-d. He'd better make time to see us."

"I'm sure he will, Mr. Pollard. But he has a previous appointment. Dr. Gerson?"

Rudy nodded. The secretary pushed a button on her intercom.

"Dr. Gerson has arrived. Mr. and Mrs. Pollard are also here and would like to see you immediately."

Pollard turned his baleful attention to Rudy. "Can your business wait?" he asked sharply.

Rudy caught an imploring glance from Mrs. Pollard. He said, "I can wait if your business is really urgent."

With scarcely a nod to the secretary, without even a thank you to Rudy, Pollard took his wife toward the door of Bradford's office. The secretary quickly pushed a button on her desk to unlock the door. The Pollards vanished behind it.

"He really seems upset," Rudy said.

The secretary said, "I can't blame them. Did you read in the papers? The Pollards' year-old son was killed by a watchdog."

"Yes, I did read about that." He was about to ask what that event had to do with Dr. Bradford when the telephone rang and the secretary answered it.

He found a chair and began thumbing through a copy of *Time* magazine. Angry voices were semiaudible from within Bradford's office. Occasional words were distinguishable. *Unusual? Is that how you describe . . .* Rudy glanced at the secretary who was still on the telephone. *Crush toys . . . a bottle in its hands. Strangle a . . . and . . .*

The voice dropped below hearing level, and when it resumed, there was a different note, almost as if the speaker were close to tears. *. . . doctor has . . . responsibility . . .*

A familiar phrase, one he had often heard from his father. A doctor has a responsibility. So said the Jewish physician Maimonides more than 700 years ago: *Oh, God, Thou hast appointed me to watch over the life and death of Thy creatures; here I am ready for my vocation.*

The secretary was off the telephone. After a few minutes the door to the office opened and Mr. and Mrs. Pollard emerged. Pollard was saying in an apologetic tone, "I guess what bothered me most, Dr. Bradford, is that Jane knew everything about our baby and I didn't. I thought she should have told me."

"You're quite right. But there won't be any reason for that next time. You're going to have a perfectly normal baby."

The voice was intimate, soft, almost embracing. The door opened to reveal fully the speaker as a large man dressed in a well-fitting dark-blue suit.

"Thank you so much, Dr. Bradford," Mrs. Pollard said. "I'm sure you'll be seeing us again."

Bradford smiled, and turned to Rudy. "Won't you come in, Doctor?"

Bradford's private office was as sparsely furnished as

the anteroom Rudy had just left. A large desk, small leather sofa, two leather chairs.

Dr. Bradford crossed to his desk. "You're Charley Gerson's son. That's why I was anxious to meet you. Your father was one of the pivotal influences in my life."

"He'd have been flattered to know that."

"A very wonderful man."

This was a verdict Rudy so often heard from strangers that he no longer had any sense of personal reality or involvement. Through the years, across time and distance, Rudy had gradually come to think of his father with compassion. A relationship with a father, living or dead, is reconstituted every day and always in a slightly different way, but the essence remains. Rudy's admiration had seemed to strengthen and deepen, and he felt now that he understood his father better than he had ever found words to say.

Bradford's next remark surprised him. "Of course, being the son of a great man can also be a burden. A heavy burden. The world expects so much more of you."

Rudy nodded. "In medical school, when some of the fellows found out who my father was, they called me Gerson the Lesser. I thought the name would stick for life."

"You seem to have adjusted pretty well."

"I can't be sure," he said. He had been altered by having Charles Gerson for his father in ways he would never comprehend. "I probably chose not to go into medical research because I didn't want to be in competition with him. It was safer to choose a career in practical medicine."

"Nothing wrong with that choice."

"My father didn't approve."

Bradford leaned back in his chair. He gave Rudy an odd half-smile. "There was a time when I had to come to the same kind of decision. Believe it or not, I was just as worried about whether Charles Gerson would approve. I gave up the study of viruses that cause tropical diseases and took up genetics and neonatology."

"I remember my father talking about that."

"Sometimes I've wondered why I did it. I would have sworn then that it was because genetics interested me more and had a wider scope. I'm not so sure now. It may have been simply that I preferred to make my own reputation in a different field."

Bradford's admission created a bond of understanding between them. Rudy, lost in reverie, recalled the moment when he heard that his father was dead. On the medicine cabinet in the bathroom he had written with a soaped finger, *Charles Gerson*. Then he had washed the words away and wept for half an hour.

He heard Bradford speak, and returned alertly to the present moment.

"Now you know why I had to meet Charley Gerson's son. Is there anything I can do for you?"

"I came to see Dr. Latolier."

"Any particular reason?"

"I referred a patient to your IVF program. Her baby died during delivery. She wants to know if the way she was impregnated had anything to do with the outcome."

"You can reassure her on that point. Once a fetus starts growing inside the womb, its chance for survival is about the same as any other. The method of conception has nothing to do with it."

"She's unwilling to have another baby until she's sure. And there's another problem. The baby was abnormal in some way."

"In what way?"

"I don't know. According to her, the doctor didn't let her see the baby."

"Was Dr. Latolier the doctor?"

"Yes."

Bradford flipped down the buzzer and told his secretary to locate Dr. Latolier and tell her someone was waiting in his office to see her. He said to Rudy, "Our experience doesn't indicate, at least to date, that there is any higher incidence of either abnormality or mortality with in vitro fertilization. But Dr. Latolier can give you the details on this particular case."

"I appreciate the trouble you're taking."

"Not at all. I'm as interested in hearing what happened as you are. Infant mortality is a very rare occurrence here at the Karyll Clinic."

They chatted for a few minutes, mostly about the publicity being given to some of the latest experiments with gene transplantation. Bradford was opposed to the government restrictions put on scientists working in their field. He compared the government's interference with the Scopes trial in the United States and the Lysenko affair in the Soviet Union.

"The experiments with recombinant DNA are a good deal safer than many laboratory procedures—the work that's being done with tumor viruses and cancer-causing chemicals, for example. Not to mention all the other science-created hazards—DDT, cyclamates, PCB and PBB, Freons, DES, and vinyl chloride."

Rudy answered, "I think what people are worried

about is that gene transplants are a first step on the road to human genetic engineering."

"That will come eventually. And why not? Looking back over the history of medicine, we are grateful to the men who pushed forward the frontiers. It's hard to imagine why they were so controversial in their own day. We have in our hands a dramatic and powerful means of changing life. Not to use it would be a criminal act."

Rudy was not prepared to argue with the acknowledged leader in the field, but he could understand why the government, responding to public apprehension, was so concerned. Scientists were dealing with an extremely intricate balance of nature that they understood all too dimly. No one really knew what the hazards in the new technology might be, nor how to guard against them. It might be wiser to defer certain experiments and to proceed with extreme caution in others.

A woman in a white doctor's smock appeared in the doorway.

Bradford said, "Dr. Latolier, this is Dr. Gerson."

"How do you do," she said. Her voice was husky and deep, like a woman imitating a man's voice.

"Dr. Gerson has a few questions to ask about a patient he referred to us."

Rudy said, "Her name is Emily Conklin. I believe you're the surgeon who delivered her baby."

Dr. Latolier nodded. "A most rare, most unfortunate tragedy. The baby was unusually large and the mother's pelvic area rather small, so I was worried about the chance for a successful vaginal delivery. When the fetal heartbeat slowed dramatically I performed an immediate Caesarean. Unfortunately, I was too late. Death had occurred from umbilical strangulation."

"I'm also told the baby was abnormal in some way."

"Gargoylism. The typical deformity. I discouraged Mrs. Conklin and her husband from seeing it because the experience would be traumatic."

"Could the gargoylism have had any relation to the in vitro fertilization?"

"None at all. If Mrs. Conklin is afraid of that, you can reassure her. It was the kind of tragedy not likely to happen again. Not one chance in a million."

Rudy nodded. In his own years in private practice and at the clinic, he had delivered stillborn babies, some with abnormalities. Medical science did not always know the answers. Fortunately, the instances were statistically negligible.

Rudy said, "Thank you, Dr. Latolier. You've been very helpful."

Chapter

5

As soon as he left Bradford's office, Rudy realized he had missed an opportunity. Part of his reason for coming here had been to see the kind of modern facilities that the Karyll Clinic had to offer. He should have asked for an escorted tour. In the corridor he paused, looking uncertainly for the elevator.

"Well, I'll be damned," a voice said behind him, "if it isn't Gerson the Lesser!"

Rudy experienced the inner twinge he had always felt during his years in medical school when he heard himself called by that name. He turned to see a stocky, bearded young man in a doctor's white smock.

"Did you ever stagger through med school?" the bearded young man asked, grinning.

"I managed," Rudy answered cautiously. The voice was familiar, and so was the mocking, challenging tone. Then he placed him—Bernie Seligson, a young man for whom everyone had predicted great things. Even as a second year medical student Bernie had been consulted by a chief resident at the hospital on differential diagnosis. Bernie was the one who had christened him Gerson the Lesser.

"I'm an o.b.," Rudy said.

"Good choice! There isn't much anyone can do to prevent a baby from being born."

Laughter did not quite take the edge off malice.

"Are you on staff here?" Rudy asked.

"One of those poor dedicated doctors who'd rather spend time treating unusual and interesting cases. We've got the finest group of professionals in the world. We've got pediatric specialists in allergies, cardiology, endocrinology, neurology, orthopedics, psychiatry—you name it. We've got doctors who can diagnose more about a sick infant from the creases in the palms of its hands and the soles of its feet than ordinary doctors can tell from a complete physical exam."

"What do you do here?"

"I'm chief of medical diagnostics. Lots of teaching, advisory and supervisory—this place is designed as much for research and teaching as for medical care. What are you doing here?"

"Finding out about a patient I referred here."

"Who's her doctor?"

"Latolier."

"A brilliant surgeon. All the difference in the world from an ordinary o.b.—as you well know."

Rudy felt a guilty satisfaction in being able to strike back. "She performed a Caesarean. The baby died."

"Really? What happened?"

He repeated to Seligson what he had heard from Dr. Latolier.

"Fascinating," Seligson said. "This will come up at our mortality and morbidity conference. Exactly the kind of thing we all like to chew over. How much did it weigh?"

"Eleven pounds."

"And not full term? Edematous?"

"No."

"Adrenal tumor or hyperplasia of the adrenal cortex is my guess. I grant you it's occasionally congenital, but it might explain the size of the little beast. Nicely complicated problem. Well, meeting you again was fun, Lesser. Keep the money rolling in. Inflict your skills on the rich."

Talking to Bernie Seligson was like sliding rapidly over ice—he had the same sense of losing control.

Nevertheless, "If you're not doing anything important right now, how about giving me a tour?"

"Can't. I've been working eighteen hours without food or sleep. Haven't been watered, haven't been fed. I'm on my way to the cafete . . ."

"Dr. Seligson! On Medicine Four," the loudspeaker announced. *"Stat!"*

"Something's popping. Have to save another life." With a short barking laugh, Seligson turned and left. After a few strides he began to run. In a hospital, no one dawdles on the way to a Stat call.

Rudy strolled down a brightly lit corridor, which intersected with other brightly lit corridors. It was like moving through the interior of a well organized, well disciplined mind.

At the bank of elevators, he pushed a down button. The elevator arrived empty. On the first floor, as Rudy tried to leave, he was stopped by a sudden influx of people. An orderly wheeled in an isolet containing a small infant of about three months. Rudy was pinned into a corner while the elevator descended to the basement. The orderly rolled the isolet out. The other passengers also left. On an impulse, just before the doors closed, Rudy got out too. He wanted a closer look at the basement regions where the operating rooms would be located.

When Rudy reached the corridor he saw swinging doors closing. The lettering on one of the doors read *ICU*. Farther on, he passed another door with a sign: *Operating Rooms—Do Not Enter*. He hesitated only a moment before pushing the door open.

Just inside was the nurse's station. Beyond were the lockers and dressing rooms; separate ones for doctors, nurses, orderlies. In those dressing rooms, street clothes would be exchanged for green surgical gowns and disposable masks, caps and shoe covers. Personally, Rudy never used shoe covers; he kept a special pair of Dr. Scholl's sandals in his locker for wear inside the operating room, and wore them over his bare feet. He believed in having everything loose and comfortable when working.

"You're not allowed in here." The nurse, at her station inside the door, looked at him sternly.

"I just wanted to see what it was like," Rudy said. "I'm a doctor, too. At Park Hill."

The nurse's stern demeanor did not relax. "No one can come in here who isn't wearing surgical garments. I must ask you to leave."

A stretcher covered with a sheet was being wheeled out of an operating room by a plump redheaded nurse. She hurried toward them.

"Coming through!"

He stepped aside, close to the wall, but the stretcher had a tight passage. Part of the sheet caught his belt buckle and was dragged partway off the stretcher.

Quickly, the redheaded nurse bent down and pushed the sheet back into place.

"You're in the way!" she told Rudy, then she looked accusingly at the nurse on duty. "Get him out of here—fast!"

Flushed, sweating, angry, she went on her way.

The nurse said, "You heard what she said. I'm sorry, Doctor, but if you don't leave, I'll have to call security. No one's allowed . . ."

"All right."

In the corridor there was no sign of the plump redheaded nurse or the stretcher. In that brief moment, as the sheet came off the stretcher, Rudy had glimpsed a small, still form beneath. Another infant on the way to the morgue. The Karyll Clinic was having a streak of bad luck.

Two days later, in his office, Rudy informed Emily Conklin of his conversation with Doctors Bradford and Latolier. Emily had come with her sister, and he had invited them both in to hear the report.

He said, "They're convinced that what happened to your baby had nothing to do with how the conception was accomplished."

"How about you, Dr. Gerson?" Emily Conklin asked. "Are you convinced?"

"They're the best in the field."

"I wouldn't believe anything they tell me. I'll believe what you tell me."

"Except for the fallopian tubes, your reproductive functions are completely normal. The in vitro process bypasses the fallopian tubes. There should be no problem."

"You haven't answered me, Doctor. Will you swear I'll have a normal baby next time?"

It occurred to Rudy that doctors were less equipped than they might be to confront legal and ethical issues. The possibility of failure had only been obscured by modern technology; it had not disappeared.

He said, "Let me put it this way. If you were my wife, I wouldn't worry at all."

"Will I need another Caesarean?"

"That's the rule. Once a Caesarean, always a Caesarean. The scar tissue is too fragile."

"Is that a danger to the baby?"

"It's nothing to worry about. The overall mortality rate is very, very low."

Emily Conklin's eyes were brimming with tears. "Do you realize what you've done, Doctor?" she asked. "You've given me hope again." Then she got up quickly and left the consulting room.

Mary Oliver said, "My sister put you on the spot, didn't she? You went out on a limb for her. That was a very nice thing to do."

"Thank you. But I'm not taking much of a risk. I really do think everything will be all right."

"I know that my sister is very grateful to you. So am I."

Suddenly the thought that he might never see her again was unbearable.

He gathered his courage. "Would it be taking advantage of your gratitude if I asked you to have dinner with me tonight?"

She hesitated, cocking her head appraisingly. Then she smiled. The smile was worth waiting for.

"I'd like that."

* * *

The telephone rang as Rudy was leaving the office for the day. Mrs. Sherwin had left, so he picked up the telephone himself.

"Hello, Lesser? Bernie Seligson. Remember that talk we had about the Conklin baby?"

"Of course."

"Did you get the name right?" Bernie's tone was nearly accusing. "I'm damned if I can find any reference to *anybody* named Conklin having been a patient here."

"Well, she was. She was in my office a little while ago."

"I can't even find her name in the computer banks."

"Somebody's slipped up somewhere. Dr. Latolier and I discussed the Conklin baby. Dr. Bradford was there too."

"I don't understand it. I've never known the people here to make a mistake like this."

"It just proves," Rudy was savoring another small triumph, "that no system is foolproof."

Chapter

6

It was ridiculous, Rudy thought, looking at Mary Oliver across the table in Maxwell Plum's restaurant. A grown man doesn't fall in love like a schoolboy.

She wore a red jacket, a white turtleneck sweater and a black velvet skirt. Her slender neck rose gracefully out of the cuff of her turtleneck, seeming to flow in a perfect curve to her chin. Her eyes were devastating. When she looked directly at him he became so light-headed that he couldn't be sure he was talking intelligibly, but their conversation seemed to move with a will of its own. Listening, he kept storing away information about her. Everything about her was worth remembering. She was apolitical and, in 1980, had decided she couldn't vote for anyone to be President. She was an industrial designer, employed by an air-conditioning firm. She was not sure she wanted to have children. Not for years and years anyway. She smoked too much and had an occasional hacking little cough.

"How long do you plan to be in town?" he asked.

"I'm going home tomorrow."

He felt a painful constriction in his throat. "So soon?"

"I'm afraid I have to. Philadelphia is where I live."

A young man appeared suddenly at their table. He was in his early thirties, with thinning light-brown hair and a stocky, compact body.

Mary put out her cigarette in an ashtray. "I don't believe this. What are you doing in New York, Sam?"

"Business. Just until tomorrow." He bent and kissed her.

A slight flush appeared on Mary's cheeks. "I'd like you to meet Dr. Rudy Gerson. Rudy, this is an old friend, Sam Dodds."

Sam Dodds shook hands with Rudy, a firm handshake that stopped short of becoming a test of strength. "Pleasure." He turned back to Mary. "I tried to call you at your mother's. She told me you were in New York staying at Emily's. So I called her and found out where you were."

"How nice."

"I don't want to interrupt your dinner. Can we arrange to get together tomorrow?"

"I'm leaving in the morning."

"I'll call you bright and early. We have a lot of things to talk about. Decisions to make." He leaned over to kiss her again. He nodded to Rudy and left. Mary's eyes followed him to the door of the restaurant.

"Have you known him long?" Rudy asked.

She regarded him speculatively for a moment before answering. "Over a year. He moved to Washington a month ago. Took a new job with the government. He's a lawyer."

"Ambitious?"

"Yes."

"Aggressive?"

"Very."

Rudy had developed an active resentment toward his departed rival. "Your sister couldn't have told him where you were having dinner. I didn't mention it to her."

"Did you tell your answering service?"

He nodded.

"Then Sam got your name from my sister and called your office. The answering service told him. Sam is very good at finding out things like that."

"Which means he knew you were having dinner with me."

"He must have. I told you he was aggressive."

She had pale green eyes and distinct, well shaped eyebrows. Her gaze was direct and open. He was sure that if he asked her how important Sam Dodds was in her life she would tell him. He did not want to know.

He said, "Philadelphia isn't the other side of the world. Will you have dinner with me tomorrow night?"

She said with a faint note of regret, "There'd be no point to it."

"They have great snapper soup at Bookbinder's."

"Perhaps I should explain. Sam and I are . . . very close. He wants me to live with him in Washington."

"Give up your career?"

She lit another cigarette. "That's the problem. Sam thinks I should be like Ruth in the Bible. 'Whither thou goest, I will go.' "

"Everyone forgets Ruth said that to her mother-in-law."

She laughed. "I'll remember that the next time he brings it up."

"How about dinner tomorrow?"

"I'm really sorry. I've enjoyed being with you. But I thought you should know how things are."

An impulse of desperation overcame him. "I know how things are, but I don't have to accept it. We've still got tonight, and there's a new Woody Allen movie playing at the Sutton. Do you like Woody Allen?"

"In his funny moods."

"At the end of this movie he's smothered to death by a dozen Italian actresses."

"I love happy endings."

They were in line outside the theater on Fifty-seventh and Third Avenue when he said, "Damn!" reached into his pocket and took out a small buzzing plastic box.

"The movie doesn't start for five minutes. Keep my place in line."

He found a phone booth at the corner and called in.

"An emergency call from Park Hill, Dr. Gerson," the answering service informed him.

"Get somebody to cover. I'm not working there until day after tomorrow."

"Dr. Tizan said it's urgent. He asked you to please get over there as quickly as you can."

Rudy groaned softly. He hung up and went back to where Mary was standing in line.

"I've got to go. It's an emergency. It must be something really unusual. I don't understand it, but I have to find out what it is. Oh, God, why did this have to happen?"

"Please don't worry. I understand."

"I'll call you in the morning. Before he does."

"You don't give up easily, do you?"

"Never," he said.

He ran out into the street, hailed a taxi and told the driver to take him to Park Hill Hospital.

Five police cars were parked outside the hospital with signal lights whirling. He took the stairs to the first floor. At the head of the stairs, a policeman barred his way into the clinic.

"I'm Dr. Gerson."

"They're waiting for you, Doctor. Right this way!"

The policeman took him to Dr. Tizan. Tizan, short, rotund, bald, was talking with a police officer in the main admissions room. This was the first time Rudy had ever seen the room empty of patients, although the room was crowded. It looked like a temporary police headquarters, with several policemen in the admissions office, others sitting on the patients' benches and standing at the doors. In the center of the room, at a large card table littered with papers and three telephones, other policemen were at work.

"Rudy! Thank God!" Dr. Tizan said.

"What's wrong? They said it's an emergency."

The police officer said, "It is. He has two nurses in there. I'm Captain Cartwright, in charge of the hostage negotiating team."

"The what?"

"A special police team trained to deal with hostage situations. We were called in by Emergency Service. They've set up a temporary headquarters and evacuated all nonpolice personnel. Unfortunately, we had a casualty. Before the negotiating team got here, a police officer tried to break in. Delgado shot through the door. The officer is in surgery right now with a busted hip. But he could just as easily be dead."

"Who did you say shot him?"

"A man named Delgado," Captain Cartwright said. "You're the one he wants to see. He's been holding the nurses as hostages until you came."

"I don't know anyone by that name."

The police captain said, "We looked him up in the files, Doctor. He came to you at the clinic with his wife a year ago. Conchita Delgado. She and Ramon are both Puerto Ricans. He's twenty-nine, she's twenty-two." Cartwright glanced at a yellow file card in his hand. "He's a combat veteran. Vietnam. We ran a check on him. He was discharged from service for battle neurosis."

"What's he want?"

Dr. Tizan said, "He walked in here and asked for you. When Ingrid said you weren't on duty tonight, he pulled a gun. Took Ingrid and Nurse Haley with him into my office. He insisted we call you at once."

Cartwright said, "He's threatening to kill both women. There are no windows, and he broke off telephone contact a few minutes ago. He won't talk to us through the door."

"What can I do?"

"We haven't found out why he wants to talk to you. It's possible that you can establish contact."

"I'm willing to try."

They left the admissions room and went down a corridor that led to Dr. Tizan's office. The door had black lettering, *Louis Tizan, M.D., Clinic Director*.

Cartwright called loudly, "Delgado!"

No answer.

"I've got Dr. Gerson here with me. He's willing to listen to anything you've got to say."

After a moment, a woman's soft, frightened voice: "He wants the doctor to come in."

"First we have to find out what he wants to see him about."

Silence followed. Cartwright nodded to Rudy.

Rudy said, "Mr. Delgado, this is Dr. Gerson. I'm willing to discuss whatever is troubling you. There may be a misunderstanding."

After a moment, the woman's soft voice: "He says you come in. Then he'll let us go."

Captain Cartwright replied, "We can't allow anyone other than police personnel to go in there."

Another silence that endured for about ten seconds. Then the frightened voice: "He says it has to be Dr. Gerson. And you only have three minutes to make up your minds."

Cartwright took Rudy by the arm and moved him back out of hearing distance. "How do you feel about it?"

"He may try to kill me."

"We'll give you all the protection we can."

"How about his wife? Can't she come here and reason with him?"

"She's at the Karyll Clinic. Under heavy sedation."

"What for?"

"Her baby died during delivery."

Rudy stared at him. "Well, that gives a pretty good idea of what he wants to talk to *me* about, doesn't it?"

"We've got a deadline. Less than a minute left. When the time's up, we'll have to break in."

"Can you get in quickly and keep him from shooting the women?"

Cartwright shrugged.

Rudy took a deep breath. "I'll talk to him—provided he lets the hostages go free."

Cartwright hurried down the corridor to Dr. Tizan's office. He returned a moment later.

"It's a brave thing you're doing, Doctor. I'm sure those two women will appreciate it. I'll be right outside if you call for help . . ."

"No one warned me that practicing medicine was such a risky profession."

"Your best chance is to let him get whatever's bothering him off his chest. Above all, don't argue."

"I won't. And I hope *you* won't waste any time coming through that door."

"Good luck," Cartwright whispered. He drew his gun and moved back against the wall, at an angle where he could shoot through the doorway when it opened.

Rudy knocked. "This is Dr. Gerson. Can I come in now?" He half expected a fusillade of bullets.

Footsteps approached the other side of the door. The door opened slowly. Rudy recognized Ingrid, the pretty young blond receptionist. Her eyes were wide with terror; no one was visible in the room behind her.

She stepped back to let Rudy enter. As he did, the door slammed and a bolt clicked.

A hard object rammed into his back. To show he was not looking for trouble, Rudy kept his hands partly raised.

"Move this way, Doctor."

Ingrid began to sob. Nurse Haley, a scrawny fiftyish woman, was sitting in a chair behind Dr. Tizan's desk. She was as rigid as Lot's wife.

Sweat began to trickle down inside Rudy's collar. His thinking processes locked around a single question:

What will happen in the next minute, the next second?

"You two can go now." Delgado motioned for Ingrid and Nurse Haley to leave. Ingrid left with a tearful glance of gratitude to Rudy; Nurse Haley marched out. As the door closed behind Nurse Haley, the gun prodded Rudy in the back.

"Lock the door."

Rudy moved to the door and threw the bolt. He hoped Captain Cartwright would not try anything rash. It would only take a split second for Delgado to pull the trigger.

"Do you know me, Doctor?"

This seemed an invitation, so he turned. The man behind him was fairly short, with an olive-tan complexion and a moustache.

"I'm afraid I don't."

A mocking little sneer came and went. The smooth, young face struggled to contain a strong emotion. "My wife wanted to have a baby. You talked her into having it at the Karyll Clinic. Our baby was made by doctors in a little saucer. Do you know what happened? My son was born dead."

Rudy studied Delgado's face. The man was perspiring slightly, and his eyes were glittering. He had the look of someone poised on the brink of an extreme action, and Rudy had no intention of pushing him over the brink.

He said quietly, "Mr. Delgado, I would like to help you. I really would. If there's any way I can help . . ."

"I am going to punish you, Doctor. You see this gun?"

"Yes."

"It is a war souvenir. I found it on the body of a

Vietcong officer. There is no way to know how many this gun has killed."

Rudy did not reply. He stood very quietly and could actually feel thoughts moving around in his head. Delgado was in no mood to be reasoned with—he would interpret any such attempt as opposition. And he was all too clearly ready to deal with opposition in a violent manner.

Delgado was muttering as he paced the room. There were times when Rudy could not make out what he was saying, and as far as he was concerned, those times were the best.

Suddenly Delgado said clearly, "You made us defy God. The priest told us that the Church would not approve of a baby made in a little saucer. But my Conchita, she believed you. She wanted to have our baby your way . . ."

"I meant no harm. You must know that."

"There were no last rites. No Christian burial with a priest." A shadow crossed Delgado's face. "The doctor said there was no reason . . . after an autopsy . . ."

Rudy asked quietly, "Who was the doctor?"

Delgado blinked, as if waking from a reverie. "The woman. Dr. Latolier."

Rudy stared. "Latolier?" The careful, fragile balance he had maintained was momentarily upset by surprise. This was the second infant death he had heard of at the Karyll Clinic in a few days. Both were in vitro births, and Dr. Latolier had been in charge in both instances. "She would never order an autopsy without your permission. No doctor would without consent of the parents."

"I would never consent. *Never!*"

"You must have misunderstood. Or perhaps your wife . . ." He stopped, realizing he had made the very mistake he wanted to avoid. His skin felt cold, and the inside of his mouth was cottony. Delgado's finger was tightening on the trigger.

Rudy cried, "Wait! I can help you find out . . ."

Whether his gambit would have worked he never knew. At that moment there was a loud knock on the door and Cartwright's voice, "Dr. Gerson, are you all right in there?"

Rudy caught an instant warning signal from Delgado, a tightening of jaw muscles. Without hesitation, he dove to the floor. The gun *bammed*. A hot breath passed his right ear. Then the door crashed open, and Cartwright catapulted across the room.

The gun went off again before Cartwright's heavy blow dropped Delgado to his knees. Cartwright's foot came up and struck him in the side of the head. Delgado went sprawling on his face.

Rudy got up shakily. Cartwright was wearing a bulky red bulletproof vest.

"A good job, Doctor," Cartwright said. "A real cool performance."

Another policeman entered the room and yanked Delgado's arms behind his back and manacled his wrists. Delgado was conscious but whimpering. His face was bloodied.

Rudy said, "Don't hurt him any more. I found out why he's so upset."

Konrad had been the caretaker in Phase Two for three years and he had never seen it fail. Whenever Dr. Bradford made his regular weekly inspection, it was always a bad day. Long after the doctor left, the creatures were restless. Who could blame them?

This morning the doctor spent most of his time in the giant pool, using various instruments to measure the mixture of salts and nutrients, temperature and pressure, and the degree of contamination. The pool was about the size of two tennis courts, and a walkway with a handrail crossed it in the middle. Standing on this walkway, Dr. Bradford lowered gauges and lifted them again. Then he made certain adjustments in the intake valves at each of the pool's four corners. He referred to this as "controlling the culture medium." When he had finished, a somewhat bitter but not too unpleasant odor rose from the pool's surface.

Konrad did not understand much of what went on. All he knew was that his creatures were being disturbed, and he wouldn't be surprised if there were more casualties. Two out of five had died this past week, and Nessie, the creature he liked best, had been strangely listless.

Today was particularly upsetting. After the usual tests, the doctor began a new experiment with Nessie.

"All chemical inhibitors have been removed. We should get penetration of the egg," he told Konrad, who understood only a little of what was said. "Of course, we don't know what is going on inside her body. Or even whether she can become pregnant with this particular sperm. The whole thing may be a washout."

Konrad nodded as though he understood. But how could Nessie or any other creature become pregnant without the assistance of an opposite sex? Nessie had neither mate nor companion. Perhaps that was why he felt so close to her. He had always been a loner. He had lost all interest in communicating with people whose interests he could not share, and was only comfortable with his pets. In their sweet presence he experienced a contentment that he never knew with his own kind.

As assistant keeper in a small zoo in his hometown in Bavaria, he had to protect his pets from unwelcome molestation by small visitors. He peered suspiciously at boys and girls trooping in. A smoldering hatred rose in him at a boy, about nine years old, who always taunted and teased the animals. Late one afternoon the boy appeared alone, just before closing. He tossed in candy to the green monkeys, who ate it and promptly began spitting blood. The candy had sharp pieces of glass embedded in it. Konrad shouted at the boy, who only laughed and danced away. The smoldering leapt in Konrad like a flame. Minutes later he was kneeling with bowed head, trembling, and the boy was dead. They had to send Konrad away for a while, and when he was released, there was no employment for him. So he left and came to this new country to work again—with other pets.

Now the experiment was done. Dr. Bradford was gone, and Nessie lay inert in her favorite corner, an area about the size of a lily pond. The giant pool was dark except for the faint luminous violet light that revealed the aquatic creatures moving within it. Nessie lay helpless, lolling, near an intake pipe, floating weightlessly in the stream like a clot of seaweed.

"Nessie," he said, feeling foolish.

Lidless eyes shifted toward him. He always had an uneasy moment when Nessie looked at him. Her eyes reminded him of the wide unblinking stare of a very young child. A slow gelatinous movement began. A flipper covered with long, thin, hairlike setae found the concrete side of the pool and quested over it. She pulled herself up until her body hovered near the top. Her body was fleshy and pink and had rudimentary breasts.

Konrad reached to touch one of the white, wrinkled flippers. Her skin felt wet and cold. Her tail flailed weakly.

"It's all right," Konrad said. "He did it for your own good." He hoped the sound of his voice was consoling.

The flipper returned to touch his hand, to slide over the back of it. Nessie's touch had a dreamy lightness.

He said, "I'm your only friend. I know how you feel."

Nessie's face, narrow and defined as the head of a seahorse, actually seemed to be listening. Her mouth made sucking noises—almost like speech.

He kept his tone reassuring. "Now you must rest, Nessie."

Nessie's head dropped. The flipper retreated over the concrete side of the pool. She moved slowly down the inside wall, making hollow sucking sounds, until she sank to the pool bottom.

"It's going to be all right," Konrad said, kneeling at the edge, looking down at her under water. Nessie lifted a face that resembled the cutting edge of an axe.

Konrad said, "It was all the doctor's fault. I don't know why he does these things. I would stop him if I could. I'm your best friend."

Chapter

7

In the morning Rudy showered, shaved and read *The New York Times* with a breakfast of orange juice, an English muffin and black coffee. The *Times* story was two paragraphs. Ramon Delgado was an "alleged suspect," charged with wounding a police officer. Rudy was mentioned as having offered himself in exchange for two women hostages.

Reading the story, Rudy felt the inside of his mouth go dry and cottony again. Never in his life had he known fear like that, nor had he ever been so close to death.

As he reached for the telephone, he muttered, "You're all right now. It's over."

He called the office. Mrs. Sherwin, his secretary, had been reading the *Daily News*. She thought the story about him was very exciting and hoped he wasn't hurt. There was a photograph of him leaving the hospital, with a caption calling him "the heroic doctor." He assured her he wasn't hurt and that he would be in the office.

Minutes later, as he was pouring more black coffee into his cup, the telephone rang. He put the coffeepot down and answered.

The sound of her voice tingled the flesh on the back of his hands.

"Rudy?"

"Yes."

"This is Mary Oliver. Did it all happen last night after you left me? I just read the story in the *Times*. Page thirty-two, bottom right-hand side. It says you risked your life to help the police."

"If I'd been killed, I might have made page one."

"Are you all right?"

"If you'll have dinner with me tonight, I'll fill in all the gory details."

"I can't."

"Has he called?"

"Yes."

He stared at steam rising from his coffee cup. "You're seeing him?"

"No. He has to go back to Washington."

Suddenly he felt warm and inspirited, as if he had just gulped down his coffee instead of looking at it.

"Marvelous. Then how about having dinner with me?"

"In Philadelphia?"

"Anywhere."

He heard the smile in her voice. "Can you come to dinner at my house on Saturday night? Mother will be there."

"What time?"

"About six?"

"Fine. I'll bring champagne."

When he hung up he was so exhilarated that he could not remain still long enough to drink his coffee. He changed into his warmup jacket and trousers. He went downstairs, and Ralph, the elevator man, said, "Hey, Doc, you're a celebrity."

"As long as they don't raise my rent," Rudy told him.

He began jogging eastward at eight miles an hour. In the past two years jogging had become an important part of his routine. Whenever he had time to spare he jogged to work. The activity cleared his mind. He entered Central Park at the 86th Street entrance. As he was moving along the park drive, he thought about the strange events of the previous night. A great deal of obstetrical surgery went on at the Karyll Clinic, fifty to sixty deliveries a day, twenty thousand a year. It wasn't too surprising that there would be an occasional infant mortality. But the Conklin and Delgado infants had both been part of the IVF program at the Karyll Clinic, and Dr. Latolier had been the surgeon in each case. That multiplied the coincidence a thousandfold. Was it possible that something out of the ordinary really was happening in the IVF program at the Karyll Clinic?

"Good morning," he said to Mrs. Sherwin as he entered the office. "Get Dr. Seligson for me in ten minutes, will you? At the Karyll Clinic."

Before she could ask about the previous night's adventure, he went by her into his private office to shower and change.

"You got your name in the papers," Bernie Seligson said over the telephone a few minutes later. "What's the real story, Lesser?"

"It had to do with a woman I referred to your clinic. Her name is Conchita Delgado. Now get this. She was in the IVF program, and her baby died during a Caesarean section performed by Dr. Latolier. Just like the Conklin baby."

"Where did you hear this?"

"From a very reliable source—the father."

"Is this some practical joke, Lesser?"

"Tell me what you know about Dr. Latolier."

"For example?"

"How many babies she delivered died in surgery during the past year?"

"None that I know of."

"I've just given you two—within the past week."

"Why are you so interested?"

"Because what happened to one of those babies damn near cost me my life."

"Careful. Your paranoia is showing. Frankly, Lesser, Dr. Latolier is as good as they come in obstetrical surgery. She delivers all our in vitro pregnancies. Dr. Bradford won't trust any other staff surgeon."

"He may change his mind about that when he sees the mortality rate on some of her recent surgery."

"Don't be a damn fool. If Gaby Latolier couldn't save those two babies, nobody else could have either."

On the four mornings a week that Rudy Gerson worked in the clinic at Park Hill, he considered lunch a luxury. This particular morning he induced labor in two patients and completed three deliveries before he started for the hospital cafeteria. He was called back to treat a young woman who was only in the first stages of labor but screaming so loudly she could be heard on the whole floor. She was a plain young girl, about nineteen, frightened to death by what was happening to her. Another demonstration of Rudy's private theory that more of the pain of childbirth happens in the head than in the pelvis.

He prescribed Demerol and Seconal to keep her mostly under, and told the nurse to give her Scopolamine. Scopolamine was not a narcotic and would do nothing to alleviate the pain, but it was an amnesic drug, and after the baby was born and the Scopolamine wore off, the patient wouldn't remember whether she had any pain or not. She would conclude that she had had a nice uneventful labor and delivery.

A few minutes later he had to write a consultation note on a chart, and then a woman, bleeding heavily, needed an immediate Caesarean. When he had finished with that surgery, the regular lunch hour was over. In the hospital cafeteria, he ordered a tuna fish and mayonnaise on white toast. The sandwich was halfway to his mouth when he heard himself being paged.

"Dr. Gerson," the loudspeaker said. Then again: "Dr. Gerson!"

He had had a tiring day. What did they want of him anyway? He put his sandwich down and went to the nearest telephone, where he was informed that Dr. Beer wanted to see him immediately in the pediatric ward.

When he arrived Michael Beer smiled at him in the way someone smiles in a rough surf when he sees a life belt land nearby. Michael was a short, wide-shouldered man of thirty, with reddish brown hair. He was Rudy's best friend at Park Hill.

Michael told him, "There's a six months pregnant woman in the ward with a weak cervix. And she's going to drop her load any time. How about helping out?"

"I was on my way to lunch. I've been on my way to lunch for several hours."

"This won't take long."

At four o'clock that afternoon, they went down to the hospital cafeteria. Nothing was left but stale Danish pastry and coffee, so that's what they had.

Michael said, "I'm having the first food I've had in ten hours and feeling well pleased with myself. I think we did a neat job."

"That makes me feel better."

"Say, I read about you in the paper. The guy must have been off his rocker."

"He was, a little."

"What was he after you for?"

"I sent his wife to the Karyll Clinic for an IVF. She lost the baby."

Michael picked up the last crumbs of his pastry. "I delivered a baby from the Karyll Clinic's IVF program right here in Park Hill about a year ago. The mother was Polish and couldn't speak a word of English. It was some time before she got an ambulance. Then the ambulance couldn't make it to Karyll Clinic. So they brought her straight here."

Rudy felt an inexplicable chill. "Everything go all right?"

Michael gave a mock shudder. "What an experience. The baby weighed fourteen pounds. Practically tore up the mother's vaginal canal. I did an episiotomy wide enough for a truck."

"Was the baby normal?"

"Not by a damn sight. I never saw anything quite like that little monster."

It was too ridiculous, the long arm of coincidence was being stretched out of joint. Three infants from the IVF program at the Karyll Clinic, and still counting.

"Do you know what happened to it?" he asked in a low voice.

"Sure. A couple of days later it was shipped back to the Karyll Clinic." Michael gave him a puzzled glance.

Conklin. Delgado. And an unknown Polish baby.

Rudy said, "Can you remember the mother's name?"

"Are you kidding? I can't remember the name of the woman whose cervix we just got through tightening up."

A half hour's search in the record room turned up the patient's chart. Michael showed it triumphantly.

"Tolczyk. I told you she was Polish."

At the counter in the record room, Rudy read over the description of the baby Michael Beer had jotted down after the delivery: " 'Rounded shoulders, longer than normal arms, an extremely small pelvis, a head supported by heavy neck muscles . . .' "

"It doesn't sound so bad when you read it," Michael interjected. "But *seeing* it!"

" '. . . a large broad face with prognathous jaw. The supraorbital bones are massive at the brow and slope quickly back to a low hairline . . .' " Rudy looked at Michael Beer. "It was apelike."

"Hair all over its body and most of the face."

"The Apgar scoring is low, but there's no indication of Down's disease. All vital signs were good. Better than good."

"Repulsively healthy."

"Then why did the baby die a couple of days later?"

"Did it?"

"It's right here on the record. It died soon after being returned to the Karyll Clinic."

"Damned if I know why. Unless it was from benign neglect. If you're trying to make a tragedy of it, it's the kind I won't shed tears over. All things considered, that was the best thing could have happened. Anyhow, I'm tired. I'm going home to start catching up on my sleep."

Michael Beer shambled out—wrinkled white coat, wide shoulders, short legs, back bent a little with weariness.

Rudy sat alone at the cafeteria table, stunned. He heard the talk around him from a greater and greater distance. Why was all this happening, all at once, and to him?

On the desk in the consulting room of his office, Rudy had a small glass ball with a tiny replica of a farmhouse and a barn, and the rear end of a cow protruding from the barn. A patient had given it to him. If he shook the ball, as he did now with one hand, a miniature snowstorm was created. Thousands of white flakes were stirred up and swirled around the house and barn, the cow disappeared into the barn, and the door shut. He liked to watch the activity in the glass ball while thinking—the action seemed to duplicate the swirl of thought in his own mind.

It was eight o'clock in the morning, and his first patient wasn't due for half an hour. At the moment he was thinking about test tube babies and the women willing to try a radically new method of conception.

Women for whom a surgical solution was not possible, increasingly despondent about their inability to have a baby. Emily Conklin had told him on her first visit that she couldn't watch television shows or movies if there were children in them. She had tried home remedies, then visited a family doctor who advised her husband not to take hot baths at bedtime because that might interfere with sperm production, and advised Emily to take her temperature every morning with a special thermometer that registered between 97 and 100 degrees. She had to keep her temperature on a daily chart to time her ovulation—as if a woman with a blocked oviduct could become pregnant by taking her temperature. When Emily finally came to Rudy in desperation, he had told her medical science knew of no way to rebuild an oviduct and the only way she could have a baby was by fertilizing outside her womb.

Snowflakes whirled. Some people thought that having a test tube baby was either a stunt or the perversion of a sacred act. A number of eggs were fertilized outside the womb but only one was reinserted into the womb, and to some people that was like aborting the other fertilized eggs. If those eggs had found a receptive womb too, they would have become human babies.

That raised a jumble of questions. No need for all those potential embryos and babies to depend for their lives on only one woman's womb. And why should research stop with a husband and wife? Very few people seriously objected anymore to the idea of artificial insemination by a male donor. That was practiced regularly. What is the compelling argument then against surrogate wombs? And why stop at surrogate wombs for women who can't conceive? Why not let any woman who does not want to undergo nine months of travail have a surrogate womb to nurture her fertilized egg? The next thing will be ovums on the auction block.

Scientists become so intent on achieving a break-through in their research that they can lose sight of the consequences. We might discover in time that this kind of fertilization results in an unusual number of human monstrosities. Bradford told him that the embryos cultured in the laboratory had not developed into deformed offspring more often than in any other means of reproduction. But this method of fertilization was just beginning, and how could anyone be sure?

Three infant mortalities. The Conklin and Delgado infants within the past week. A third, Tolczyk, about a year ago. Three deaths within a year. Considering how few in vitro births were recorded, this was well beyond normal parameters. And suppose there were more than three? That would present an even more dangerous statistic.

Two of the infants had suffered from strange abnormalities. Gargoylism was the Conklin baby's problem. The Tolczyk baby was like a little ape or Neanderthal. And Delgado? No mention of abnormality, but a suspicious autopsy had been performed, possibly without the parents' permission.

He watched the snowflakes settle. Plain lies, damned lies, and statistics. In every generation there is a certain number of mutations, called the genetic load. Twenty-five years ago in industrial countries this amounted to four percent of the population. Now the load had reached almost twelve percent, due to the increase of mutation-causing substances in the environment. Every year more damage was being done to the biological basis of man's existence.

The possibility could not be excluded that an unusual number of abnormalities and mortalities in the IVF program was simply a prediction of what was to come in ordinary human reproduction. A frightening thought.

Why hadn't an alarm been sounded? He could think of several possible answers. The doctors at Karyll Clinic might consider it a simple bulge in a graph that would flatten out in time. Or they might stubbornly be continuing to experiment with in vitro technique simply for the sake of experiment—a situation not unknown in medical history. The temptation was so great. Scientists like to play God, to hear their own voices out of a burning bush. If one sets out to perfect an entirely new way of conceiving human beings, where does one stop? A scientist raised to the level of a divinity feels he can create a new world in any image desired. Human error becomes magnified to a cosmic dimension, to the final unimaginable pairing of a supergalactic ovum with the Milky Way.

No reason to delve into fantasy when there were more practical explanations. To protect the Karyll Clinic's reputation. To gain time to find out what was going wrong in order to avert a scandal that might put an end to the in vitro fertilization program. Every hospital in the country was besieged by women who wanted to have babies on the program. Over one million American women had the kind of infertility that the IVF procedure could help. The cost of each treatment, with delivery and aftercare, was over two thousand dollars. That multiplied to a potential market of at least two billion dollars. If word leaked out that the rate of mortality and abnormality was too high among the IVF babies, the market could vanish overnight.

Rudy shook his head impatiently. Money might be a sufficient motive for many doctors, but he could not imagine Peter Bradford doing anything for venal purposes. The pursuit of knowledge was his passion, not the pursuit of riches.

The last flakes settled in the glass ball. The barn door slid open and the cow's rear end protruded. Rudy reached for his private telephone and began to dial Mary Oliver's number.

He stopped dialing as Mrs. Sherwin opened the door to his office. "There's a Dr. Seligson to see you," she said. "He has to talk to you right away."

Chapter

8

A different Bernie Seligson came through the door. There was the same half-mocking grin twisting his lips behind the beard, there was the familiar half-slouch with his hands in the pockets of a corduroy jacket that he wore over faded jeans. But Rudy sensed a clear difference in his attitude.

Bernie slumped into a chair opposite Rudy's desk. "I didn't make an appointment because I knew you wouldn't believe it."

"What?"

"I am here by way of making an apology." He put one leg up casually over the leg of his chair and became the perfect picture of someone trying to be at ease. "Pretty incredible, right? Mister Know-It-All eating crow."

"I'll try not to enjoy it too much. What's on your mind?"

"I'd like to check out a few items with you first. Take a look at this."

Rudy glanced at a folded paper that Bernie handed him. It was a duplicate death certificate for Baby Girl Conklin.

"Xeroxed it myself," Bernie said. "Read it."

Rudy skipped over routine questions about the deceased, with the overtones of tragic irony. (*Citizen of what country? Married; Never Married; Widowed or Divorced? Usual Occupation?*) In Part One, the cause of death was listed as Respiratory Failure. The question of *Due To, Or As a Consequence Of* was answered by: Fetal Accident; Umbilical Cord Strangulation.

The certification was signed by Gaby Latolier, M.D., and there was an additional certification from the Medical Examiner. Attached to the death certificate was a copy of the autopsy report. He glanced over the Clinical Resume and the Gross Autopsy Description, External Examination. Neither there nor on the succeeding pages that described the Internal Examination was there anything inconsistent with the explanation of what caused the death of Baby Girl Conklin.

"Where did you finally locate it?"

"The one place records are kept that hardly anyone thinks of checking. The OR roster."

Every operating room in the country had such a record. The chief nurse kept a daily schedule of the surgery to be performed, entering it on a large desk calendar and transferring each page to a logbook when complete. That record was on file in the operating supervisor's office in the surgery department.

"What do you make of it?"

"Somebody's gone to trouble to have Conklin's name removed from the usual records."

"How about Delgado?"

"No problem there. Found it first place I looked—in the computer files. She checked out of the hospital today. That's the second document. Read it."

Bernie was coiled in the chair, watching Rudy as he

studied the death certificate and autopsy report on Baby Boy Delgado.

Rudy's voice sounded a bit high in his own ears. "It's very interesting. Almost a duplicate of the report on Baby Girl Conklin."

"Two in vitro pregnancies, both with the same cause of death, within a few days. And with the same surgeon."

Rudy leaned back in his swivel chair. "I can give you one more. Tolczyk, Karin."

"Jee-sus!"

"She was an IVF patient at Karyll Clinic about a year ago. Her baby was delivered at Park Hill because the ambulance didn't have time to get her to the Karyll Clinic. The doctor who delivered the baby described it as practically simian in appearance."

"Did it live?"

"Karin Tolczyk and her baby went back to Karyll Clinic for treatment. The baby died there."

Bernie observed glumly, "We've got the best hospital in the country. But all it takes is something like this to wreck everything. Peter Bradford will have to be told."

"Not right away."

Bernie looked at him suspiciously. "You don't think Bradford's involved?"

"No, I don't. But it's still possible that we're dealing with a coincidence. We don't know whether the Delgado baby was abnormal—just that it died. And while we know the Tolczyk baby was abnormal, we don't know *how* it died. We need more proof."

"I can find out about Tolczyk."

"And check out Delgado's signature on the hospital admission form, or a Blue Cross application. It must be in the records. We'll check it against the signature on the autopsy report."

"Good idea." Bernie unscrambled himself from the chair. "I'll report to you."

Twenty seconds after Bernie left his office, it struck Rudy that Bernie had not called him by the familiar name. Not Lesser. Not once.

At thirty-four, Bernie Seligson considered himself at the threshold of a brilliant career. He had wanted to be a doctor since, as a boy of eight, he had visited his dying grandfather in a hospital and was impressed with the respect everyone had for doctors. On the way to his chosen vocation, he became intolerant of anyone who did not put study and achievement at the top of his list of priorities. He had a mild contempt for those who cultivated friendships, pursued women, attended movies or read anything not directly connected to becoming a man of medicine.

What he particularly resented was a doctor like Rudy Gerson, who had somehow survived the rigors of medical school without imposing on himself the harsh discipline needed to achieve excellence. That was why Bernie never missed an opportunity to snipe at him—and why he had tagged him as Gerson the Lesser.

The next afternoon at Karyll Clinic, he began his investigation. The admission records had a copy of Ramon Delgado's signature. It appeared to be the same kind of unsteady scrawl appended to the autopsy report. Bernie was no handwriting expert and had no way of telling if the signature was a forgery.

He turned his attention to the Karin Tolcyzk case. In the large computer room with its ceiling-high gray filing cabinets and its long counter along the left, he filled out a request for the Tolczyk medical chart, adding his name and the name of the department to be billed for computer time.

Tolczyk was not listed.

"There has to be a mistake," he told the woman at the desk. "She had a baby at Park Hill Hospital and was transferred here. Maybe that put her in a different category of patient."

"We don't file by category. If a Karin Tolczyk was here, she'd be on our computer."

"Maybe you got the spelling wrong."

"This is the way you spelled it."

"I could have made a mistake."

"I can ask for alternate spellings."

They tried every possible variation.

"Would you like to speak to someone in the administrator's office?" the woman at the desk asked.

"No. Never mind."

By then, Bernie had a strong feeling of *déjà vu*. At the deputy administrator's office, he looked through microfilm copies of the Mortality and Morbidity Review. The death of the Tolcyzk baby had not been reported for review by the staff members. That left only the operating supervisor's office, where he had found Emily Conklin's name in the roster, but there would be no mention of Karin Tolcyzk because the baby had been delivered at Park Hill Hospital. Nevertheless, he went through the OR roster carefully, beginning fourteen months ago and working up to as late as ten months ago. No Tolczyk. During his search, he was struck by a pattern of improbabilities. When he finished copying down the names in alphabetical order, he studied them.

Clark, Deborah and William.

Goodman, Beverly and Frank.

Martino, Teresa and Anthony.

Wilder, Barbara and Max.

These four parents had lost their babies during the period he checked. A period of four months. Add to these the death of Baby Tolczyk. Five deaths. This couldn't be a statistical aberration.

He returned to the computer room and asked for charts on the new names. The only medical chart returned to him was for Wilder, Barbara and Max.

"No record for the others you gave me," the clerk told him.

"Could there be a mistake?"

The clerk gave him a pitying look. "Of course not."

The Wilders' baby girl had died of cardiovascular disease shortly after birth. Gaby Latolier was not the obstetrical surgeon, nor was Roy Harrison the anesthesiologist, and the Wilders' baby had not been conceived on the IVF program. He crossed that name off his list. It was probably a legitimate, unavoidable infant fatality. Perhaps the only one.

Where were the missing charts for the other four patients? They had to be kept somewhere in the hospital.

Somewhere was probably Dr. Gaby Latolier's office.

At five o'clock, when he knew that Dr. Latolier was making her final rounds, he stopped by her office. A thin-faced secretary with wide-rimmed glasses was typing in the anteroom.

The secretary looked up while her fingers kept typing.

"What can I do for you?"

"Is Dr. Latolier in?"

"I don't expect her back for at least an hour."

"Perhaps you can help me."

She stopped typing, pulled the completed page out of her machine and swung around in her typist's chair to face him.

"Glad to, if I can."

"Dr. Latolier has some charts that aren't on file in the computer room."

"You mean IVF patients?"

"Yes, those are the ones. I'm Dr. Seligson. I'd like to have a look at them."

"You can't. She keeps them under lock and key in her office."

"I just need a quick look. We're compiling statistics for a comparison with the IVF program at other hospitals."

"I wish I could help you. But I have strict orders." Her hand rested protectively on the left side of her desk. "I can have her paged for you. She'll have to give permission."

"It isn't that important. I'll ask her later."

He could not imagine getting Dr. Latolier's cooperation. Obviously, she was trying to keep the records of certain IVF patients out of the usual channels of information. That was a strange procedure. He intended to find out what was in those secret files.

He went down to his car in the parking lot, and from the tool kit in the trunk chose a heavy duty screwdriver. Nonmedical personnel always left promptly at five-thirty. He returned to wait in the corridor until he saw the secretary leave Dr. Latolier's office. She was wearing her coat.

As soon as she got into the elevator, he went to try the door to Dr. Latolier's office. It was locked. He slipped a plastic credit card into the crack of the door and used it to push back the lock. Then he turned the knob and the door opened.

The secretary's desk was neatly cleared, the typewriter covered. The center drawer of the desk opened easily. Nothing there interested him. Other desk drawers also opened easily. Only the top left-hand drawer was locked. That was where her hand had rested in an instinctive protective gesture. He needed less than a minute with the screwdriver to force the lock and open the drawer. Inside he saw a functional clutter: typewriter ribbons, paper clips, rubber bands, a roll of postage stamps, a Scotch tape dispenser. And a circlet of keys. The second key on the ring opened the door to the inner office. A tall gray steel filing cabinet was in the corner. The smallest key fit a lock that opened all four drawers.

In the top drawer, in a section marked IVF, he found a folder with a master list of forty-four patient's names, with dates of arrival, insemination, departure, return to the hospital, delivery, and a final notation: either *Normal, No Complications,* or a cryptic *Special Reference.*

He went directly to the *Special Reference* folder and found the charts. They were in alphabetical order. The entries followed the usual format for a patient's chart. There were separate pages for background data, diagnosis, the admission form containing the first interview, and the Physical Examination Form. The Continuation Record was a log of the patient's condition at each examination up to and including delivery. Attached to these was a medical history, a Doctor's Order Sheet that listed drugs prescribed, a Medication Record with the daily dosages. There followed a Pathology and X-ray Report, a Record of Vital Signs that recorded the patient's blood pressure, pulse and respiration, a graph of the temperature, and Nurse's Notes indicating the behavior of the patient as observed by the nurses in attendance. There was also a clothing and personal property record, and a Voluntary Request For Surgery Form that had to be signed to authorize a Caesarean delivery.

Under the final heading, *Disposition of the Case,* the real meaning of the *Special Reference* file became apparent. All of these infants had died.

He busied himself copying out salient facts from the patients' charts. There were seven charts in all. He began with Tolczyk because Rudy had asked him to look into that case. Then he moved to the top of the list and began to copy data from the chart of a patient named Deborah Clark. Preoccupied with his task, he did not notice that he was no longer alone.

"What do you think you're doing, Dr. Seligson?" asked Gaby Latolier.

Bernie looked up and blinked. A thrilling sensation vibrated in his chest, as if a great ponderous bell had been struck.

Gaby Latolier stared at him in silence.

"I've been going through your files," he answered, standing up. He folded the notes he had been writing and put them into his pocket. Then he closed the open folder on the desk.

Dr. Latolier pointed to the top drawer of the filing cabinet, open, its handle bent outward from the pressure exerted on it. "If you can't give me a satisfactory explanation, I'm going to call the police."

Bernie said, "I was gathering information that isn't available anywhere else in the hospital."

"I *am* going to call the police." She moved toward her desk.

Bernie said quietly, "They may have more questions to ask you than I."

She put her hand on the telephone. "I can't imagine what you mean."

"I don't blame you for hiding these medical charts. There has been an unusual number of bad results among the babies born in the IVF program. And you've been covering it up."

He watched her hand move slowly away from the telephone.

She regarded him gravely. "Have you thought about what would happen if the news did get out?"

Until that moment, he had hoped that she would supply some other convincing explanation. Now he thought: *My God, it's true.*

She appeared to hunch her shoulders a little higher. "Think it through, Doctor. What will happen if this leaks out? The government will probably ban all further in vitro fertilization. We're engaged in a long-term systematic research project. For the first time in history we are studying the actual beginnings of life. We can't let all our work go down the drain at the first setback."

"What about the hospitals all over the world with IVF programs? They have to know about this."

"Dr. Bradford has been keeping them informed."

"Bradford knows about this?" He found that almost as shocking as the evidence of the cover-up itself.

Gaby Latolier nodded. "We're relying on him to find out what's gone wrong. He's close to a solution. It may have to do with overcoming the hormone imbalance in the women's bodies at the time of implantation."

"How?" Bernie couldn't help being caught up in the problem.

"Dr. Bradford thinks that by omitting all hormone treatments and just watching for a hormonal signal from the patient that an egg is about to be released, we can avoid the imbalance."

He could be right, Bernie thought. The signal would come from the special tissue that forms when an egg is ejected from its sac in the ovary—the corpus luteum that manufactures the hormones essential to a successful pregnancy. By waiting a short time—thirty hours—to harvest the egg, they might avoid the hormonal imbalance.

Another thought occurred to him.

"What happens meanwhile? You're taking a chance every time you fertilize another woman."

"We're all taking a risk. Everyone connected with this may have his or her career ruined. And the Karyll Clinic—you know how important it is to Dr. Bradford. This place isn't a part of his life. It *is* his life. You might also consider what it will mean if the IVF program around the world is set back, suspended or ended forever."

"Perhaps it should be—if these are the results you've been getting."

"Dr. Bradford doesn't think so. He's certain that all we need is a little more time. We can't afford to have a scandal break now."

"Suppose he's wrong—and he doesn't have the answer. How can you justify what may happen to the babies that are being born?"

"There's nothing we can do to stop them from being born. But there haven't been any further in vitro fertilizations. And there won't be until we know it's safe. Perhaps we came to the wrong decision in keeping this a secret—but we did it for what seemed to us the right reasons. Is it too much to ask that you help us keep the secret a little while longer?"

"I don't know."

"At least promise to do nothing until you can talk to Dr. Bradford."

He wanted very much to talk to Dr. Bradford. There were many questions he would like to ask, and only Bradford knew the answers.

"I can promise that," he said.

From Dr. Latolier's office, he went directly to his own room in the wing of the hospital reserved for staff members. The room was small, painted white and equipped with metal furniture. A narrow bed was set against one wall beneath a projection that gave it the appearance of a recessed Pullman berth. The wall projection was a closet. There was a steel desk and a chair, and a compact bathroom.

As Bernie took off his jacket he saw in an inside pocket the notes he had copied from Karin Tolczyk's and Deborah Clark's medical charts. Somehow the plain documentation made his conversation with Gaby Latolier seem a bit unreal. True, the consequences of exposure could be terrible for Bradford and Latolier and the Karyll Clinic—even for the future of IVF research. But when a large scale medical experiment goes wrong, the potential for harm is nearly unlimited. He had no right to keep what he knew to himself, not even until he spoke to Bradford. At the very least he owed it to Rudy Gerson to let him know.

In the hallway he found a telephone. He dialed 9, waited, and dialed Rudy's number. The telephone rang twice before Rudy's voice cut in. It was a taped message saying he was not at home, but if, at the signal, the caller would leave his name and number, he would call back. He didn't want Rudy to call back tonight. It would be easier to place another call to him in the morning. Then together they would decide on the best course of action. He needed to consult with someone who could help him define his own feelings before he spoke to Bradford.

He took the notes and put them in an envelope, wrote Rudy's name and address on it, sealed it, and affixed a stamp. There was just time to put the letter in the express mail pouch that left the Karyll Clinic every evening.

He went back to his room. It was early evening, but he had been a day and a night without sleep. He was exhausted. He lay down on the narrow bed without undressing and closed his eyes.

Chapter

9

Peter Bradford's mood was growing more dispirited as the long evening ebbed away. He had been all day with his mother in her room, trying to come to terms with the fact that she was going to die. It was foolish to hope. Aleukemic leukemia had progressed beyond any medical remedy. The end was only a day or two away, perhaps only hours.

She was more resigned than he was. Only today while they were talking about his work—he confided everything to her—she suddenly interrupted:

"You've mentioned Gaby Latolier's name often. Apparently you depend on her a great deal."

"Yes, I do."

"How old is she?"

"About thirty-five."

"Attractive?"

He smiled. "Look here, Mother, I hope you're not thinking along those lines."

He had tried marriage once, and that was enough. Captivated by her grace and beauty, he had fallen in love with a young woman from the rarefied echelons of South Carolina society. When she left him she declared, "I refuse to be your second-best love; or even your third," referring first to his work and then to his mother. Their marriage had been a brief, unhappy interlude.

"Your first wife never understood you," Mother said. "Gaby Latolier might be more suitable. How does she feel about you?"

He was aware of Gaby's feelings. "I think she would welcome a closer relationship."

"Then don't wait. Very soon now you will need someone to take my place."

He wondered what she would say if she knew Gaby's background. His mother was a genteel snob who, above all, abidingly disliked what she considered to be "common."

"I'm not sure I can make her happy," he said.

"What has that to do with it?" she replied with asperity.

To her, personal happiness was irrelevant. She had no patience with the concept that life was designed for the gratification of desires. Excellence was the only possible goal.

The nurse came to the door. "Telephone," she said in a hushed murmur. He had not heard it because all the telephones were muted in order not to disturb Mother. The nurse took his place at the bedside. He went to the nearest telephone, in his adjoining bedroom.

"Peter?" Gaby said. "Something has happened here at the clinic that I thought you should know about."

She told him about Dr. Seligson finding the IVF files in her office. Consternation rippled over the surface of his mind. He reminded himself sternly that the application of intelligence to a problem, no matter how insurmountable, could reduce it to sensible proportions.

"We have to discuss this," he told Gaby. "I'll return at once."

"Your mother?"

"I'll explain to her."

He returned to her bedroom. His mother had fallen asleep. He signaled the nurse to leave. He wanted to be alone to say what might be his final goodbye.

He stood for a moment looking down at his mother, wondering how to explain without revealing too much. She was unbelievably frail. He could almost trace the faint pulsation of blood through the thin shrunken veins. He decided it would be easier to leave her undisturbed. There was no necessity for last words between two people who shared the same vision, the same hope, the same commitment. This was one of the very rare moments in which he was aware of feeling a truly profound emotion. He might never look at her living face again.

The nurse was waiting outside the door.

He said, "When my mother wakes up, tell her I had to return to the clinic. Explain that it's terribly important. I'll call tomorrow and tell her all about it."

If she has a tomorrow.

He drove back to the Karyll Clinic that night. He hoped that the drive would help him clear his mind to deal with the problem waiting for him. But his thoughts stubbornly remained with his dying mother, the only person with whom he had shared an unreserved, unquestioning intimacy. During the inevitable times of doubt, of faltering, when he had needed the compass of another mind, she had been his surest guide. How could he possibly replace her?

He remembered standing beside her, as a small boy, at the gravesite where his father had just been buried. She had said merely, "He meant well. He was a nice person." Her husband had never been of the first importance in her life. All her hopes were in her son. She bred him to be an overachiever, whose sole need was to know; always to know. She taught him to sacrifice the common experience of living, the minor pleasures and temptations, in order to achieve greatly. It seemed to her—and later, to him—a small price to pay.

Now what Gaby Latolier had told him over the telephone added a new and frightening dimension of danger to what he had achieved. Five years ago he had been having serious problems with the Ethics Advisory Board set up by Congress to oversee research in reproductive genetics. The Board had enforced federal regulations barring further work on test tube fertilization pending a decision on the ethical questions involved.

He went to Washington to appeal that decision. He warned the Board members that their shortsighted policy would give away this country's lead in laboratory fertilization and artificial implantation of human embryos. In a year, at most two, he promised them the first great breakthrough in this field. If their foolish edict prevented that from happening, it would simply happen somewhere else.

The Board turned him down. In their view, no achievement, no matter how miraculous, could erase the unethical character of such experiments. It was not possible, they said, to view nascent life as a mere "product." With continuing research there would have to be failures, near-misses, discards. Each of these might involve fertilized eggs that could mature into healthy fetuses.

Against such specious argument he was powerless. When he openly disobeyed their order and went on with his research, the Board used its authority and cut off all federal financing. He couldn't pay those working with him, so one by one they had to abandon him to make their living. Soon there was no money even for equipment. Private funds had dried up. He spent all his own money, and Mother heavily mortgaged the house to raise more. But at last every possible resource in friends and credit was exhausted, and he stood face to face with ruin.

Then he received the invitation.

He would never forget the vellum envelope with an unembellished card within on which was written in a spidery thin hand, *Dr. Bradford, I would very much like to discuss something important with you at dinner on Thursday of this week. My chauffeur will pick you up promptly at seven o'clock.*

The note was signed: *Hector Karyll.*

At the designated hour a Rolls-Royce limousine was waiting outside Bradford's East Side apartment house. A chauffeur, immaculately attired in uniform, boots and visored cap, held the limousine door open for him, then took his seat behind the wheel. A pane of opaque glass discouraged communication. Forty-five minutes later the limousine rode through an iron gate onto the grounds of a magnificent twelve-acre estate in Westchester. The mansion was a Gothic splendor, with turrets, small secluded balconies, iron-barred stained-glass windows on the ground floor. A butler greeted

Bradford at the entrance and indicated that Hector Karyll would receive him in the library.

The man seated in a chair by a large fireplace wore a silk shirt open at the throat and a pair of maroon velvet trousers. He was small and slender, with sparse gray hair combed back from a wide forehead. He had a finely boned face with taut skin stretched over it that resembled a death mask.

He did not rise as Bradford entered the library, but removed the stopper from a decanter of Baccarat crystal.

"I've been looking forward to meeting you, Doctor," he said in a soft, husky whisper. "Will you share a brandy?"

As he sipped his brandy, Bradford's gaze strayed to the table before him where a large folder lay, embossed with the initials HK. Hector Karyll did not refer to it.

"The science of genetics has always been my secret passion," he remarked. "Now that I am nearing the end of my life I realize that only genetics can provide a fundamental solution to the world's problems. Political remedies are only temporary palliatives."

"Politicians can make a lot of trouble for scientists," Bradford said with a rueful smile.

Karyll's small, well shaped head nodded in agreement. "Particularly in a system like ours, where the voice of the people is always heard. Political leaders must sell their souls to the mob. And the mob perpetuates the monstrous lie that all men are born equal, that man is only what his environment and upbringing make him."

"That view is biologically mistaken," Bradford said. "It ignores the crucial element of heredity."

"Precisely. It's possible to improve the genetic makeup of humankind. But that requires procedures not politically acceptable within the framework of a mobocracy. Instead, our medical scientists devote their energy to improving public health services that only lead to a deterioration in our genetic makeup. I believe you wrote a paper on this very subject."

"Not too many people have read it."

Some years earlier, when he was only a brash junior associate of Charles Gerson, he had published an article in which he argued that the preservation of relatively unfit genotypes increased their representation in the general population. He pointed out the danger of attempting to restore a specific type of diseased patient, a diabetic for example, to a condition approaching normal health. Whatever elements of the diabetic's genetic makeup may have contributed to the disease were therefore disseminated more widely in succeeding generations. The entire apparatus of modern therapeutics was increasing the future number of debilitating hereditary diseases in the population.

"I've gone to pains to find out all I can about you, Doctor. In my opinion, that thesis represented the place at which you began to follow a road that diverged from Charles Gerson. His work was directed toward improving medical procedures, without regard to the wider question of human genetics. You saw much more clearly what had to be done. I asked you to come here tonight because I've come to the conclusion that you're the man I've been looking for. I want to make a proposition to you."

The proposition was breathtaking. Karyll would undertake to build a mammoth hospital and research facility devoted to every aspect of reproductive biology. Peter Bradford would be in complete charge. And he would continue his experiments without fear of government interference.

Karyll said, "You will no longer be hobbled by all the senseless rules and regulations that govern other scientists, because there will be no government financing. All the money you need will be made available."

"I-I don't know what to say."

"Then you accept?"

He nodded. "I have only one suggestion. The hospital should be named after its founder."

Hector Karyll cackled with delight.

Later that evening, as Bradford was leaving the mansion, he delayed for a moment in the doorway.

"There are many exciting discoveries to be made, a limitless horizon before us," he told Hector Karyll. "For all we know, tonight may have altered the future course of human existence."

Karyll smiled. "I admire arrogance. It's a quality essential to success. Pride may be the sin by which the angels fell—but it's the virtue by which men rise."

"I'll try to remember that."

"I'll make the final arrangements tonight—including a bequest in my will to assure that after I'm gone the clinic will be supported as it should be."

A year before the clinic opened on the grounds of the Westchester estate, Hector Karyll was dead. In a last letter to Peter Bradford he expressed his regret that he would not be around to witness all the wonderful discoveries in genetics that would be made. But he hoped Bradford would continue with his research "in order to perpetuate the ideas we both believe in."

Now, racing in his car toward the Karyll Clinic and a fateful meeting with Gaby Latolier, the memory of that past event somewhat obscured Peter Bradford's attention to the present. He was gazing through half-closed eyes at a narrow roadway leading him across a bridge when headlights suddenly leapt at him.

He had veered partly across the dividing line. Swiftly he turned the wheel to the right. At the same time he hit his brakes and the rear of his car skidded. Tires squealed. The bridge railing became abruptly clear in his headlights. The skid seemed to go on and on, an impossibly slowed-down movement. Bradford held his breath, waiting for the terrible impact when the car would be precipitated through the railing into the river.

Then his headlights swung back to the road. In his rearview mirror he glimpsed the red taillights of the other car dwindling in the opposite direction.

He had been spared.

The night was full of stars, luxurious gleams on black velvet, subtle radiances from distant suns. He should have known that nothing could happen to someone who was about to change the future course of man's existence.

Gaby Latolier was standing near the window of his office looking out over the parklike estate below.

"It's a very awkward time for this to happen," she said. "I never should have kept those records in my office."

"What do you think he will do?"

"He doesn't understand all the implications. How could he? But he is aware that something is wrong. I'm sure he'll demand a complete investigation of the IVF program."

Bradford doodled with a pencil. "I could point out to him the importance of what we're doing, the damage that would be done by premature disclosure."

"I don't think that would change his mind."

"No, I guess not." Bernie Seligson was one of the new breed who would not rest until they proved that the perfect pesticide is a carcinogen, the marvelous new detergent isn't biodegradable, the new miracle chemical that preserves food also pollutes water. And the IVF program at the world famous Karyll Clinic is killing babies.

Gaby said, "We can't allow a threat to your work to continue."

These were not the kind of problems he had trained himself to deal with. Looking back now, he saw that the first mistake had been to let the Pollards take their infant home. He had been sure the mother would let the baby remain at the hospital for observation and testing. The unfortunate publicity that surrounded the baby's accidental death had taught him to be cautious.

On the whole, luck had certainly not been with them. The Tolczyk baby was delivered in a different hospital, the Clark baby in a remote Ozark town by a midwife. They had learned from those misadventures. Now questionnaires were given to couples before an in vitro pregnancy that tried to anticipate such problems. Only those with stable living styles were accepted, and only the most promising of these were chosen for the select list. The clinic's ambulance service was carefully instructed in procedures, and an intern from the clinic rode with any ambulance answering a call from an IVF patient. Telephone calls from any names on the select list were put through instantly to Gaby Latolier or him.

But there was still no way to guard against the unforeseeable—Delgado going berserk, for example. More publicity, more questions, a widening circle of people were becoming involved. And now a new danger had surfaced on the medical staff of the clinic.

He was being forced to venture into riskier areas simply to proceed with his work. Would the dangers keep mounting until there was no way to protect his achievement? He was gripped with an anxiety that made breathing difficult.

What he was about to sanction was incredible. He comforted himself that he would never do it for his own benefit, nor in his own defense. Hard experience had formed him into a rock—unshakable.

He closed his hand, as if crumpling a sheet of paper. "Do what has to be done."

Gaby nodded. "I'll talk to Delaney."

After she had gone Bradford stood in his office, looking at his reflection in the window, pale and drained beneath the lights, a bit faded-looking, like someone in an old photograph. Suddenly he was reminded of Dorian Gray looking at his unchanging reflection in a mirror, aware that his portrait hidden in a closet had just added another wrinkle of malevolence, a small evil flicker in the eyes.

Chapter

10

Rudy had dinner with Mary Oliver and her mother in Philadelphia. He brought two bottles of Moët et Chandon clinking against each other in a paper bag.

Mrs. Oliver was a formidable woman with a formidable set of opinions. He sat in the living room and sipped champagne, listening to Mrs. Oliver and nodding agreement occasionally. When you are courting the girl of your dreams you also have to court her mother. The next time he came to Philadelphia, he suggested, he would take them both to the restaurant of their choice, then to a play that was having a preBroadway tryout. That pleased Mrs. Oliver. He discovered that she did not approve of Sam Dodds, and that endeared her to him.

Mary wore a flowered caftan that did interesting things for her slender figure. Whenever he looked at her his heart began to speed up and deliver more oxygen to a brain that seemed to him to consist of only a few molecules of thought floating in a jar of eroticism.

He tried to concentrate on amusing Mrs. Oliver. He

told her about a pregnant woman's husband who had warned him that he did not want a girl baby.

"What did you tell him?" Mrs. Oliver asked, unsmiling.

"That his wife didn't have much to do with it, that it's entirely up to the father to determine the sex."

"Oh, I don't believe that," Mrs. Oliver said. "Everything isn't so cut and dried."

Rudy considered trying to explain about chromosomes X and Y, and decided not to.

Mrs. Oliver said, "I don't think we should probe into things better left to nature." Then she cleared her throat, a preliminary to a change of mood. "You were my daughter Emily's obstetrician. There is something I'd like to ask you."

He sensed trouble. "Go right ahead."

"What happened to Emily's baby? I know it was . . . stillborn . . ." Her voice faded a little, as though having trouble getting around an obstruction in her throat. "But that's very unusual in this day and age. There must be *something* doctors could do with all their medical knowledge . . ."

"That isn't always true unfortunately." He explained what had gone wrong with Emily's baby, ending with: "Accidents will happen, Mrs. Oliver. I know it isn't much comfort to say the accidents are getting fewer and fewer."

By then her hand was pressed hard against her cheek. "My children were all delivered by a plain old country doctor who carried everything he needed in a little black bag."

"Mother," Mary remonstrated.

Mrs. Oliver took out a handkerchief and blew her nose.

Rudy said, "You know what they say about obstetricians, Mrs. Oliver. They may not do much good, but they can't do much harm."

Mary looked at him gratefully.

A bit tremulously, Mrs. Oliver said, "Well, it's God's will. What can't be mended must be endured."

A few minutes later, quite recovered, she was telling Rudy how her father, Mary's grandfather, had helped to build the house so her mother could move in on their wedding day. In turn, Rudy told about his father. "I was supposed to follow in his footsteps. Instead, I've lived in his shadow. I never developed the right sort of obsession."

On the way into the dining room, Mrs. Oliver sailed ahead of them like a stately flagship.

Mary whispered, "If I'd had a strong domineering father like yours, I'd have grown up a dependent little thing, always trying to please, unable to make my own decisions. If you'd had a strong domineering mother like mine, you'd probably have been bisexual."

"I think we're both lucky," Rudy said. "Freud's in his heaven, and all's right with the world."

After dinner Mrs. Oliver retired to her room. He and Mary did a crossword puzzle, sitting on the sofa, shoulders almost touching. She got the three-word answer to: *Who fought for Emperor Nero?* Lions and Christians.

"How did you know that?" he asked.

"It's the only thing everybody knows about Nero, except for his fiddle."

He said, "I don't believe that story about lions and Christians. If it's true, how come there are so few lions today and so many Christians?"

A moment later she asked for help: "Human birth in eleven letters, starting with a *p*, with a *u* and an *r* in it." He answered, "Parturition." She gave him an approving look.

They finished the puzzle some minutes later. In the lamplight, he saw a smooth tightening of her cheeks.

"What's the matter?"

"Oh, it's Sam. We quarreled because I was seeing you tonight."

"He's rather possessive, isn't he?"

"Quite. In fact, he oinks."

"Oinks?"

"Sam's a bit of a male chauvinist pig. He won't admit it, but it keeps showing through. Basically, he thinks women shouldn't be independent. They should all work as receptionists or waitresses until they get married. And then settle down to be nice obedient housewives."

He grinned at her. "You don't have any right to like him."

"I can't help it."

"Try me. I'll make up a whole list of our areas of compatibility."

"For instance?"

"For instance, I think women have a perfect right to be anything they want to be. Including housewives. And I'm very sexy."

"Hmm."

"Try me."

Her shoulder was touching his, and he put his arm around her. The sensation of holding her was incredibly sweet. She drew away slightly. For a moment his will and his body were at opposites. Then he reached up to touch her hair. He pulled her gently toward him and kissed her. As their mouths met he felt the rapid, fluttered beating of her heart.

Mrs. Oliver called from an upstairs bedroom: "It's nearly ten o'clock. Dr. Gerson will have to leave if he's going to catch his train."

Mary slowly disengaged herself. She looked at him with widening eyes.

"I don't have a train," he said mildly. "Anyhow, there are trains running all night."

"It is getting late. And Mother won't go to sleep until she hears you leave."

"When can I see you again?"

"Call me."

He couldn't let it go at that.

"How about Saturday night? Dinner at Bookbinder's?"

"Sounds lovely."

"Then it's a date."

"Yes." She seemed to be holding herself in check. Now, suddenly, accepting the remarkable thing that occurred in the past few minutes, she smiled. "Sam always took me to health food restaurants. I nearly OD'ed on health foods."

A few minutes later, at the door, they kissed goodbye. And it happened again. The same swift arc of passion.

"I'll get you out of Mother," she whispered.

He didn't understand what she meant until he remembered his invitation at the dinner table while searching for some not-too-unstable foundation on which to build a two-way conversation with Mrs. Oliver.

"I didn't mean . . . Of course she's welcome if . . ."

She touched her forefinger gently to his lips, and said firmly, "Mother won't mind."

*   *   *

On the long train ride back to New York he was foolishly happy, in a state bordering on exultance. Just thinking about Mary started erotic impulses flowing into his nerves and muscles.

When he reached the great old-fashioned stone apartment building that fronted on Riverside Drive it was past midnight. He entered the lobby and went into the small adjoining mailroom. He used his key to open the mailbox. There was the usual formidable amount of advertisements from pharmaceutical houses. Like Bogart with his letters of transit in *Casablanca,* as long as he had an M.D. after his name he would never be lonely. No one is a more faithful correspondent than a pharmaceutical house.

In his apartment, while glancing through the mail, he turned on the message recorder to listen to the telephone calls.

There was his daily message from Mrs. Golden. Despite three normal deliveries of perfectly healthy children and the fact that she was uneventfully six months into her fourth, as Mrs. Golden's pregnancy progressed she developed stranger and stranger symptoms. She suffered from every possible ailment. Any day now he expected her to call up to complain that she had undescended testicles.

He switched off the message recorder in the midst of Mrs. Golden's latest symptom. In his mail he had found an envelope scrawled in a nearly illegible hand. The return address was the Karyll Clinic. Above the printed return address was scrawled *Seligson.*

Rudy opened the envelope.

*   *   *

Early in the morning he called the Karyll Clinic.

"May I speak to Dr. Seligson?" he asked the operator.

"Just a moment, please."

After a minute a man's voice: "May I help you?"

"I'm calling Dr. Seligson."

"Are you a patient?"

"No, I'm not. I'm a friend."

"I'm afraid Dr. Seligson isn't available."

"Is he operating, or what?"

"We can't discuss this over the telephone."

"What are you talking about?"

"It's hospital policy. If you require further information, you'll have to come here in person."

The telephone connection broke off. Rudy stared at the receiver as though it had just done something annoying.

What he had heard over the telephone could scarcely be more alarming, but there had to be a mistake. He ran two blocks to his garage. The drive to the Karyll Clinic in upper Westchester passed in a long blur of apprehension.

He drove through the gate into the visitors' parking lot and ran into the entrance lobby of the hospital. The woman at the desk said Mr. Foster would speak to him in his private office.

The private office was small and so was its occupant—a soft, unctuous little man.

"I believe you are the gentleman who called before. May I ask your name?"

"Gerson. Dr. Gerson. Now what is this about?"

"What is your relationship to . . . uh . . . Dr. Seligson?"

"Look, what's happened? Why all this runaround?"

"It was all so unexpected. Everyone is still very

upset. Dr. Seligson was found dead this morning."

Rudy looked at him, stunned.

"An accident?"

"He died in his bed sometime during the night."

"What of?"

"I really can't discuss that. You might speak to Dr. Hartley."

Dr. Kenneth Hartley was a lean, lanky black man. He had been resting in his room when Rudy entered. Now he sat on the edge of his rumpled bed, a beam light on the wall behind him. His eyes were deeply set and his face haggard.

He ran splayed fingers through bushy hair. "I guess I'm still in shock, Dr. Gerson. Bernie was my best friend here at the hospital. He helped me with a patient just the night before . . . God!" A shudder ran through his body.

"What was the cause of death?"

"Heart failure."

"Heart failure—in a man his age! Who found the body?"

"There was a call for him at seven-twenty and he didn't answer. I went down to shake him up. He didn't answer my knock, so I went in. He was lying in his bed, on his back, his mouth open. Not breathing. Already cold. There was nothing I could do for him. Nothing!" Kenneth Hartley's voice choked. He sat, shaking his head, unable to speak.

"Who certified the cause of death?"

"I did."

"How do you know it was heart failure?"

Hartley replied slowly, "I didn't know what to think until the path lab confirmed the diagnosis."

"Can I see that autopsy report?"

Kenneth Hartley got off the bed. "Sure. You can see his body if you like."

"There wouldn't be any point to that after an autopsy."

"No. I guess there wouldn't." They left the room. "How long did you know Bernie?"

"A long time. We only became friends quite recently."

"He was a great guy. And a really fine physician. I'm going to miss him. Would you like to see his room? It's over there."

The door was closed but unlocked. Hartley opened it. Rudy stood beside him inside sterile enclosing whiteness. The sheet and blanket were turned down on the bed, wrinkled and creased as if Bernie had gotten out of it a few minutes before. The pillow was dented irregularly where Bernie's head had lain. There was no light in the room except for the small desk-lamp that cast a wan illumination and made the walls look almost gray. A small calendar was on the desk, a ball-point pen athwart it.

Hartley was standing with his back to him, looking down at the bed. "He was sleeping here last night," he said in a monotone. "Came in and lay down and drifted off—and never woke up. It's ... so ... damn ... stupid!"

Rudy put his hand lightly on his shoulder. "We can go now."

"His clothes are hanging in the closet. Christ! As a doctor, you see so much death. You see death every day. But when it happens to someone close to you, like this . . ."

Rudy preceded him out of the room. Hartley followed, closing the door softly behind him, as if there might be someone inside whose slumber he did not wish to break.

Chapter

11

At five o'clock that afternoon Rudy left the Karyll Clinic. It had begun to rain. Hartley waited at the canopied emergency entrance at the rear of the central hospital. When Rudy drove up he got in, and moments later they were underway. The tall buildings of the hospital complex receded, losing their color in the gray teeming.

For the first minute or two they said nothing at all. Then Hartley spoke. "You said you wanted to talk to me privately."

Rudy nodded. "Suppose something is wrong with the IVF program at the Karyll Clinic?"

"What do you mean?"

Rudy told him about the Conklin and Delgado infants. "Bernie Seligson was checking on another woman named Tolczyk. And just before he died he sent this to me." He showed Hartley the notes taken from the Tolczyk and Clark medical charts. "Quite a coincidence. What are the odds that a young healthy man should die just when he did—of natural causes?"

"What the odds are don't matter. He's dead. What other explanation is there?"

Rudy considered himself to be a sensible man, attuned to a world of light and reason in which dark events had no place. But he could not believe that Bernie Seligson's death was in any way natural.

"Murder."

He expected Hartley to dismiss that suggestion with a pragmatic chuckle. Instead, Hartley's eyes flicked from the streaming window to his face. "I don't believe you really believe that. It's crazy."

They passed the long concrete slip of a train station and Rudy caught a glimpse of a rainwashed sign: *PORTCHESTER*.

"Does the name Pollard mean anything to you?" he asked suddenly.

"I don't think so."

"There was a story in the newspaper not long ago. A couple whose year-old baby was killed in a fight with a neighbor's watchdog."

"Yes, I do remember now."

"According to the newspaper story, the baby killed the watchdog too. That isn't possible—not by any ordinary standards of what a year-old can do. Unless it was some kind of a . . . freak."

"I don't see what you're driving at."

"The Pollards' baby was born at the Karyll Clinic. Suppose their baby was also conceived on the IVF program. Suppose it became some kind of mutant, possessing far more strength than any normal infant?"

"That's just wild speculation."

"But if I'm right, it would be another important piece of evidence that something is seriously wrong with the IVF program."

"That's a big if."

"As I recall, the Pollards lived in Portchester. That's where we are now."

Puddles leapt up to assault the car. They drove past houses huddling close together against the downpour, like cows in a pasture. Hartley stared ahead through a streaming windshield and busily clicking wipers.

"Why would they talk to us?" he asked. "People who have a tragedy like that can't be anxious to discuss it with strangers."

"I'll think up a reason." Rudy was silent for a minute. Then he said, "I think I may have one."

He explained his idea to Hartley, who listened carefully before he shook his head. "I still think it's crazy."

"But you'll come along?"

"Can you give me one good reason why I should?"

"Because you were a friend of Bernie Seligson."

After a moment Hartley said resignedly, "Okay."

Rudy found an open drugstore. The sky was getting lighter, but rain still drummed on the car roof and windows. He hurried into the drugstore and looked up the Pollards' address in a telephone directory.

The Pollards' house was the kind that anyone would describe as a nice place to bring up children. It was a large modern ranch house with a comfortable enveloping look, a wide lawn and an oversized garage. Rudy drove up a narrow circular drive to the front door.

A young girl about twelve years old answered the doorbell. She was dusky-skinned, slant-eyed, with broad flat cheeks and a wide flaring nose.

"We called a few minutes ago," Rudy said. "Is your mother in?"

"Mom! It's for you."

A moment later a young woman appeared, wiping

her hands on a towel. "I was making biscuits." She glanced at Rudy, then at Ken Hartley. "You said you were doctors. What did you want to see me about?"

Rudy gave her his business card. "We're doing a feature story for the magazine *Medical World News*. The editors think their readers should know about the Karyll Clinic's in vitro fertilization program."

Mrs. Pollard looked doubtful. "In that case, you ought to speak to Dr. Bradford."

"The editors are interested in the human interest angle. They want to hear from parents who actually were enrolled in the in vitro fertilization program." He paused, waiting for some denial.

Mrs. Pollard merely continued to look doubtful. "I'm afraid you can't talk to my husband. He's in bed with the flu."

"What we'd really like to know, Mrs. Pollard, is the whole story from the beginning. Just as it happened."

"I wouldn't know where to begin."

"Anywhere you like."

In the living room there was a fireplace and overstuffed armchairs near the sofa. The chairs and sofa harmonized with flowered draperies that hung on either side of mullioned windows.

Rudy and Hartley sat in the armchairs, facing Mrs. Pollard on the sofa. Rudy could sense emotion flowing from her before she began a long rambling account of how they had moved to this house in Portchester because they had always wanted a large family. After two years they had gone to a doctor and discovered she had an infertility problem. That was the first of many fruitless visits to specialists. She had become miserable and depressed. Finally they decided on adoption.

They adopted a Vietnamese girl who had suffered injuries in a napalm bombing. They paid for corrective surgery, including a good deal of facial remodeling. And they learned to love her. "But we still wanted a baby of our own. I suppose you could say it became an obsession with us. I wanted to experience what it was like to give birth to a child of my own."

Rudy waited patiently, recognizing that she was putting off the more painful part of her story. At last, with a sudden pulse of energy, she began to describe how she and her husband Tom first heard of the Karyll Clinic's "test tube baby program." They were among the earliest to enroll. She told of becoming pregnant, and the timbre of her voice deepened to convey the marvelous excitement of knowing a child was inside her body. For her, pregnancy was moving and beautiful, powerful with meaning. Then the strength drained from her and words came reluctantly as she told of the birth of her baby. She seemed almost to be talking to herself when she said, "Dr. Bradford warned us not to take him home. I had to fight him to get permission, and he said I didn't know what I'd be letting myself in for. And he was right. I wouldn't have believed an infant could do the things he did. He was exceptionally strong. I had to cover his bottle with a washcloth because he held it so tightly it sometimes cracked between his fingers."

"What happened on that last night?" Rudy asked gently.

Mrs. Pollard glanced into the fireplace as if she could find there the dead embers of an unsettling memory. "He shook the bars of his crib so hard they broke.

That's how he got out and crawled over to the window." She made a helpless movement with her arms. "I know that sounds like something he couldn't possibly do, but he did it."

"Do you think your baby's abnormal strength had anything to do with the fact that he was a test tube baby?"

"Dr. Bradford didn't think so. He said the way he looked had nothing to do with it either."

"How he looked?"

"After a while I sort of got used to it, but my husband never did."

"Can you describe him?" Hartley asked, speaking for the first time.

"He had kind of a sloping forehead. A small hump in his back. And all that hair. Head to foot. After a while I got to thinking of him as *furry*—and that helped." She stared at them, and said quietly, "I'm really sorry. I can't talk about it any more."

Rudy stood up. "Thank you for giving us so much of your time."

She did not reply. The rain had stopped, and a faint breeze stirred the fronds of a large potted palm standing between the windows.

"You've been very helpful," Rudy added.

She remained quiet, passive. "You're welcome, I'm sure."

As they drove away from the house, Hartley said, "She's a nice woman. I wish you'd been more honest with her."

"If I had been, she wouldn't have let us into the house."

"What good did it do, having her rake up all that again?"

"We added one more name to a steadily growing list of abnormal infants conceived on the IVF program."

"And what does *that* prove? It might be nature's way of handling the problem. If a woman miscarries, that's often a sign the fetus was imperfect. Can't the same thing be true here? Those other babies were born dead. The fact that they didn't live might be nature's way of handling them *after* they're delivered."

"What about the attempt to cover up the deaths?"

"Hardly worth making a stink about. Bradford is probably aware of what's happening and he's taking steps to correct it. You can't make a big conspiracy out of that."

"And what about Bernie Seligson?"

"Frankly, your idea that he was murdered is nuts."

"He mailed me those notes from the medical charts of two women—Karin Tolczyk and Deborah Clark. Why would he do that?"

"I'm a doctor. Not a mindreader."

Rudy gave Hartley a measuring glance and then shook his head. That rationalization, so seductively easy, did not take into account the number of suspicious circumstances. Each one might be inconclusive in itself, but there were too many. He had not been wrestling, like Jacob in the Bible, with mere shadows and images. The conviction that he was right, and the knowledge that he hadn't convinced Hartley, set up in him a distrustful tension. He became angry as if he'd been deliberately tricked.

"You don't want to look at the facts," he said accusingly.

"You don't have any facts worth looking at. Take my advice and stop playing ersatz Sherlock Holmes. Go back to being Dr. Watson. You're a doctor, not a detective. You have no right to put nice people like Mrs. Pollard through an emotional wringer because you've got the wind up about something that doesn't exist."

Rudy's bitterness was growing. He was appalled at the obtuseness of an otherwise intelligent man like Ken Hartley. That someone at the clinic wanted to keep the facts about the IVF program from getting out was perfectly clear. There was no convincing alternative explanation.

He deliberately called a halt to the rush of his indignation. This was time for clarity, not for emotionalism. Hartley could not refute the fact of a cover-up, but he was able to explain it away. How? Because a circumstantial case had not been established. A pretty powerful case would have to be made before Hartley, or anyone else who hadn't lived through the events of the past few days, could be persuaded that murder might have occurred. Murder was an alien act; it never happened to a friend.

Looked at in this way, Hartley's attitude was easier to accept. To infer that murder had taken place in order to cover up a few instances of unusual births in the clinic might appear to anyone as nutso facto reasoning. Rudy had loosened the reins of caution too soon—letting his conclusions run away with him.

His indignation was leaving him. "Could you keep an open mind for twenty-four hours?"

"About what?"

"Bernie took notes from the chart of a woman named Deborah Clark. She was on the IVF program but didn't have her baby delivered at the clinic. She went to a midwife in some little town in Arkansas."

"Where her baby was probably born perfectly normal and is still living."

"I intend to go down there to check it out. If the Clark baby's alive, I want to examine it. If nothing is wrong, I'll chuck this whole thing."

"That's being sensible."

"On the other hand, if the baby is dead, or suffering from the same syndrome as the Pollard and Tolczyk and Conklin and possibly Delgado babies, I think you ought to admit that we're dealing with something a lot worse than a coincidence."

"And if I do admit it? What then?"

"I'll want your help."

The next morning Ken Hartley was working beside Gaby Latolier in Operating Room D, desperately trying to save the life of a woman seven months pregnant who had been brought to the emergency area suffering from a gunshot wound in the chest. After five hours the mother's condition turned critical, and Gaby Latolier decided to get the embryo out while there was time. She performed a Caesarean, and the premature infant was rushed to an isolet in the intensive care ward. The mother was wheeled into the emergency ward and placed on a Bird respirator.

"I hope she makes it," Ken said.

Gaby Latolier stripped off her gloves. "Nothing gives more satisfaction than saving lives. That's what medicine is all about."

Ken watched her go down the operating room corridor. From the way she walked he could tell that she was in a state beyond weariness. At that moment yesterday's errand with Rudy Gerson seemed to him more foolish than ever.

He left the OR area and placed a call on a house phone.

"Dr. Bradford's office," a pleasant female voice replied.

"Dr. Hartley calling."

"Can you tell me what this is in reference to?"

"I have to see Dr. Bradford right away. It's important."

"I'm sorry, Dr. Hartley, Dr. Bradford has a very full schedule. I really can't make any more appointments."

"This is urgent—a security matter."

A trace of cool annoyance: "Mr. Delaney is in charge of security. I can transfer this call."

"No, no, it has to be Dr. Bradford." Ken began perspiring. The need for confession was swelling in him, drumming in his skull. "You can tell him this much. It's about the Pollards . . . and Dr. Rudy Gerson."

"The Pollards and Dr. Gerson," she repeated with the faintly remote air of someone repeating an instruction while writing it. "I'll give your message to Dr. Bradford. I'll call you to confirm any appointment."

"Thank you," Ken said. As he hung up he was sure he had done the right thing.

Later that afternoon, he heard himself being paged. He was being asked to report to Dr. Bradford's office.

Peter Bradford stood up from his desk and motioned Ken to a club chair. A wooden plaque was on the wall, with a quote from Thomas Jefferson: *I have sworn an oath upon the altar of Almighty God to combat every form of tyranny over the mind of man.*

Bradford sat down again behind his desk. "My secretary said you wanted to see me about something urgent."

"Do you know Dr. Rudy Gerson?" Ken began without preamble.

"Yes."

"I was with him the other night at the home of a Mr. and Mrs. Pollard."

"Thomas and Jane Pollard?"

"Yes."

Bradford turned a pencil from point to eraser on his desk blotter. "May I ask why?"

Ken felt his cheeks starting to burn. "Dr. Gerson was very anxious to find out if their baby was conceived on the IVF program here."

"Please go on."

"He and Dr. Seligson apparently had the idea that an unusual number of deaths and abnormalities were occurring among babies conceived on our IVF program."

"I see." Dr. Bradford kept looking at him. "Is that all?"

Blood came singing up into Ken's ears. "When Dr. Seligson died so suddenly, Dr. Gerson thought there might be some connection."

"Connection?"

"It sounds silly, I know, but he isn't convinced Bernie Seligson died of natural causes. He thinks it may be an attempt to cover up . . . God, I feel ridiculous saying this."

"Dr. Seligson died of a heart attack."

"Dr. Gerson asked me some questions about that. The next thing I knew he was telling me about this conspiracy, or whatever you want to call it. I tried to tell him it was nonsense, but he talked me into going with him to interview the Pollards. He told the Pollards we were writing an article for *Medical World News*."

"This entire episode strikes me as bizarre."

"At the time, with Dr. Seligson's death so fresh in my mind, I went along. I can't explain why."

"Did the Pollards make you believe there *is* anything wrong with our IVF program?"

"Not at all. I told Dr. Gerson as much. As for Bernie Seligson dying so suddenly, well, that was . . ."

Bradford said calmly, "Dr. Seligson had a rheumatic lesion, chronic type, that resulted in a narrowing of the mitral valve."

Ken was stunned. He blinked, tried to reply, but couldn't think of anything to say. "He never mentioned anything like that to me," he said finally.

"It wasn't a thing he confided to everyone," Bradford replied, his tone intimate, embracing and rich with assurance. "When he came to work here he asked me to keep his medical record in strictest confidence. During the past year he suffered several episodes of pulmonary edema and hemophysis after exertion. Under the circumstances, I think it's fair to say the fatal attack was not unexpected."

Ken was not entirely sure how to react. His heart was beating strongly in response to his shocked incredulity. "Under the circumstances, I'd have to agree."

He was aware of Dr. Bradford looking at him closely.

That night in the pathology lab, Ken watched the autopsy on a recent patient, the woman that he and Gaby Latolier had tried so hard to save. The cause of death turned out to be internal bleeding due to the gunshot wound.

As casually as he could he asked, "Did either of you do the post on Dr. Seligson?"

"Sure, that was mine," one of the two pathologists volunteered.

"I glanced at the report. But I didn't notice any mention of a rheumatic lesion."

"There wasn't any."

"No narrowing of the mitral valve?"

"Nope."

"I could have sworn Seligson had that problem. What *was* the cause of death?"

"We couldn't find anything really wrong. The plain fact is, his heart just stopped. It happens that way sometimes. Were you a friend of his?"

"Yes," Ken said.

"Too bad. I understand he was a nice guy."

Chapter

12

A twin-engine Cessna brought Rudy from Louisville to a small private airfield that consisted of a long paved runway, a large hangar, and a level field on which a dozen planes were parked. Three other passengers disembarked from the eight-seater plane. One was tall, with a sallow complexion and mournful expression. The other two were a man and woman in their fifties who must have been married; they had not spoken to each other during the flight.

The tall mournful man walked beside Rudy.

"From this part of the country—or visiting?" he asked.

"Visiting," Rudy said.

"Ain't much to see. My territory covers nearly a thousand square miles. I'm in the tractor business—sellin' em. Where you headin' for?"

"Missoula."

"Missoula? *Real* backwoods. Nothin' in Missoula."

"I'm going to rent a car and look around."

"Try the gas station half a mile from here. Tim has bought himself a new Chevrolet he's willin' to rent. I'm goin' in that direction, so I'll drive you."

The tall man had a station wagon parked near the airfield. He drove Rudy to the gas station, waved to a man in overalls and drove off.

The man in overalls was deeply tanned, and his eyeballs were startlingly white. He was sitting on a wooden stool tilted against the gas station wall.

"I understand you have a car to rent," Rudy said. "The gentleman who dropped me off said something about a new Chevrolet."

"How much you willin' ter pay?"

"Tell me what you think is fair."

"Don't do business that way. Name me a price. I'll tell you if I take it."

"Twenty dollars for the day."

The man nodded. "You'll need gas. Not included." As he was filling the gas tank on the "new" Chevrolet, actually a two-year-old Impala, he asked, "Come fer the fishin'?"

"Visiting. Came to see a family named Clark that lives in Missoula."

The man held the gas line, watching the gauge. "Jeremy? Didn't know he had friends outside the county."

"Can you tell me how to get there?"

Slowly the man removed the gas line and screwed the cap back on the Chevrolet's tank. He turned to Rudy with a squinting appraisal before he answered, "See that paved road yonder? Foller it about a mile or two, then take the dirt road off to the left. Roads don't have no name. Folks around here know where they goin' to. The Clark house don't have no name either."

"How'll I know it when I find it?"

"Big kind of rambly house. Brown shingles. Red barn

on the right as you come to it. Jeremy has an old black Ford sedan out front."

After a mile, Rudy turned off onto a rutted dirt track that was unworthy of the name of road. At ten miles an hour he was jolted roughly, and the car wheels spun up dust. The sky clouded over, it began to rain and then the wheels churned up mud. It seemed to Rudy that of late he had done a good deal of driving in the rain.

He turned on the car's headlights. In the diminishing light, he wasn't sure he could find the Clark house. He passed a small, tidy house with a mailbox in front. Peering through the car's side window, he read aloud: "*Nora Atkins, Rooms To Rent.*" He decided to ask directions.

He left the car and ran through the pelting rain. An orange light glowed in a front window.

The woman who opened the door to him was small, dark, and wore a kerchief tied over her hair. She was about sixty years old.

Rudy said, "Pardon me, I'm looking for Jeremy Clark's house."

She looked at him with surprise. "You're turned around. Jeremy Clark's place is back the way you came. A good thing you stopped when you did. Nothin' up ahead for miles but the county fairgrounds."

"The gas station told me it was in this direction."

"Station at the airport?"

Rudy nodded, and Nora Atkins stepped back a little to allow him in out of the rain.

"That was Tim Clark," she said. "Nephew." Thunder rumbled with great rolling reverberations. She said, "Anyhow, it'd be dark afore you got there."

"Do you know the Clarks?" Rudy asked.

"Should think I do. I helped to birth poor Debbie's baby."

Rudy made a sudden connection. "Are you a midwife?"

Nora nodded. "Delivered near everyone in this county the last twenty odd years."

What a stroke of luck, Rudy thought.

A gust of wind shook the house and torrents of water spattered against the windows.

"I don't see how I can drive anywhere tonight," he said. "Can you put me up?"

"Cost you six dollars. Dinner and breakfast included."

"That's fine."

She looked out at the car being washed over with rain. "Any luggage with you?"

"Just a small suitcase."

"Bring it in."

When he returned, Nora had gone to the woodbin in the kitchen to get wood for the fireplace. She got a fire going.

He said, "That Clark baby you delivered is the one I came to see. I'm a doctor, an obstetrician." He dipped again into his bag of disguises: "I'm writing a book about strange and unusual births."

"How'd you hear about Debbie?" She was not challenging, just stolidly curious.

"At a hospital in New York."

"Jeremy Clark don't hold no friendly feeling for anybody from New York."

"Why is that?"

"It's where Debbie went and got herself pregnant. Jeremy blames her goin' there for what happened to her. Can't say he's wrong. Never would have happened if she'd stayed under his roof." Nora stood up. "Set a while. I've got to get started on dinner."

Dinner was corned beef and mashed potatoes. Rudy praised Nora's cooking. After dinner she retreated to a rocking chair in the living room, and picked up some needlework.

"So you came here to see Debbie's queer baby," she said. "He's something to see. Has the mark, clear as I ever saw."

"The mark?" Rudy said.

"I've been midwifin' babies into this world for a long time. Never saw the like of that one. Hair all over. Slopy head. Real scary to look at. The Clarks are Godfearin' folk, and Jeremy said it was Debbie's punishment."

"Her punishment?"

Nora's round cheeks lifted until they seemed to pack closely around her nose. "Took up with a divorced man in New York. She got herself with child to make him marry her. But he wouldn't. Said it wasn't his, 'cause he'd had himself fixed so he couldn't never father a child. Poor Debbie."

Poor Debbie, indeed. Unable to become pregnant by her divorced lover, she must have hit on the idea of having an in vitro baby, then found someone willing to show up at the Karyll Clinic and pretend to be her husband. The scheme hadn't worked.

"She sat right here in this room," Nora went on, "tellin' me all about it one day. Cryin' for to die. She was pregnant then, and ready to deliver. Big as a barn. Her man had walked out, and she'd come home to birth her baby amongst her kin. After the baby was born she couldn't stand to look at it, but Jeremy made her nuss and mother it."

"Have you seen the baby recently?"

"Nope."

"Have you talked to Debbie about it?"

"Couldn't hardly do that. Debbie Clark is dead and in the ground."

"Dead?"

"The way I heered it, she fell down the stairs and broke her fool neck. She always was a wild one, not like her sister Sara. Sara got married here 'bout a year ago. Nobody was even invited to her weddin'. Jeremy Clark didn't want no strangers around."

"Debbie's baby. What happened to it?"

"Don't rightly know. The Clarks are close-mouthed folk who keep their business to theirselves. I reckon Sara's lookin' after it." Nora Atkins got up. "It's bedtime for me. If you're stayin' up, you'll have to poke up the fire when it gets cold."

"I will. Thank you."

He woke in the morning to the smell of frying bacon. Slowly he became aware of the unfamiliar room. He was cold under his thin blanket. He had slept in his underwear. Quickly he slipped on trousers and a shirt, and went down to the kitchen.

Nora Atkins was flipping over bacon in a pan. "Breakfast'll be ready in ten minutes. Go back upstairs and take your bath."

He sniffed. "Smells great."

She turned over the last slice of bacon. "You better get here in two jifs if you want to get fed."

Rudy went upstairs. The old-fashioned bathroom

was spacious. Even while taking a bath he could smell the bacon frying. He hoped it tasted as good as it smelled.

Nora brought him a second cup of coffee to go with homemade bread and bacon. He waited patiently for another chance to open a conversation.

"I should be getting underway," he said finally.

"Where to?" Nora asked.

"To have a look at Debbie Clark's baby."

"You're goin' on a fool's errand. Jeremy won't let you near that child. Could even be dangerous."

"Dangerous?"

"Jeremy's father was a moonshiner. Never asked questions of anyone snoopin' around. Jest reached for his rifle. And Jeremy's a lot like his father."

"I won't be snooping. I just want to see the baby. I'll try to explain matters when I get there."

"Do as you please." Nora got up, wiping her hands on her apron as if washing her hands of his problem. Then she said, "Oh, my, I forgot the county fair's openin' today." Her mouth pursed thoughtfully. "Jeremy won't leave anyone home but the youngest boy Abner. Could be you'll have an easier time gettin' around him than old Jeremy."

Twenty minutes later, Rudy was driving along a road mined with potholes from the previous night's rain. In the clear gray morning light the houses he passed were somber, without a glint of welcome. After a few miles the first car appeared, a black Ford. Then he passed several of the Ford's cousins. The people in the cars were hard-countenanced, wearing their go-to-meeting finery. One car's front bumper bore a sign: *County Fair*.

Cars began coming in a steady procession before he reached the huge gaunt elm tree and flat-faced rock where Nora Atkins had told him to turn off.

The car gave a sudden jolt that sent him bouncing to the roof. He felt his head gingerly. And he didn't notice the black Ford sedan that made a U-turn and followed him into the turnoff.

Chapter

13

Smoke rose in a lazy spiral from the chimney of the Clark house. But there was no sign of the old Ford the nephew at the gas station told him would be here. The Clark family must have driven it to the fair.

There were two small windows, but nothing moved within the quiet dimness. A locked screen door and a plain wooden door barred entry. Rudy knocked. There was no answer. He knocked again, more loudly.

A dog started to bark inside. A moment later a young voice said from just inside the door, "What d'you want? No one's home."

"I'm from the state health board," Rudy said.

"You better git before my Daddy gits back." The dog started to bark again, rapidly. "Shut up! Shut up before you git *her* goin'!" A sudden howl as if the dog had been kicked.

Rudy rapped on the door again. "I have to come in," he said.

This time, slowly, the door opened to reveal a teenaged boy wearing overalls. He stared at Rudy sullenly.

"I ain't gonna let you in because my Daddy says I can't."

Rudy said, "I heard there's a baby here with a case of smallpox."

The boy looked at him challengingly. "Ain't nobody sick here."

"It'll just take a minute to look around."

A wail sounded from the rear of the house.

"Oh, dang it! You got her goin'! And once she's started there's no stoppin' her." He moved several paces back. "You better *git!*"

He turned and hurried away. The wailing continued, an infant's wailing.

Rudy went inside the house. To the left was a room with nondescript furniture, several plain chairs, a table, a Franklin stove. The staircase was on the right, leading up from the kitchen to the second story. The kitchen had a wood-burning stove, and laundry hanging from a line.

The wailing was not coming from upstairs, but from the shadowed rear of the house. He passed by several small bedrooms, each with a narrow cot and a small table with a white pitcher on it.

"Dammit! Stop that yellin'! *Stop it!*"

In the back bedroom the young boy was leaning over a plain handmade wooden crib on rockers. He was snarling, "You'll drive me crazy! I oughta wring your little turkey neck!" He turned, saw Rudy, and his anger crumbled into a cautious nervousness.

Rudy told him, "Don't be frightened, son. I just want a look at that baby to see if he's all right . . ."

"*Her.* She ain't sick. Look how she's hollerin'!"

"I think I can quiet her." He moved to the crib; the boy stepped back.

The boy said uncertainly, "Once she gits started, there ain't *no* stoppin' her!"

The wailing continued unabated. Inside the crib, a baby, wearing only a white diaper and a white soiled undershirt, raised tiny chubby arms. Its whole face, red with anger and frustration, was as tight as a clenched fist.

Debbie Clark's baby would be a year old. This was a newborn infant. There had to be another baby in the house somewhere.

The boy had disappeared, and Rudy was alone with the howling infant. He heard footsteps come down the corridor. The boy looked in, then withdrew. A man entered. He was rangy, gaunt, with graying hair and deep cleft-lines in his cheeks.

He held a shotgun pointed directly at Rudy.

"You ain't gittin' away with it this time."

The gaunt man's eyes were small, red-veined, and he had a pale stubby beard. His expression was slightly vacant and dull, but with a hard bright underlay of savagery. He held the shotgun in the casual practiced manner of a man who knew what to do with it.

He motioned, and they went into the living room, Rudy first, the gaunt man and his shotgun following, the boy trailing.

"I'm not trying to get away with anything," Rudy said, turning to face him in the living room.

"He said he was from the health board," the boy said shrilly.

"Git his wallet," the gaunt man ordered.

The boy slid behind Rudy and deftly removed the wallet from his hip pocket. He handed it over to the gaunt man.

Cradling the shotgun in his arm, still aimed at Rudy, the gaunt man opened the wallet. He studied the cards in a plastic folder.

A slow grin revealed crooked yellow teeth. "I figgered you'd be a doctor."

He thumbed through the money in Rudy's wallet, then removed it and stuffed the bills into his pocket. He tossed the wallet away.

Rudy said, "Obviously, you've got me mixed up with someone else." He was having trouble keeping his eyes off the shotgun dangling negligently from the man's arm.

"Don't take me for dumb, mister doctor. Jeremy Clark ain't dumb."

"I made a mistake telling your son I was from the health board," Rudy said. "The truth is that I was at Nora Atkins's house last night, and she mentioned your daughter Deborah's baby. I couldn't help being curious. I'm not only a doctor, I'm an obstetrician." He saw Jeremy Clark's blank expression, and added: "I deliver babies. I became curious when Nora Atkins described what your daughter's baby looked like."

"That story ain't hardly nearer the truth than the other one. You don't fool me none. You didn't have to get no look at Debbie's queer baby. You're the one come down here and took it."

"The baby isn't here?"

"You damn right. You had to kill Debbie to git it. I figgered you'd come back someday to git Sara's baby too."

"Why would I want to do that?" Rudy asked.

"I've heard of doctors like you who put babies up for sale. Git a mighty good price for 'em."

"Certainly not for the kind of baby your daughter Debbie had."

Jeremy looked briefly uncertain. His small eyes blinked. "Hennie said your woman was with you last time. But it don't matter none. You could be in this with others. Could be lots of you workin' together."

"You can call the hospital in New York. I'll pay the charges. They'll tell you who I am. It's the Park Hill Hospital at . . ."

Jeremy said sourly, "Ain't got no phone and wouldn't call anybody if I did. If I let them know you's here, they'll come around later askin' questions."

Obviously there was no way he could convince this man of anything. Jeremy's last remark, about people coming around later and asking questions, clearly implied that Rudy was not going to be around to answer questions. If he intended to leave here alive, he had better think of a way to do it. And fast.

Rudy felt the back of his neck starting to sweat. Fear was such a riveting emotion that he couldn't seem to feel anything else.

He stalled: "You can't keep me here against my will."

"Cain't I? You was trespassin' on my propetty."

"All right, I admit that. Call in the law."

Jeremy sniggered. When his lips drew back a string of saliva hung suspended from a tobacco-brown incisor. "You're real smart, ain't yuh?" He jerked the shotgun up, jamming the barrel tightly against Rudy's chest. The hard steel muzzle moved down, down, scraping. Rudy felt the track it was making on his skin.

Jeremy's tongue licked his lips. "I kin blow your fuckin' balls off, y'know that?" Still looking at Rudy, he pulled the barrel away and swung it in a vicious semicircle.

A bright yellow flare of pain shot through Rudy's head. Then he was on his hands and knees. His head hurt and his brain was clouding over. I can't let myself go under. I may never wake up again.

"I'm goin' to make it easy for you, mister. I'm jest gonna blow your fuckin' head off."

A table was near Rudy. He got one hand to the top and clasped the leg with the other to steady himself. Somehow he pulled himself up, all fifty tons of him, along the table leg. His head was full of broken gravel, he was climbing out of a deep dark canyon. Jeremy watched with amusement until Rudy got the palms of both hands on the table, and lifted his torso up on it for support.

Still trying, with nothing to lose, he muttered thickly, "I can prove I'm not who you think."

He pushed down on the table to raise himself further. The table tilted. Something toppled and fell to the floor with a crash. For an instant he thought Jeremy had fired. A pungent odor filled the room. Rudy was still leaning on the sharply tilted table with one elbow and part of his body. A bright yellow rivulet sprang up from the broken kerosene lamp. The rivulet raced across the floor, leapt onto the boy's overalls. He screamed.

Jeremy tossed away his shotgun and began to beat at the boy's legs.

Rudy moved toward the door with painful deliberation. If he tried to move faster, his legs would fold under him. Jeremy was busy beating out the tiny tongues of flame on the boy's overalls.

Black smoke accompanied Rudy out the door. He kept moving, traveling forward on momentum. He reached the Chevrolet. As he got in and wriggled across to the driver's seat, the intense pain in his head began to let up a little. He pulled the car door shut.

Jeremy Clark appeared out of the smoke in the doorway, holding his shotgun. Rudy slid far across on the seat. He heard the *blamm* of an explosion, and the car windows shattered. He opened the door on the other side and plunged out onto the road. In a crouching run he reached the Ford. The keys were in the ignition. The engine sputtered.

Jeremy ran toward him, reloading the shotgun.

Rudy pushed down hard on the accelerator. With a rattling roar, the Ford pulled away. Moments later he heard another shotgun blast, but he was out of range.

When he glanced back, Jeremy Clark was beside the Chevrolet. The car was leaning at an awkward angle, its tires blown out on one side. Coiling black smoke still drifted out the doorway of the farmhouse.

At thirty miles an hour, he was jounced so hard he could hardly hold the wheel. The Ford apparently had no shock absorbers, and each jolt was like a separate knife thrust into his aching head. He passed a telephone pole and a line connecting to a farmhouse. As soon as Jeremy or the boy reached here, they could send out an alarm. A mile farther, he saw a small wooden pointer on the road with the single word *Airport* scrawled on it. Then he remembered that he no longer had his wallet. No cash, no credit cards, no return plane ticket.

He reached into his pocket. He had a little over thirty dollars. Not enough for a plane ticket to New York.

As he drove by Tim Clark's gas station, a hand-lettered sign stood in front of the gas pump: *Back later*. He had left a deposit on the Chevrolet, but there was no way to get that money back.

The Ford rattled to a stop in front of the airport office. He smoothed his hair back. A bump was starting to form on the scalp, but it was hidden by his hair. He got out of the car. A small bowlegged man with thick gray hair and a seamed tanned face came out to greet him with a questioning smile.

"When is the next plane leaving?" Rudy asked.

"One's going in a few minutes."

"What's the first stop?"

"Fayetteville."

As soon as he reached Fayetteville he could call Mrs. Sherwin and have her wire him money.

"How much for a ticket?"

"Twenty-six dollars."

Rudy pulled three ten dollar bills from his pocket.

The man's smile became a little pinched. "Isn't that Jeremy Clark's car you're driving?"

Rudy said, "I rented his nephew Tim's Chevrolet, but it broke down. Jeremy lent me this to get back to the airport."

"How much luggage you taking?"

"None on this trip," Rudy said.

The small man grunted, turned, and went into his office. He was on the telephone as Rudy strolled in.

"Any problem?" Rudy asked.

"Just checking with Tim Clark at the gas station." He held on for half a minute. "Don't seem to be any answer."

"Isn't that my plane?" Rudy asked, pointing to a

six-passenger prop plane warming up about a hundred feet from the office. He held out the three ten dollar bills.

The man eyed them and hung up the telephone. "We don't get too many people 'round here with no luggage who don't seem to care which way they're goin'."

Rudy managed a laugh. "I just came here for the day. To see my old friend Nora Atkins."

"Nora? She a friend of yours?"

"She delivered my wife's baby a few years ago."

"You don't say." He seemed relieved. "Well, well."

He began writing out the ticket.

Ten minutes later the telephone rang in the airport office.

"Hiya, Tim. I was tryin' to call you a little while back. Wanted to check up on somebody drivin' your uncle Jeremy's car. The Chevy you rented him broke down and Jeremy lent his Ford . . ."

"Stop him!"

"What are you talkin' about?"

"Jeremy didn't lend his car. He stole it!"

Through the side glass wall fronting on the airfield, the man could make out a small speck dwindling in the western sky.

"Ain't no way I can stop him now. You tell your Uncle Jeremy that there ain't nothin' for him to worry about. His car is right here, safe and sound."

Chapter

14

Sitting in bra and panties before the dressing table mirror in her bedroom, Mary Oliver wondered: How is it possible to know when you're in love? Love is a shortsighted emotion in which perspective is lost. You lose the ability even to analyze your own feelings. You just go bobbing along like a frail raft over turbulent white water.

A few men had appeared with a look of meaning in their eyes only to fade away. You had some lovely times, but the end was always the same. She said: Thanks for everything, darling, I really am fond of you. Goodbye.

Her first lover was a tall, gangly pole vaulter on the Temple University track team. He did not take her virginity—they performed the service for each other. She felt as if she had accomplished something particularly pleasing, as if she had vaulted with him over a hurdle.

That immature man—a face remembered through gauze—proved no match for Sam Dodds when he appeared in her life. She had gone with her young man to Veteran's Stadium to watch a green-shirted Phila-

delphia Eagles football team play on Sunday afternoon. The young man knew Sam and invited him over.
That same evening Sam called her. The next day she
had dinner with him.

After the first time they made love, she hoped they
would find other things in common. He worked for the
law firm that represented the Philadelphia Eagles.
Although she did not particularly care for football, she
saw every home game that winter. They went out a lot.
Sam liked big cocktail parties, the kind where she
spent most of the time standing in a corner and
pretending to be a lamp. He also liked card tricks and
practical jokes. That summer they spent a month at
Harvey Cedars on Long Beach Island. The month was
June. They had lobster cookouts on the beach, made
love frequently and went for swims at dawn.

That autumn, back in Philadelphia, she often wanted
to throttle him. They quarreled about a wide range of
subjects. She had a strong will and he had an over-
mastering ambition. He supported charter reform that
would have given Mayor Rizzo a third term as mayor of
Philadelphia because "a lawyer needs a friend at City
Hall." When she reproached him he accused her of
being unrealistic. Everybody had to compromise with
conscience now and then. Anyone who didn't was a
fool—and would only come to grief. She began, not
wholly in jest, to refer to him as "Honest Sam," and
suggested he might do well in politics. He did not find
her amusing. He had very little sense of humor. "I've
got to be me," was his favorite expression. She observed crisply that most people who went around saying
that didn't have much of a "me" to be. He accused her
of trying to dominate him. They quarreled, but made

up in bed where their relationship was at its best. He posed in front of the bedroom mirror and flexed his muscles. He had a superb physique. She began to realize that they were arguing so much because if the arguments stopped, they would have nothing else to talk about.

When Sam decided to accept a job offer in Washington he invited her to come down there to live with him. That would mean giving up her job. She might have been tempted to do it, but she was too annoyed that the sacrifice involved did not even occur to him. She put him off and continued living at home with her mother. Her contribution enabled Mother to pay the mortgage and taxes on the house. On the day she left, the house would have to be sold.

She heard a knock at the bedroom door. Mother had been taught, after much effort, to give warning of her approach.

"Come in."

Mother opened the door. "I was just wondering if you were going to watch television tonight."

Mother was devoted to all the programs in the top twenty of the Nielsen ratings; she laughed along with the canned laughter.

"I have a date."

"Who with? That nice young obstetrician from New York?"

"Sam Dodds called me at my office this afternoon. We're having dinner tonight."

"I thought that was all over."

Mother was right of course. That was sad in a way. She and Sam had spent two Christmases and New

Years together. There *had* been a kind of excitement in the beginning.

Mother's mind was working along predictable lines. "Hasn't Dr. Gerson called?"

"Not yet."

"He will."

"I'm seeing him Saturday."

"Oh. That *is* nice."

Mother retreated downstairs to her television.

Mary put final touches on her makeup, adding a touch of lip gloss, heightening the color in her cheeks, giving her hair a last brush. In spite of everything, she wanted to look her best for Sam tonight. Let him carry away a flattering image, a portrait of her in his mind like a cameo in a locket. No danger he would grieve. He suffered from too much self-reverence to feel anything but compassion for a woman he left behind.

Dear Sam. It was her fault, not his, for trying to fit him into a mold that he did not fit. As a young girl, she had dreamed of sitting in a room when in walked this man and the whole world went zap. She had not lived long enough yet to be really wise about men, but she was learning. There was a lot more to be said for simple communion, sharing, emotion requited. A secret and irrepressible smile crept across her face. Rudy was so uncomplicated, so sincere, so sweet.

Downstairs she heard the doorbell ring. She glanced at the ashtray on her dressing table. Four cigarette stubs. She was usually not this nervous. What was the matter with her? All she had to tell him was that she'd found someone she liked better. It happens to everyone all the time. Sooner or later it had to happen to Sam Dodds.

She slipped into the simple, understated, but elegant, black dress she had chosen for the evening. No matter what, they were not going to a health food restaurant tonight.

As she started out of the room the telephone rang.

"About Saturday night," Rudy said, "I have to ask for a raincheck."

"Is anything wrong?"

"I've just come back from a trip. You won't believe what happened to me." An unnatural tension stiffened his voice. "I can't tell you about it now, but I will as soon as I make sense of it myself."

"Are you all right?"

"Yes. I know this must sound peculiar to you."

"Mysterious. Not peculiar. When will I see you?"

"I'm not quite sure. I'll call."

He had not sounded so perturbed on the morning of the Delgado incident when he had narrowly escaped from great personal danger.

"Is there anything I can do to help?"

"No. Forgive me for breaking our date, and, oh, yes, I've decided that I'm in love with you. If that sounds like a reckless, unconsidered statement, I can't help it."

He hung up. She replaced the phone but kept her hand on it as though further communication were possible without wires. She could hear his voice saying, *I'm in love with you. If that sounds like a reckless, unconsidered* . . .

Not at all.

When the right man walks into your life, the world does go zap.

*   *   *

Rudy was awake, staring at the ceiling in his bedroom. It was six-thirty in the morning. The ceiling was a screen replaying for him extraordinary events. He saw Jeremy Clark's gaunt, haggard face, heard the deadly blast of his shotgun. The man had been possessed with rage, and there must be a reason for it. His tale of a baby being kidnapped must be real, as real as Nora Atkins's description of what the baby looked like.

But why would anyone kidnap an abnormal baby? That didn't make sense, even as part of a cover-up. The kidnappers could as easily have left the baby in Missoula, where its existence would remain unknown to all but a few close-mouthed kin. Not even Nora Atkins, the midwife and a neightbor, had known if the Clark baby was alive or dead.

He had gone there to find out if the Clark infant suffered from the same syndrome as the others. In finding the answer, he had aroused a gnat-swarm of new questions, including the puzzling death of the baby's mother. She had fallen downstairs and broken her neck. Drunk? Or a suicide? Or was her death involved in some way with the kidnapping of her baby? That would provide further motivation for Jeremy Clark.

Rudy had no idea if any of his speculations made sense. But at some point it became easier to believe in the likelihood of a central purpose at work than to keep multiplying unexplainable "accidents."

He had his customary orange juice, toast and coffee while sitting in robe and pajamas at the kitchen table. Then he donned his jogging outfit and laced up his Adidas. Minutes later he jogged across to Central Park West. His body moved gracefully, each step taken

deliberately, striking the ground first with his heel
and rolling forward, slightly flexing his foot, taking off
from the ball of his foot to the next step.

But this morning not even jogging could dispel the
cobwebs. He remained perplexed and anxious. He moved
forward in a straight line, like the pendulum of a clock,
but his thoughts revolved in an unending circle. In all
fairness, Ken Hartley now ought to concede the circumstances suspicious enough to warrant further investigation. But suppose Hartley was still skeptical?

Something inside him snapped, a last barrier of
objectivity. He was not willing to accept that he was
pursuing an implausible theory. There had to be some
explanation that would gather up all the loose ends
into a credible knot. His body, mimicking argument,
was not moving now in its accustomed rhythms. He
was running on the balls of his feet, putting excessive
strain on the tendons and muscles of his ankles. His
arms were too high—as though warding off criticism—
and he moved them too much, causing his body to sway
and twist.

When he became aware of it he slowed down to a
walk.

Then he noticed a car moving slowly up Central
Park West on the other side of the avenue. The car was
not quite parallel with him.

The car's slow progress was what drew his attention.
Traffic moved by in a swift stream as the car proceeded
sedately down the avenue. The driver must be looking
for a parking space.

Then he saw the car pass by several available parking
spaces.

It was a green Mercury Monarch sedan.

He began jogging again and left the car behind in traffic. As he reached the 86th Street transverse, he turned in to run on the narrow strip of sidewalk that bordered the road. He heard the roar of traffic fade slightly. Then he glanced back over his shoulder and saw the green Mercury Monarch turn into the transverse too.

A stone staircase led up from the narrow strip of sidewalk into the park itself. On impulse, he turned quickly off the sidewalk toward the staircase. At that instant the Mercury sedan veered sharply inward. It climbed the sidewalk and the front of the car made a grazing contact with the stone wall where Rudy had just been. Instantly, it turned off the sidewalk back onto the road and sped off. Rudy saw it disappear into the traffic maneuvering along the transverse.

Brakes shrieked and a car pulled to a stop nearby.

"I saw that crazy bastard," the driver shouted from the car window. "He could've killed you!"

Rudy stared at him. "Yes, I know," he said in a numbed voice.

"Did you get his license number?"

"No."

"Crazy bastards like that shouldn't be allowed on the road!" The driver shook his head in disbelief. "You sure had a close call." He drove off.

Rudy leaned back against the stone wall and took a deep breath. If not for his quick intuitive move, he would have been lying crushed on the sidewalk, drawing his last breath in agony. Stop it, he told himself. Stop it. He detested the feeling of fear that set a pulse thumping in his temples.

Stop it.

*   *   *

Rudy did not clearly remember how he got back to his office. When he arrived Mrs. Sherwin was in her accustomed seat behind a reception window in the anteroom.

"I'm glad to see you, Doctor. Did they find the man who stole your wallet? I wired the money you asked for."

He had to wrench his mind around to understand what she was saying. Oh, yes. He had told her that story on the telephone after arriving in Fayetteville with no money and no wallet.

"I got it, thank you."

"There've been some phone calls. Mrs. Golden has been calling. And Dr. Beer wanted to know if you'd be at the game this evening."

This was a biweekly poker game in which Rudy occasionally participated. Out of a pool of ten possible doctor-players, rarely more than six showed up because of crowded schedules.

"Tell him no. Is that all?"

"Dr. Hartley has telephoned several times. He seemed especially anxious to talk to you."

"Get him for me right away."

His loose sweatshirt was stained with perspiration. Ordinarily he would have taken a shower and changed into one of the suits in the closet in his private office. But he was anxious to talk to Ken Hartley.

When he heard the buzzer he picked up the telephone.

"Ken?"

Ken said abruptly, "Can you meet me here at the clinic? It's really important."

"Yes."

"I have a room down the hall from where Bernie Seligson lived. I'll be looking for you."

Rudy put down the telephone. He was still under rigid control, waiting for his nerves and muscles to calm down and stop warning him about a danger that had passed. After a moment he buzzed Mrs. Sherwin and told her to cancel his appointments for the morning. He showered, changed and took a taxi to his garage. On the drive to Westchester he ignored the speed limit. In thirty-three minutes he was at the gates of the hospital. Visiting hours had not begun. The guard at the sentry station glanced at the Porsche's MD license plate and waved him through.

Few cars were in the parking lot. He drove through one empty tier after another to reach a section nearest the main entrance. He entered the immense lobby through wide glass doors.

On the residential floor, Ken was waiting outside the open door to his cubicle. His room was a duplicate of the one that had been home to Bernie Seligson, sterile, depersonalized, neat, functional, completely devoid of litter. That kind of room had negated Bernie's personality, who in life had been rumpled and careless of personal appearance. Ken Hartley appeared more suited to it.

Ken closed the door to his room and locked it before he turned to Rudy.

"I told Bradford about our visit to the Pollards."

Rudy felt a twinge, a tiny flicker of the fear he had known earlier. An image came to his mind: a car leaping toward him over a sidewalk.

"Why did you do that?"

"I didn't go along with your idea that there was a cover-up in the IVF program. It seemed crazy." Ken spread his hands and raised his eyebrows, as though offering an apology. "Then we got to talking about Bernie's death."

"Well?" Rudy asked.

"Bradford said that Bernie's death wasn't unexpected because of his heart condition."

Rudy said slowly, "I didn't know he had a heart condition."

"According to Bradford, he had a rheumatic lesion with a narrowing of the mitral valve. He'd already had several episodes of pulmonary edema and hemophysis following exertion."

"Pretty serious."

Ken Hartley's sad, soft eyes showed anger. "Bernie and I played racquetball together," he said. "I've seen him play three real tough games one right after the other."

Rudy drew a quick breath.

Ken asked, "What would happen to a man with that kind of heart problem?"

"It would kill him."

"Exactly. Just to make sure, I checked with the doctor who did the post on him. Bernie had no heart condition."

Reflexively, Rudy's heart began to beat strongly. "How could Bradford expect to get away with it? If the autopsy report showed . . ."

"Who knows what the report showed? It could easily have been changed."

Rudy was silent.

Ken said, "After that, a number of things began to

make more sense. There *were* too many deaths on the IVF program. And too many suffering from the same kind of abnormality."

"Welcome to the club."

Ken pushed one hand back through his bushy hair. "Tell me what happened on your trip. Did you get to see the Clark baby?"

Rudy told him about the midwife Nora Atkins's description of the baby. He added that the baby had been kidnapped a few weeks after its birth. About the same time the mother had died—of a broken neck.

By the time he finished his account, perspiration had formed on Ken Hartley's forehead. Ken got up, went into the bathroom to pour himself a glass of water and gulp it down. He returned to the room and sat down.

His dark face was troubled. "Back home we have a saying. When something in a woodpile smells like a skunk, there's usually a skunk in the woodpile. Looks to me as if someone's gone to a lot of trouble to keep this smell from getting out."

"I agree."

"What do we do? Call the police?"

"That thought has occurred to me. But if they just barge in and start asking questions about the IVF program, Bradford will give them more than enough answers to prove nothing's wrong."

"Do you realize what you just said?"

He looked at Ken, puzzled, trying to recall his last words. Then he did. He had referred to Peter Bradford as a prime mover in the cover-up. Peter Bradford, one of the world's leading men of medicine—a former colleague of his father.

"Bradford is in it up to his eyeballs," he said firmly. "Why else would he lie about Bernie Seligson?"

"It's just so damn hard to accept. I don't understand it. Why should he risk everything to cover up a few mistakes in the IVF program?"

An unsettling question, to which there was a logical answer.

"There must be more to it."

"Like?"

"What else is going on that they might really want to keep under wraps?"

"Everything here is open and above board as far as I . . ." Ken struck his fist against the palm of his hand. "The off-limits building!"

"What?"

"Everyone calls it that because it really is off limits. To everyone but the people who work there." As Ken became excited, his words began to tumble over each other: "It's the Genetics Research building and it's divided into sections. Phases One, Two and Three. Not even the people who work in Phases One and Two know what's going on in Phase Three. That's where the real advanced stuff is done. And it's where Peter Bradford spends most of his time. Dr. Latolier is there a lot too—I never did figure out why—except she and Bradford work so closely."

"What would the chief of surgery do in a place like that?"

"That's just the point. There's got to be a link between the IVF babies and Phase Three in the off-limits building. I know one place that could connect them. Operating Room K. That's where all in vitro babies are delivered."

"Nothing unusual about that," Rudy said. "Steptoe and Edwards introduced that idea in England. Only one operating room for all in vitro deliveries. Kept sterile at all times."

"I think Operating Room K is part of an experiment being conducted at the off-limits building. I don't know what kind of experiment. But Bradford and Latolier would both have to be involved. That would account for her being over there. She's the link between the in vitro babies and what's going on in Phase Three."

"Where does that leave us?"

Ken gave a sigh of exasperation. "If they're doing research on those dead little babies, it's illegal to experiment with humans."

"We'd have to prove that first. Do you know anyone who works over in Phase Three?"

"Not even a nodding acquaintance. They don't socialize. The way I understand it, they're all handpicked for their jobs. By Bradford himself."

"Can you get into the building?"

"That's easier. Phases One and Two are under tight security but not all that tight."

"That would be a start. You might figure a way to get into Phase Three and have a look. But it would be risky. You could be walking into a lot of trouble."

Ken Hartley grinned. "They wouldn't bother anyone of my color. That'd be interfering with my civil rights. Besides, I work for this hospital, and it would look natural for me to be in there. I can plead dumb curiosity. Most people at the central facility would love to get a peep at that place."

Rudy placed his hands gently against Ken's arm. "I don't like the idea of your sticking your neck out."

Ken's grin faded. After a moment he said, "Bernie Seligson was my friend. You reminded me of that once. Now I'm reminding you."

"Okay. But in God's name be careful. We both know the kind of people we're dealing with."

Rudy left the hospital by the employee's entrance and found the Porsche in the parking lot. A yellow sun was almost overhead as he drove onto the narrow asphalt road that led to the Hutchinson Parkway. The road sparkled with motes of light. He squinted ahead while his thoughts returned to his conversation with Ken Hartley. This was not a problem for two well-meaning young doctors. But who else could they turn to? There wasn't enough evidence of a crime to satisfy the police.

Rudy didn't even know what Bradford was doing, or why. Bradford would not go to such lengths without reason, which indicated the scheme was important enough to cover up—even at the price of a man's life.

He was a mile from the parkway entrance when he heard the pulsing of a car engine approaching. He steered slightly to the right and glanced in the rearview mirror.

His scalp prickled.

The car behind him was a dark green sedan.

He pushed down on the accelerator. The Porsche leapt ahead and swung into the turn. When he glanced at his rearview mirror again, heavy maple trees with dense limbs and branches were obscuring the view. The dark green sedan had vanished.

He relaxed a little, smiling at himself. He had overreacted. The green sedan had probably not been a Mercury Monarch. If you live in a climate of fear, the weather of your mood is affected. He was oversensitized to danger. If he kept on this way, paranoia was only a hop, skip and jump . . .

The dark green sedan was back.

It hurtled out of the turn behind him like an oncoming missile. The driver had timed his move perfectly, hurtling out of the concealment provided by the turn and the obscuring trees.

Rudy couldn't speed up in time to elude the speeding car. To his right was a steep embankment covered with heavy underbrush. The road had narrowed to where two cars could scarcely pass abreast of each other. He swung the car toward the middle of the road. Then the steering wheel was knocked from his grasp by a tremendous jolt.

The little car seemed to rise, taking flight. Everything around him seesawed. A brazen clangor rang in his ears. He grabbed the wheel in time to hold the battered car steady on the road.

The entrance to the Hutchinson Parkway was half a mile away. If another car appeared suddenly on the other side as he whipped into the next turn, that would be his finish. The driver of the car behind him would get him one way or another.

The Porsche was rammed again. He heard a terrible *thwocking* sound, and the little car rocked and swayed. The force of the collision nearly propelled it onto the embankment. At this speed there would be no chance of survival.

He twisted the wheel, throwing his weight hard to the left. The Porsche keeled over as centrifugal force pummeled it. Trees and road and sun whirled in a giddying kaleidoscope.

He hung suspended in terror for a long instant before the car regained its balance. Its scorched and shredded tires gripped asphalt. Its wildly racing engine took hold to yank the car from its slide.

Rudy's body settled back into his seat. He was faint from the shift of pressure. He could hardly see. The faintness passed, his sight cleared. He gripped the wheel firmly, pressed down hard on the accelerator, and sped in the opposite direction.

Unable to duplicate Rudy's sudden maneuver, the driver of the sedan kept plunging ahead.

Rudy stared at the rearview mirror. He felt emptied, a wind-filled sack, a puffed skin of emptiness.

Enough of this, he thought. I'm going to the police.

Chapter

15

Monroe Thorpe had a wide face, marcelled hair and eye corners over which too many crows' feet had walked. For twenty-one years he had been police chief in the community known as Plinth's Landing (pop. 1843).

He took down the vital statistics patiently, name, address, age, occupation, year and make of car ("How do you spell Porsche?"). He jotted all down on a sheet of yellow foolscap.

Then they went over the incident in detail, replaying it in the very slow motion of description, questions, answers. Thorpe painstakingly copied the facts onto the record.

"Another thing," Rudy said. "I've seen this car before."

"Where?"

"In New York City. Just this morning."

Thorpe's pen stayed poised a moment over his notes before he looked up.

Rudy said, "At the 86th Street crossover into Central Park. A late model Mercury Monarch, dark green, moving about five miles an hour on the other side of Central Park West. When I started into the transverse, it made the turn with me and tried to run me down."

Thorpe put his pen down carefully crosswise on the foolscap. "How do you know it was the same vehicle? The odds are pretty high against a car you saw in New York coming up all the way to Plinth's Landing just to get involved in an accident with you."

"It wasn't an accident. The driver was coming after me. Deliberately trying to force me off the road."

Thorpe pulled at his tufted eyebrow as though picking a glass splinter out of it.

"Well, now, that puts a different face on things. That's a very serious charge." Thorpe stared at the sheet of foolscap on his desk before he picked it up, folded it carefully in thirds, and put it into the breast pocket of his blue shirt. "Let's go have a look at the place where it happened."

They got into a dusty police cruiser, and during the drive Thorpe did not ask questions. He found the road Rudy had taken leaving the Karyll Clinic and followed it for a short distance. They passed the sign indicating that the entrance to the Hutchinson Parkway was a mile ahead.

"This is where I first saw the car coming," Rudy said.

They drove on a short distance.

"Around that next turn," Rudy said. "That's where it raced up behind me. Really barreling."

Heavily drooping maple branches almost blocked the view at the point where Thorpe braked the police car to a stop. They got out and walked along the asphalt road while Rudy described what had occurred at what point.

"Everything must have happened pretty fast," Thorpe said. "A car traveling sixty is going eighty-eight feet every second. How fast were you going at this point?"

"About forty. Maybe less."

"Maybe he didn't see you in time. He wouldn't have more than a second or two coming around that curve."

"He saw me all right. He was trying to kill me."

"Couldn't he have been drunk? We had a car hit a fellow late at night on this very road. Knocked him out of a pair of laced shoes. In real high-speed accidents that can happen. The driver was drunk right out of his mind." Thorpe stopped, looking at where tire marks veered wildly in a tight circle. "This must be where you turned your car around."

"Yes, it is."

Thorpe stooped to examine the marks on the road. Little shards of rubber were in the tire tracks.

"How many people were in the other car?"

"I think the driver was alone."

"But you're not sure?"

"Not entirely."

"Was the driver a man or a woman?"

"I'm pretty sure it was a man."

"But not entirely?"

"No."

"But you are sure it was the same car you saw in New York City?"

Rudy felt himself flushing. "Yes."

"Do you know why anyone would want to harm you?"

What could he say that would sound convincing? That there was a conspiracy at the prestigious Karyll Clinic in which the world-famous Dr. Peter Bradford was involved? If the choice were between levels of improbability, it was a lot easier for Thorpe to believe in a motiveless killer than a conspiracy.

"No one that I know of," Rudy said. "Look, I know it sounds unlikely. But who would drive eighty miles an hour on a road like this? And look where he caught up. On a section of road where he could come at me with no warning."

"It would help if we had a license plate number. Even one letter."

"Sorry."

Thorpe's smile was a parting of the lips with no meaning. "We don't have much to go on. But we'll do everything we can. I won't kid you that we've got the manpower in our town. But we've got a working arrangement with White Plains. Their accident investigation unit is first rate."

Rudy felt a cold hatred growing in him for the unknown enemy who was trying to kill him. "What will they do?"

Thorpe said, "They could alert the highway patrols to look for a dark green Mercury Monarch with a dented fender or bumper. They could even put it through a computer and get a line on all vehicles of that make and model in the state. Then narrow it down until they find the vehicle they're looking for."

"But they won't, will they?"

The wrinkles deepened at Thorpe's eye corners. "They may not want to go to all that trouble for a vehicular accident where nobody's been hurt. Thank you for your time and trouble."

That evening Rudy was sitting in the black leather reclining chair in the living room of his apartment. His slippered feet were resting on a hassock. The stereo was tuned to station WNCN and playing softly, and he was reading the *New England Journal of Medicine*. He was trying to keep darker thoughts at bay, shutting off channels through which the memory of recent events might reenter his mind.

The doorbell rang and he got up to answer it. When he looked out the peephole his mood instantly brightened.

He opened the door. "This is a nice surprise."

"Is it all right to come in?" Mary asked.

"By all means."

She was wearing a smart-looking white suit with a rust-colored Coach bag over one shoulder, and she carried a small attaché case. She put the case down on the black-and-white checkered linoleum of the hall-way, slung her bag off her shoulder and put it on the chair beside the hall telephone stand.

Rudy said, "There's a bottle of Moët et Chandon in the refrigerator that I've been saving for a special occasion."

"How nice. I like your apartment. Is there more to it?"

"See for yourself."

As he popped the cork on the champagne, she returned from her tour, oohing-and-ahing about the view. Her tone was brisk, cheery.

He poured champagne into two glasses. "You missed sunset. Sunsets here should not be missed."

They sat on the sofa, a little apart, facing the stereo and the uninhabited black leather chair under the isolated reading light. The *New England Journal of Medicine* was lying open on the hassock where he had left it.

She sipped from her glass. "I was going to dinner with Sam Dodds when you called last night. You sounded pretty upset. And you didn't give a very good excuse for canceling our date."

"It wasn't the sort of thing I could talk about over the telephone. The whole experience was pretty bizarre."

"Let's talk about it."

Once he began to talk he couldn't stop. He told her what had happened in the little town in Arkansas and went on to what happened since, including the near-accident on the road leaving the Karyll Clinic.

The clock made a peculiar whirring sound as it struck the hour. Ten o'clock.

"Well, that's it," he said. "I don't know whether Hartley will get into the off-limits building or not. Either way, I expect him to call."

She had both hands locked around her knee, rocking a little. She said with utmost seriousness, "It's much too dangerous. You shouldn't get mixed up in this. What can you hope to accomplish?"

"I'm not sure myself. All I know is that I can't shrug my shoulders and walk away from it."

She put her hand gently on his. "Do you remember what you told me on the telephone? About how you feel? Well, I feel the same way."

"Would you mind repeating that?"

Instead, she leaned over and kissed him. It was not just a kiss to say hello.

"Now I want you to repeat that," he said.

"First I want to explain what I'm doing here tonight. When I had dinner with Sam I told him I'd found someone I liked better."

"You're not only beautiful. You have good judgment."

"And now that I've found you, I have no intention of losing you."

"You couldn't."

"You've had two pretty close calls."

"I'm open to suggestions. What do you think I should do?"

"It's not your problem. If the police aren't interested, forget it."

"The other side doesn't seem to be in a mood to forget. Whoever killed Dr. Seligson has just as good reason to get rid of me."

"You don't have to scare me. I'm scared."

"What can I do? I can't stand around and do nothing until they take another shot at me."

They were both silent, and he realized that in the past hour something had happened that was important and unfathomable. It was hard to believe that they had met such a short time ago. When he first saw her he had recognized how attractive she was, but now he would never see her in the same way again, for his feeling about her had become subjective: Everything about her was beautiful simply because she was Mary Oliver.

As he stared at her, thinking about the significance of all this, it occurred to him: My God, I might not have been home tonight.

He said, "It's Saturday night. We're having our date after all. Are you staying with your sister in Riverdale tonight?"

"She doesn't even know I'm in town."

The volcanic eruption of sunset over the Jersey hills had faded hours before, but some of its fire seemed to transfer itself to this room.

She said, "That attaché case is my overnight bag. I have a very sexy negligee and a very fetching outfit to wear tomorrow. I can't wait to show them to you."

*   *   *

In the negligee, low cut, close fitting and silky, the skin of her arms and neck and throat appeared translucent. The soft prominence of her breasts rose and fell with each breath.

She sat beside him on the bed in the darkened bedroom. The scent of her perfume was exciting and elusive. When he kissed her everything turned into sensation. His fingertip traced her fine slender clavicle. Silk within silk. He removed the delicately appliqued straps of her negligee and rubbed his cheek against her partially revealed breasts, then folded back an edge of silk to kiss the roseate stain of each nipple. It was like kissing velvet.

She lay back on the bed, her dark hair splayed against the pillow. At the first contact of their bodies, a liquid fire ignited in his brain and turned his body molten. She began to quiver beneath him. All thought ceased, all words failed as he held her close.

A sharp twinge wakened him. Vivid dream images began to subside. Another sharp twinge.

He translated the feeling into sound. A telephone ringing. He saw the clock on the night table. Past midnight.

He fumbled, had it. "Hello."

"Rudy?"

"*Ken!* What?"

"I had to wait until the switchboard closed to call direct. I got into the off-limits building, but Phase Three is wrapped up tighter than Fort Knox. I couldn't get near it."

"That's okay." He remembered what Mary had said. "Maybe it's for the best."

"I did pay a visit to Operating Room K. Just to look over the setup while no one was around." Ken's voice dropped to hardly more than a whisper. "And something's peculiar. Damned peculiar."

"What is?" A chill that was like an invisible presence washed over him.

Ken's voice became a breath, almost too insubstantial to be heard: "The conveyor in the utility room. And in a cabinet drawer . . ." His voice stopped, then came back rushed: "I can't talk any more."

Rudy asked quickly, "Where can I meet you?"

"You can't." The voice was so faint now it was unreal, but Ken's fear was audible. "I may be in trouble. Real trouble."

The broken connection seemed to leave an echo behind: a small startled exclamation?

"Ken!" Rudy said. He heard the deep passage of breath through his lungs and out through his clenched teeth and lips.

There was no answer.

Mary was lying on her side in bed, watching him.

He trembled with a high strange current of excitement, the kind of feeling that sends a man into danger without properly reckoning the odds or understanding the risks.

Suddenly the situation in which he found himself seemed incredible. It was someone else who sat here, sinking deeper and deeper into the bottomless pit of inevitability. He was convinced he had to do something, but far from convinced of the wisdom of what he was about to do.

"I have to go," he said. As he spoke he was sitting up on his side of the bed and turning on the light.

Chapter

16

Earlier that evening, Gaby Latolier entered the nursery playroom on the top floor of the Genetics Research Building. She found Alma trying to play clap hands with three hairy little apes. Actually, they were Sendais, but at this stage of their development it was difficult to distinguish them from apes.

Alma was having no luck getting the Sendai infants to clap their hands. They watched Alma with pale, torpid eyes and did not know what was expected of them.

Alma was short and plump with a solemn face. She wore a gray starched uniform. When she saw Gaby she looked relieved to stop what she was doing. She got up from her knees.

"Are the others coming?" Alma asked.

"Later tonight. We're expecting a new one in a few hours. Then we'll transfer them all together. I think you'll find them quite a surprise."

"In what way?"

"They aren't the same." Gaby indicated the three hairy infants with a wave of her hand. "They look much more—human."

178

She knew that Alma was locked into the old-fashioned notion that to create a hybrid, something new, like the genes of a different species, had to be introduced into the process of reproduction. Alma thought the Sendais were created from a union of human and a lower species like the primates. Her human superiority would be affronted by the truth, that in such a union the human chromosomes were driven out almost as soon as the cells began to divide, and the lower species tended to prevail.

"I'd like to see the weekly report," Gaby said.

"I'll have Geraldine bring it."

Geraldine was a five-foot-ten-inch black woman whose hair was like an enormous bushy helmet. Gaby glanced through the three separate charts to note the results of tests and observations. Everything was proceeding exactly as Peter Bradford predicted. They were showing far more rapid physical development. At one year and a month, the Sendai infants were the size of five-year-old human children.

She handed the charts back. "I want you to begin keeping the same records for the new ones when they arrive. Estelle and Janet will be detached from duty in Operating Room K. They can help out."

Alma said, "We can handle it without any help."

These two didn't want strangers intruding into their domain. Two lovebirds perfectly happy to twitter together for the rest of their lives. Alma and Geraldine had worked together previously at a center for retarded children, but when the nature of their relationship became known they were asked to leave. They were perfect for this job, experienced, secretive, desiring no company but their own.

Geraldine asked, "How many more are coming?"

Gaby told her, "Five, including the new delivery."

A new kind of life. Peter Bradford had penetrated farther than anyone before him into the mechanisms of life at the most detailed chemical level. His achievement would rank with the great scientific discoveries of the century.

A hairy female Sendai picked up a tattered Raggedy Ann doll, held it by one leg, dangling head downward. Suddenly she lifted it and began to batter it on the floor.

"Stop that!" Geraldine ordered.

She tried to snatch the doll away, but the Sendai held on to it. The resistance was merely instinctive, for her placid pale eyes stared at Geraldine without expression. Geraldine could not wrest the doll away. At last, the doll's legs began to tear, and ripped away from the body. Geraldine held only the torso and head.

Gaby looked at the doll's tangled hair and button eyes and comical red-painted mouth.

She said, "We must try to teach them not to be destructive. That's very important."

The incident forced Gaby to remember some things she did not want to. In a small, dark walk-up apartment in the Fourth Arrondissement of Paris, she had played on a bare floor near a gray-streaked window with a floppy stuffed doll rescued from a trash can. She called her doll Annette. She and Annette played their own amusing game when Mother was entertaining a friend. Gaby would turn Annette's head to listen to the sounds from the bedroom. Gaby would mimic the sounds, and Annette's head would wobble helplessly with laughter.

Gaby was at school one morning when a policeman came to the classroom. The teacher called Gaby by name, and she got up and went with the policeman, who was very kind to her. He told her not to be frightened, that a "terrible thing" had happened at home and she would have to be brave.

A neighbor had identified the bodies of her mother and father, but the other man, the one lying nude on the bed with eyes staring up at the ceiling, was unidentified. Gaby recognized him as one of the men who frequently came to visit her mother. Her father had shot him. Then he had shot her mother and himself.

Gaby was sent to an orphanage. At fourteen she ran away with a young gardener who worked there. She stayed with her lover a few months. One morning she told him she was pregnant. The next day he was gone. He left without a word or a note, and Gaby accepted his leaving without regret. She had not liked him very much.

There was only one way she knew to survive. Standing on a corner, posing provocatively, she smiled at any likely customer, and one thing invariably led to another. In three weeks she earned enough money so she could go to a doctor in town. André Latolier was sixty-two years old. He had a thick body, white hair, and a seamed ugly face. He asked her politely to undress, gave her a thorough physical examination including tests for syphilis and gonorrhea. Then he kissed her breasts, made her stretch out on the table where he would shortly take the baby from her, and made love to her.

Two days after the operation, when she returned for an examination, white-haired Dr. Latolier told her she must come to live with him in his house.

Dr. Latolier smiled. "It will be a pleasant arrangement for us both. I will adopt you as my own child. I am a widower—my wife died eight years ago. You will be very happy with me."

That evening she moved into Dr. Latolier's home. He lived in a gray frame house of ample proportions in a nice respectable section of the working class suburb of Passy.

Her life was not unhappy. André was a heavy drinker, and when drunk he beat her, but at other times he was very kind. He discussed patients with her in the evening when she brought him his nightly glass of brandy. They chatted about patients' symptoms and diagnoses until it was time for them to go to bed.

On one occasion, a pregnant woman who was being examined in André's office suddenly began to have her baby. With Gaby's help, André got her up onto the table. Gaby handed him the proper instruments with quick, sure precision, and the birth was completed without incident.

André, however, was not grateful for her help. He seemed to resent it. That night he got very drunk and was particularly abusive to her.

A few months later a male patient arrived at the office, still clad in pajamas with an overcoat over his shoulders. During an argument, his wife had stabbed him with a pair of scissors, puncturing his trachea. André had left a few minutes earlier on an emergency call, so there was no one in the office but Gaby. She saw that the man would die without immediate medical

treatment. There was no time to send for an ambulance. Gaby performed a tracheotomy to create a breathing opening in the neck, and by the time André returned
to his office the patient was resting comfortably on a
cot in the anteroom, his wound bandaged. He had been
treated with a professional competence almost equal to
André's own.

André was furious with Gaby. Didn't she realize she
could have got him into very serious trouble? What she
had done was against the law. She had practiced
medicine without a license. If anyone talked, there
might have to be an investigation. He worked himself
into a rage and gave her a severe thrashing.

André never again discussed his patients' symptoms
with Gaby. He was not aware how many hours she
spent reading his medical reference books. Nor did she
inform him when she arranged to take the entrance
examination at a medical school at Nanterre, on the
western outskirts of Paris. She qualified with the highest
mark ever registered by any applicant at the school.

When André found out, he refused to let her go. He
threatened to write the director of the school. If she
tried to leave, he would make up a story about her
stealing from him and have her prosecuted for theft. To
enforce his threat, he beat her so severely that she had
to spend a day in bed and wear a high-necked dress
with long sleeves to conceal the bruises.

One week later, while Gaby was away at the market,
a fire completely destroyed the frame house where
André Latolier lived and worked. The official investigation decided that André had been drinking heavily
and smoking. A cigarette he dropped had smoldered in
the carpeting, caught, spread to the draperies, and

within minutes there was no possibility of escape. Fortunately he had been suffocated by smoke long before the flames reached him.

The official verdict might have changed if the police knew that André had given up smoking when alone because he feared just such an occurrence. Gaby, as André's legal heir, was awarded the "house and other assets," but the house was totally destroyed, the land worth less than the mortgage, and the fire insurance did not begin to cover the difference. "Other assets" consisted mostly of unpaid bills, and became uncollectible at his death. The shrewd French workers and farmers, whose wives had been his patients, saw nothing to be gained by paying good money to a dead man.

Gaby had no money to support herself, so she had to apply for a scholarship at the Nanterre medical school. In return for free tuition, she did "scut" work for the hospital where she was being trained. She wheeled patients to X-ray and operating rooms, did white and red blood cell counts and urine and stool analyses. This took up so much time that she missed medical lectures. But that did not matter. Everything was so absurdly easy for her, so elementary, she felt like a fencing master being drilled in how to stand and how to lunge. Her main interest was in surgery. A chief resident at the hospital, who heard her discuss the treatment of various surgical conditions, began to consult her on differential diagnosis.

One day the chief resident told her, with awe in his voice, that Peter Bradford was coming to their hospital to give a lecture. Bradford was a leading researcher in modern genetics and the biochemical mechanisms of disease. Gaby begged the chief resident to sneak her into the lecture, and he agreed.

That afternoon in the lecture hall became a turning point in her life. Listening to Peter Bradford, she knew that her future was settled once and for all. She had a sense of excitement, of kindling impatience.

That very night she sat down and wrote him a letter. Because she knew he would not be susceptible to flattery, she included hard, challenging questions that indicated why she could not entirely agree with him. He replied, and that began a correspondence that eventually led to his invitation to come to the United States to work with him after her graduation.

The day after she graduated, she booked passage to the United States.

Gaby left the nursery room at the off-limits building and returned to the central hospital. She went immediately to check on her patient. A fetal monitoring system was recording vital conditions in her womb. A cardiometer was connected to the fetal scalp by a thin wire introduced through the vagina and the cervix. A fluid-filled tube was connected from the uterus to the monitor to record the frequency, duration and pressure of any contraction. The fetal heart tones were regular and the vital signs were within normal limits: 98.6 temperature, pulse averaging 80, respiration averaging 18. Blood pressure was 120/80.

The patient, however, was in a dangerous state of tension. She complained of moderately severe cramps and pain in the lower back.

"You mustn't worry," Gaby told her. She placed her hand on the swollen, hard belly and felt movement within. "We're going to do a Caesarean, but it won't be difficult."

"Why can't I have my baby normally?"

"It would be a long difficult delivery. "You're a prime-ip—a first pregnancy. And there are complications. The baby is very large and positioned feet first. Monitoring indicates it would be born face up. That's a difficult position. Less flexibility because the baby can't be bent downward in a natural curve. It has to be a Caesarean."

"What does my husband say?"

"He's signed the release form."

At that moment Gaby was summoned outside. Delaney was waiting.

"I'm sorry to bother you. I tried to reach Dr. Bradford first."

"He's in his lab. Not to be disturbed."

Peter had gone there when he received word of his mother's death. For him, work created endorphins in the brain, nature's own painkiller.

"We have a problem with Dr. Hartley. One of the security guards noticed him trying to get into Phase Three."

"What was he doing there?"

"We're not sure. I've been following your orders: Watch him but don't interfere. The guard let him go with a warning. He came back here—and went to Operating Room K. He was there about twenty minutes. He returned to his room a little while ago."

"Tell the switchboard we'll monitor his calls. He'll try to get in touch with Dr. Gerson."

"We can put a stop to that."

"Why should we? He won't know he's being monitored.

We'll hear what he's found out. Maybe he'll bring Gerson here. One way or another, we have to get rid of both of them."

"Leave it to me."

She understood Delaney. In his way he was a perfectionist. Efficient, heavy-handed, cruel, but with his own pride.

She spoke slowly, adding emphasis to her words: "Let's not bungle it this time. You've failed twice before with Dr. Gerson."

A tiny edge of white appeared at his mouth corners, as if they had been touched with dry ice.

"It won't happen again."

"I hope not."

She watched him go off down the corridor, his back stiff with resentment. He was a man who added up to a certain total, and there weren't many who did that. A violent man, surely, but violence was present at all levels of society in slightly different forms.

She accepted the world and the absolute necessity of self-defense.

Chapter

17

The man at the garage brought down the Porsche. "You know, Doctor, your car has a bad dent in the rear bumper and part of the trunk. It didn't happen here."

"I know it didn't," Rudy told him.

"If somebody rear-ended you, I hope you notified your insurance."

"I haven't yet, but I will."

On the highway to Westchester he encountered little traffic. He drove at seventy-five miles an hour. If a state trooper stopped him, he might have trouble persuading him he was a doctor. He didn't look like one in leather lumberjacket, sweater and corduroy slacks.

He had dressed this way for a reason. Even at this hour of the morning he couldn't walk in the main entrance to the hospital. They must be expecting him to show up sooner or later, but they were not aware that he knew they were expecting him. He was counting on that.

He had decided to gain admittance through the emergency entrance. Confusion reigned there at almost any time in any hospital; it would be very difficult to station enough security guards to keep watch on everyone coming and going. And they had no reason to think he would try to slip in that way.

As he drove through the gate toward the emergency entrance he saw an ambulance parked under the bright-lit canopy. Just ahead of him a Ford station wagon was pulling into a parking space. Rudy parked beside it. A woman and a man got out. The woman was very pregnant. She was stooping forward as she walked, leaning on the man's arm, and she left a trail of spattered blood behind.

Rudy caught up and took her by the other arm. "Here, let me help."

Inside, the waiting room was crowded. Rudy helped them to find a space on a bench.

"Stay with her," Rudy told the man. "I'll check her in."

The man nodded. As Rudy left, he was saying to the woman, "It isn't as bad as it looks. They'll take good care of you."

Rudy was fourth in line, directly behind a woman holding a squawling red-faced baby, a very fat woman drawing wheezing breaths and releasing them with a curious whistling sound, and an authoritative bespectacled woman who was describing in a loud voice to the nurse the unpleasant symptoms that required her to seek maternity aftercare.

Rudy went to the front of the line. A security guard was in a chair to the right of the desk. "Can you help me?" Rudy asked him. "There's a woman who's hemorrhaging."

He indicated the bench, where a pool of blood was already forming on the floor.

"I'll get someone right away," the guard said. He jumped up and hurried off.

Moments later the guard and an orderly reappeared with a cot. They helped the woman who was hemorrhaging onto the cot and wheeled her away.

The nurse at the admissions desk looked at Rudy. "I'll need the clinic number and a history of that patient. Do you have it?"

"I'll get her husband."

The nurse handed him a form. "Give him this and tell him to fill it out and bring it back to me."

Rudy gave the form to the man sitting forlornly on the bench. Then he drifted toward an open alcove where refreshments were vended. Several large machines offered soft drinks, coffee, candy and snacks. A sturdy-looking young woman was pulling the lever for an orange drink. A paper cup came down and was held in place by clamps while a spigot filled it.

Her pink perspiring face turned to Rudy. "If you want a Coke, it's empty. If you want a Seven-up, it's empty. I hate orange, but I'm dyin' of thirst. The rest is all diet." She wiped her forehead with her sleeve and left, sipping her orange drink.

Just beyond the alcove there was a hallway. Rudy followed yellow directional arrows on the floor until he reached a door with an inset glass pane that looked into an emergency ward with at least twenty cots. A young woman, no more than seventeen, wearing a kerchief over her hair, and a young man who wore a yamulke, were sitting beside a patient in the first bed.

A nurse pushed a wheelchair through the door. The nurse was gaunt and thin, and the woman in the wheelchair was rosy-cheeked and blooming. Rudy held the door open for the wheelchair to pass through.

"Thank you," the nurse said with a wan smile.

"Can you tell me the way to the A-block elevators?" Rudy asked.

"Straight to the end of the hall. Turn left."

A-block elevators led to the residential area for hospital staff. The elevator took him down to the now-deserted, dim area, and he found his way to Ken Hartley's cubicle.

At the door he asked softly, "Ken, you in there?" There was no answer.

He tried the knob and was surprised that it turned loosely. He stepped quickly inside the room. "Ken, it's me. Rudy Gerson."

Silence. He closed the door and turned on the light. The room was just as he had seen it before, immaculate and sterile. A coverlet was neatly turned on the bed. A telephone was on the projecting shelf that served as a desk. He examined it. The telephone's gleaming surface was not marred by a single smudge. It appeared to have been wiped clean.

Lifting the receiver gingerly, he heard an infrequent clicking, not even a dial tone. On the base of the phone a thin red label carried words in yellow lettering: *After midnight dial 9 for an outside number.*

Rudy replaced the receiver in its cradle and looked about the room. He tried to imagine Ken Hartley on the telephone to him. Had Ken spoken in a whisper because he feared being overheard?

He went back to examine the loose knob. The lock had been forced. Some kind of instrument had been used. Tiny scratch marks were visible.

He went into the diminutive bathroom. A half-filled

glass of water was on the sink. A toothbrush and a tube of toothpaste were nearby. The bristles of the toothbrush were still damp. Whoever had cleaned up the room had not bothered with the bathroom.

Rudy was sure he could retrace Ken Hartley's movements. After he had tried and failed to get into Phase Three, he had returned to the main hospital. He had made his solitary inspection of Operating Room K, and come here to his room to wait for the switchboard to close at midnight. When he picked up the telephone to make a direct call someone was outside listening. During the call something had warned Ken, perhaps subliminally. But it was too late. He was surprised, overpowered.

Where had they taken him and what did they intend to do with him? Rudy felt a surge of helplessness. He searched the room again, but there was no clue. Not a hair, not a stain. Once, as he straightened up from searching under the bed, he was startled by the sight of his own face in a small mirror on the wall. He looked ghastly.

I may be in trouble. Real trouble.

He left the room, turning out the light. The corridor was still dim and deserted. He heard the sound of a distant elevator and waited until the sound ceased. No one appeared.

He took a moment to orient himself on this subterranean level. The residential area was near the OR area. He found the main corridor and followed it to the passageway that led to the OR area.

Operating Rooms. Only Authorized Personnel Beyond This Point.

Near the entrance the nurse's station was empty.

There was no need for a guardian at this hour. Beyond
the nurse's station a line of doors stretched along the
right side. In a hospital this large, allowing for the
usual ratio of one operating room for every fifty beds,
there should be about twenty-five ORs.

His footsteps were muffled as he moved slowly down
the hall. A sliver of light showed beneath two doors.
Muted sounds of activity came from within. Between
each pair of operating rooms was an unlettered door.
These were the utility rooms, with instrument sterilizers,
washer sterilizers, work counters, storage shelves and
scrub sinks.

He stopped in front of Operating Room K. No light
showed here. The door opened into darkness. As he
entered, the ceiling light turned on. The room was
standard size, about twenty by eighteen feet with a
ten-foot-high ceiling. The walls were of glazed tile to a
point five feet below the ceiling, then became a surface
of light green plaster.

He took a quick inventory. There was an individual
transformer to supply electricity, and a hygrometer to
control the proportion of moisture in the air, an intercom
system with speaker microphones at each of three
outlets. There was also a wired telephone device for
dictating operating notes, an ultra-high-frequency radio
system for paging other areas, a central pipe system for
oxygen, and a central vacuum cleaning system.

The operating table had conductive rubber pads and
an attached surgical lamp of the new type that allowed
several operators to work simultaneously in a deep
small cavity. The lamp also had a camera attachment
for taking TV pictures.

Just then Rudy heard something he did not want to hear.

Over the paging system: "Nurses Blakely and Haywood to the OR please. Operating Room K. Stat!"

He turned off the light with a wall switch and hurried into the adjoining utility room. He intended to continue on to the next operating room, but a blank wall confronted him. This utility room was not shared. It was strictly for the use of Operating Room K.

Moments later footsteps ran down the hall. Rudy had no choice but to remain where he was and look around for a hiding place. He decided to sit with his back to the metal counters dividing the scrub area from the rear of the room.

Seconds later overhead lights went on. Then faucets in the scrub sinks turned on as microsensors signaled someone's approach. Sitting with his back pressed hard against the counter, Rudy felt the vibration of running water.

The two persons who entered must be doctors. They were beginning the scrub. He rehearsed in his mind what they were doing as the seconds kept ticking by. They had taken little plastic squares out of a cardboard box and squeezed the plastic squares until they popped open. Inside were sterile brushes, with bristles on one side and a sponge impregnated with iodine on the other, and a small plastic file to clean their nails.

Now they were scrubbing up their arms, starting at the elbow and working down over their hands with straight short strokes. Now they were scrubbing all four sides of each finger.

One doctor spoke for the first time. Over the running water Rudy recognized the low voice of Gaby Latolier.

Most of what she said was inaudible over the running water, but a question came clearly: "Nitrous oxide, Dr. Harrison?" The reply was, "Of course."

Odd. Even Caesarean deliveries were accomplished with the use of a simple anesthetic that bathed the spinal column and rendered the nerves numb so the patient would not feel anything from the point at which she was injected. Inhalants were avoided because through the bloodstream of a pregnant woman they can reach the placenta. The only reason to administer nitrous oxide would be to make the patient "stargaze"—be out of contact with what was happening.

The scrub was a laborious, painstaking process that took ten minutes to complete. Then, holding their hands high, both doctors shook their elbows over the sink. A few drops splattered over the counter onto Rudy's face.

Microsensors turned off the faucets as the doctors stepped back from the sinks. Moments later the access door into Operating Room K swung open and two masked and gowned doctors left the utility room. On the other side, a scrub nurse would be waiting to give them sterile towels to dry their hands before slipping on their sterile gloves.

The lights in the utility room went out as soon as the access door closed. In the operating room next door sounds of activity increased. Rudy listened to it for several minutes while his eyes began adjusting to the darkness. Then he began a leisurely search of the room.

Suddenly he drew in a long, long breath. He felt like someone on a high cliff who has suddenly glimpsed a terrifying chasm yawning beneath.

Blinking against the darkness, he forced himself to look again. From a partly open cabinet in a work counter opposite him a tiny hand projected, as if making a grotesque plea for help.

It was a baby.

At that instant, he heard its wailing cry.

He felt cold, and shock was like a pain in his chest.

Then with a warm gush of relief, he realized that the cry came from the operating room next door. The population had just been increased by one.

He approached the counter and pulled out the drawer. The infant lay on its side. Its eyes were closed, lashes resting with a silky softness on full pink cheeks. Its head had a scanty coating of blond hair. Its arms were small, chubby, perfectly formed.

Lying so peacefully, its resemblance to a newborn baby *was* startling. But this was only a replica, life-size, lifelike, unalive. Why? The question sounded almost spectral with incredulity. He felt as if he had the key to a mystery and didn't know where the lock was.

Ken Hartley had been in this room earlier. He must have found this replica of a baby. Perhaps that was what Ken meant when he had whispered, *Something's peculiar, damned peculiar.*

Quickly Rudy pushed the drawer shut, making sure the baby's hand was no longer caught. He glanced at his wristwatch. He could time what was going on next door by the luminescent hands. At most he had a few minutes left to discover what else Ken had seen in this room.

Now they're sucking out the baby's throat and mouth. Now they're administering oxygen and positive pres-

*sure, if needed, and assigning the one-minute Apgar
score.*

The utility room was equipped just as he expected it
would be. He encountered no surprises until he examined the conveyor that connected Central Supply with
the utility room.

All conveyor systems connected only two rooms, with
a single button that summoned it from one station to the
other. This one had two button controls.

*Vital signs are being checked before the three-minute
Apgar score. And they'll be looking for prematurity,
congenital malformation, birth injury, for anemia and
infection.*

He opened the top and bottom panels of the conveyor.
The space inside was larger than in any others he had
seen. Why? A conveyor was only needed to transport
special equipment from the supply room below.

*Now the baby was being given a vitamin K shot, plus
two drops of silver nitrate in its eyes to prevent gonococ-
cal infection.*

He heard someone approach the access door. He
scrambled to hide himself—this time on the far side of
the scrub sinks, crouching almost directly beneath the
basin.

Lights went on. A nurse entered and went directly to
the conveyor. He risked a quick glance. She was plac-
ing something in the conveyor. Her body blocked his
view, but the object resembled a baby warmer. He
ducked back quickly.

The conveyor ground into motion.

A cabinet door creaked open and shut.

The nurse returned to the operating room. Lights
went out in the utility room.

Rudy left his hiding place. The grinding noise of conveyor pulleys in the shaft stopped. He opened the cabinet drawer that had held the replica of a baby.

It was empty.

If all goes well, the floater nurse takes the newborn baby wrapped in a blanket to a nursery—either regular, special observation or intensive care.

A dead baby is taken to the morgue.

That's what the replica is for, he thought; to show any nurses, orderlies or doctors who might be around that a baby actually was taken from the operating room.

But what did they do with the real baby?

He returned to the conveyor on the side wall. Why two control buttons if only one was needed? The conveyor only had to go to the supply room and back. One push on the button would send it, another bring it back.

Unless the conveyor went somewhere else.

A grinding noise began again in the shaft. The conveyor was returning. Someone must have sent it back.

When the conveyor stopped he opened the top and bottom panels and looked in. The interior was empty. Whatever the nurse had put inside was gone.

Almost at the door connecting to the operating room he heard Dr. Latolier say clearly, "I think Dr. Bradford will be pleased, don't you?"

"I know he will," a man's voice replied.

They would be coming back to the utility room in a moment, and neither of his previous hiding places would work. At this angle, entering through the access door, they would be sure to see him behind the metal counter. If he tried to hide near the scrub sinks, they would see him as soon as they got there.

He climbed into the conveyor, drawing his legs up after him. It was a tight fit. He barely managed by holding his shins and drawing them in close to him, keeping his elbows pressed to his sides and his head and shoulders bent down sharply. Fetal position.

He pulled the conveyor panel shut just as the lights went on in the utility room.

For the next few minutes he maintained a very cramped position. To keep his mind off the discomfort, he tried to analyze what was causing it. His muscles were composed of small areas of tissue which contracted or shortened when chemically activated. When a muscle contracted, carbon dioxide, heat, water, and lactic acid were produced. Increased blood flow to a muscle or heat dissipation by sweating would carry these metabolites away from the muscle area. But in his case the muscles were under unnatural stress, and the oxygen was not sufficient to diffuse the metabolites. Lactic acid built up to cause the ache in the strained muscle. If he had to stay in this position much longer, he would really be hurting.

Through a tiny opening between the panels he saw the light in the utility room go out.

Cautiously he opened the top panel of the conveyor. He reached out and his finger found the top button. He pushed it. Then he pulled the panel shut. The conveyor started up with a grinding of pulleys.

He had no idea where he was going.

But he was on his way.

Movement stopped one floor above the utility room. He opened the top panel and saw a room lit by two rows

of parallel ceiling lights. One row was fluorescent
bulbs, and the other consisted of ultraviolet lamps
giving off a faint greenish light. The room had no
furnishings except for several clear plastic boxes resting on top of solid metal tables.

Isolets. Self-contained islands of life.

Each containing an infant.

At the isolet farthest away from him a plump redheaded nurse, wearing dark-lensed glasses against the
low level ultraviolet rays in the room, was bending
over a newborn infant. The infant lay on its back, its
little hands making vague circles in the air and its legs
rubbing each other. The nurse attached three wires,
one to each chest nipple and another near its umbilical
region. The wires were connected to an oscilloscope
screen above the isolet. As soon as they were attached,
a yellow light began flashing on the screen with each
pulse.

The nurse straightened up and looked directly at
him.

He swung quickly out of the conveyor. As he did, he
slipped one hand into the pocket of his lumberjacket.

"Don't make a sound," he commanded. "I won't hurt
you if you cooperate." He added, on an inspiration: "I'm
a policeman."

He wasn't sure she believed him. But that didn't
matter as long as she remained quiet. The infant in the
nearest isolet was a girl whose unfocused eyes indicated an age of less than six weeks. Yet she weighed at
least thirty pounds. There were gauges to measure the
temperature and oxygen content, a small blinking TV
camera shutter and a lamp that illuminated the
interior.

He moved closer to read the ID bracelet around the baby's ankle.

Conklin.

Keeping his hand in his pocket and a wary eye on the nurse, he moved on to another isolet. The fretful infant inside was flinging its arms in uncoordinated movements.

Delgado.

Both babies had been reported dead at birth. Their parents were told they were dead. Yet here were both infants—*alive!*

He was immobilized by shock, but the redheaded nurse wasn't. She made her move. She reached into the isolet and snatched away a connecting wire. Instantly the light inside dimmed and brightened, the shutter on the TV camera started blinking rapidly, and on the greenish blue oscilloscope screen a warning pattern flashed.

The nurse ran for the door. Before she got there, a big florid-faced man pounded into the room.

The nurse screamed something to him, pointing to Rudy. The big man's face showed surprise and anger.

"Damn!" he said.

Rudy timed his rush at him perfectly. He drove his fist hard at the big man's jaw.

It was like hitting solid cement.

Everything happened then in slow motion. The big man's fist drove into Rudy's groin. White flame shot through his body. He bent double, choking. A terrible concussion, like the blow of a hammer, struck the back of his neck. He went down.

Someone else hurried into the room.

Gaby Latolier said, "That alarm. What was it?"

The nurse said, "I disconnected a monitor. I had to do something."

Ignoring Rudy, Gaby Latolier went directly to the isolet where the baby was wailing. "Seems all right," she said after a moment. "No significant interruption. But I'll double-check the vital signs."

Rudy felt as if the top of his head had been blown off. He could not catch his breath. Exquisite bursts of agony kept exploding in his groin.

He heard Gaby Latolier as if from a great distance. "You should have caught him earlier. He shouldn't have got this far."

A voice that sounded like rocks shifting underground replied: "Damned if I know how he did. But I'll find out."

"Never mind that. Bring him to the off-limits building and we'll question him there. Let's get the transfer underway. Dr. Bradford wants it complete within the hour."

Rudy's brain was throbbing. He was slowly becoming disconnected from the pain in his body. This is it, I can't hold on.

"Can you handle him alone?" Latolier asked.

"*Him?*" the gruff voice replied scornfully.

"I don't want anything else going wrong. We've had quite enough of that tonight."

In a tiny corner of Rudy's brain the last wink of consciousness winked out.

Chapter

18

In Rudy's apartment that morning, Mary heard the clock whir at the hour of seven. She was staring at the telephone and willing it to ring. Rudy had promised to call her as soon as he made contact with Dr. Hartley. It shouldn't have taken this long.

She tried to make allowances. There might not have been a telephone at hand. He might not want to risk a call from the hospital. He might have wanted to check out for himself what Dr. Hartley had seen in Operating Room K that was so "damn peculiar."

But after every allowance was made, including possible delays on the road, he should have called before this. He would have called if he were able to.

Why didn't the telephone ring?

All she needed was his dear sweet voice on the telephone saying he was all right.

She had felt a premonition when he left her to answer that postmidnight call. Now she was sure something had happened to him.

The telephone call might have been setting a trap. Rudy had no doubt that the voice belonged to Dr. Hartley. How could he be sure? A disembodied voice over the telephone assumes a new and different personality. Even if the call were from Dr. Hartley, why had he suddenly broken off?

Ten minutes past seven.

She had to be realistic. Discount the possibility that everything had gone smoothly. Only in the *Reader's Digest* does everything end happily.

What was left? At times she had regretted acting in haste, but there were more times in which she had regretted not acting at all.

She couldn't sit here waiting for a telephone call that might never come.

She dressed in the same outfit she had worn when she arrived at Rudy's apartment last evening, a world of time ago. She stood up, gave the telephone twenty seconds longer to ring. It did not. She put on her suit jacket and went out.

At West End Avenue she hailed a cab that took her to Grand Central Station in time to catch the 7:54 to Westchester. She got off at Plinth's Landing. A cab was parked outside the railroad station. The driver was an older man, wearing a checkered cap and a heavy workshirt.

"Take me to the police," she told him.

He looked at her with interest, but she said nothing.

Police headquarters was in a building that also housed the town hall and the post office. A woman, wearing a pale blue shirt and a dark blue skirt, was at a desk with a typewriter, a small computer terminal and two telephones. A silver badge was pinned above her shirt pocket.

She listened to Mary, then picked up a telephone. "Chief, this is Connie. A young lady's here with a missing persons report. . . . Maybe you'd better talk to her."

She handed Mary the telephone.

"Chief Monroe Thorpe," a voice announced. "May I help you?"

"I hope so. I want to report a missing person."

"What is the person's name?"

"Dr. Rudy Gerson."

"Dr. Gerson? I talked to him yesterday in connection with an accident report. What's happened to him?"

"I don't know. He left his apartment to go to the Karyll Clinic. He promised to call me as soon as he could. I haven't heard."

"When was that?"

"He left just after midnight."

There was a silence at the other end.

"You mean a few hours ago? We don't report a person as missing until he's been gone at least two days."

She tried hard to keep control of her voice. Lack of control always implied an element of irrationality.

"I know he's in danger."

"What makes you say that, Miss . . . uh . . ."

"Oliver. Mary Oliver. He got a telephone call shortly before he left. From a doctor at the Karyll Clinic who said he was in trouble. He wanted Rudy . . . Dr. Gerson to come right away."

"What kind of trouble?"

She thought about it and decided he wouldn't believe her. "I-I'm not sure I can explain."

Monroe Thorpe's tone was that of someone trying to be patient. "In my opinion, this doctor was calling him about some kind of medical emergency."

"No, it wasn't that at all."

"Whatever it was, I'm sure Dr. Gerson will turn up. There's nothing to worry about."

"You don't understand. His life is at stake. You've got to do something!" She could hear the strain in her voice.

"Why don't you call the Karyll Clinic?" Thorpe asked soothingly. "Talk to this other doctor. He'll tell you where Dr. Gerson is."

She realized it was hopeless. Thorpe would never come with her to the Karyll Clinic to search for Rudy. Not on the basis of her story.

Only a few days ago, leaving her office, she had seen a group of pickets outside a public health clinic. They were carrying placards and shouting slogans and carrying on heated discussions with passersby and persons entering or leaving the clinic. Everyone became quite emotional, and the police were forced to intervene.

"I haven't been telling you the truth," she said. "Dr. Gerson is part of a group opposed to what they're doing at the Karyll Clinic."

Across the desk from her the young policewoman sat up a bit straighter.

"What they're doing?" Thorpe asked with a slight edge to his voice.

"You know, tampering with human birth, letting women have babies in test tubes, committing abortions. I belong to the same group. We had to take extreme measures to stop them."

"I don't understand."

"That's why Dr. Gerson went over to the Karyll Clinic. Now I'm afraid he's in trouble." She took a deep breath. "He's planted a bomb!"

The policewoman opposite her looked stunned.

"He did—*what?*" Thorpe barked into the telephone.

"That's why I'm so worried about him. Something must have gone wrong."

Thorpe said, "Now, listen, young lady, Miss Oliver, or whatever your name is, if you're making this up . . ."

"I swear I'm not! I'll go with you if you want me to."

"Put Connie on the phone," Thorpe said crisply.

Mary handed the policewoman the phone. Now I've done it, she thought. No matter what happens I can handle it, as long as I know that Rudy is all right.

Connie said tensely, "Yes, Chief. No, I wouldn't say she is . . . I was as surprised as you when . . . Hold a minute." She held the phone and looked hard at Mary. "The police chief wants me to remind you that filing a false report is a crime. You can go to jail."

"I realize that," Mary said.

Connie said into the phone, "She realizes that . . . I don't think there's any choice. If a bomb goes off and people are hurt or killed . . . All right, Chief. Right away . . . Yes, I know the number."

She hung up the receiver, then lifted it again and quickly dialed. "Hello, White Plains? I'm calling for Chief Thorpe at Plinth's Landing. Get your bomb squad over to the Karyll Clinic right away. The chief will meet you there. It looks like we've got a terrorist plot." She hung up, looking at Mary as if she were an alien being who had just arrived on a flying saucer.

Mary met her gaze defiantly.

A few minutes later Monroe Thorpe arrived. He wore a bulky blue woolen jacket over a blue shirt with a gold badge pinned to it. He gave Mary an intent appraisal, as if sizing her up for a report. "You're coming with me. Let's go!"

Ten minutes later, siren screaming, they drove up in a police car to the main entrance gate of the Karyll Clinic. As they entered the main lobby, a security guard moved quickly to intercept them.

"What's going on?"

Thorpe flashed his identification. "Police. We have a tip a bomb has been planted in this hospital."

"Who told you that?"

Thorpe jerked a thumb at Mary. He went past the guard on the run. At the elevator he whirled impatiently to Mary. "Where to?"

"Operating Room K," she told him. "That's where he was going."

Thorpe turned to the guard who had caught up with them. "Get on the pipe and tell everyone to clear out of that area."

"I have to inform Mr. Delaney."

The guard hurried off to the telephone and returned a few seconds later. An elevator took them down to the subterranean level. They were running along the main corridor when another man headed them off.

"I'm Delaney. What's this all about?"

"Police emergency! Did you start clearing the area?"

"There's nothing wrong here. You can't just barge in and . . ."

"This young lady says a bomb was planted in the hospital."

Delaney shot a look at Mary. "She's lying."

"We can't take that chance."

Thorpe raced down the connecting passageway to the operating rooms, with Delaney and the guard just behind him. Mary brought up the rear.

In Mary's eyes Operating Room K appeared premonitory. She wasn't sure whether this was because in rooms like this the struggle between life and death was at its sharpest, or because she knew they were not going to find any bomb.

She watched them search the room. As soon as they finished searching, they would question her again. That man Delaney was sure that she was lying. He would probably convince Thorpe of it.

She backed out of the doorway and ran along the passageway. She passed a door that was slightly ajar, and ducked through into a small room lit by an overhead globe. Stacks of footstools, piled-up basins, a refuse container. A large linen hamper. She closed the door behind her and turned the lock. On counters there were heaps of housekeeping supplies, paper towels, cleaning utensils, gauze packing and sponges. On the topmost counter half a dozen bulletin boards were lined up in a neat row.

She turned off the light.

A minute later she heard someone approach. The knob of the door turned.

"Locked," Thorpe said.

"Supply room," Delaney growled.

"Can we get a key?"

"At the nurse's station. But she isn't in there."

"Then where is she?"

"She's left the hospital."

"Why would she pull a crazy stunt like this?"

"Why do people turn in fake fire alarms? Or call airlines to say they put a bomb on board? She's the same kind of nut."

Thorpe gave a discouraged sigh. "If I find her and arrest her, I'll have to testify at a preliminary hearing and again at the trial. *If* the D.A. doesn't drop charges. Even if there's a trial, the judge will probably give her a suspended sentence and release her in the custody of some friend or relative. *Jesus!*"

Footsteps clattered up. "Bomb squad," said a breathless voice. "Where is it?"

Thorpe said, "We're screwed, boys. There isn't any bomb. Some crazy woman told us there was. But she's disappeared."

"Don't feel bad. It happens. We get a lot of crank calls, but we have to check each one out. Show us where the bomb was supposed to be."

All the footsteps moved away.

Mary turned on the light in the supply room. A long, wide shelf in the back of the room was loaded with white cotton suits, surgical greens, cotton dresses and spare uniforms for nurses and orderlies. She went through the nurse's uniforms until she found one her size. The skirt was a bit tight around her hips, but otherwise the fit wasn't bad. A pair of white lisle stockings did nothing to improve the look of her legs. She couldn't find a nurse's cap or shoes. After a few minutes she gave up looking for them.

She listened at the door before turning the lock. No one was in the passageway. She moved out to the main corridor. If she turned right, she would reach the main elevator bank that would take her back to the lobby.

She turned left. A door at the end of the hospital corridor opened, and a gaunt man in his thirties emerged. He wore a white doctor's smock and had a clipboard in one hand. He walked steadily toward her. A short distance away, he stopped and his gaze traveled down to her feet.

"Interesting," he said.

She was wearing her street shoes.

He asked, "What's your name?"

"Mary." After a brief hesitation, she added: "Dodds. Mary Dodds." Sam owed her an alias.

"I haven't seen you before."

"I'm new here. Just reporting for duty." She smiled. "And I think I'm a little lost."

"Looking for the nurses' lounge?"

She nodded, still smiling.

"I'm Dr. Roy Harrison." He began to stroll with her down the corridor. "Where did Old Lady Barnes assign you?"

"That isn't quite settled yet."

"The nurses' lounge is right in there."

Mary opened the door into a spacious area surrounded on three sides by lockers. A large table in the center was littered with empty plastic coffee cups, a pair of pink slippers, an opened cosmetics case, a pair of amber-colored sunglasses and scissors. In a corner of the room was a blackboard with scribbled chalk messages, and bulletins and announcements and clippings pinned to its wooden borders.

A heavyset black woman in a white slip was pouring from a large-size commercial coffee maker in the middle of the table. One leg of the coffee maker was propped on a battered magazine. She filled the coffee cup, looked up and nodded to Mary, then took the plastic coffee cup with her into the shower room.

A young woman was dressing at an open locker. She had short blond hair and a willowy figure. A pair of discarded pantyhose lay over one corner of the table atop scattered sections of the New York *Daily News*.

"Welcome to GHQ," she said to Mary. "It isn't much to look at, but the reason it looks this way is because we *like* it this way. It's the only real dump in the whole hospital. The only place to relax. Where did you get those shoes?"

"I've just been hired. I'm not working today. I just came to look around."

"Where are you assigned?"

Mary said promptly, "Old Lady Barnes hasn't made up her mind."

"Old lady who?"

"Barnes."

"Never heard of her. Mathieson is the supervisor, and I never heard anybody call her Old Lady." Miraculously the young woman was fully dressed, in a light blue pants outfit, a colorful scarf around her neck, and high-heeled wedgies. Her locker was wide open, her nurse's uniform hanging next to a red sweater.

Mary said, "I might go to work in Phase Three."

"Don't let Mathieson assign you to that building. Everything's hush-hush and creepy. They pay more, but it isn't worth it."

"Thanks. I'll bear that in mind."

After she left, Mary looked around. Several lockers were partly open and crowded with street clothes. She heard the rushing noise of water in the adjoining shower room.

Suddenly, just outside the door, a voice said: "I spotted her as a phoney right away."

Dr. Harrison.

Two sharp raps on the door. "Security. Everybody decent in there?" another voice asked.

Mary sped into the shower room. A mist of steam

was emerging from one of the tiled stalls. Quickly she ran to the far end and got into an empty stall.

Two more sharp raps on the door to the shower room.

"Security."

The shower kept running.

Knocking grew louder. "If you don't answer, we're coming in!"

The throaty roar of water continued. A door opened and closed.

Seconds later Mary heard a startled shriek.

"Creeps! *Perverts!*"

"I'm sorry!"

"Get the hell out of here! Dumb morons!"

"We're looking for someone. The doctor says . . ."

"There's nobody in here but me, you stupid peeping toms! Who gave you the right to push in here? *Move it!* Nobody belongs here but *nurses!*"

Dripping with indignation, holding a skimpy towel as insufficient armor, the heavyset black nurse kept shouting until the men retreated. From the stall in which she was hiding, Mary glimpsed her savior's damp naked buttocks quivering with righteous anger.

Mary waited until the indignant black nurse departed. When she emerged from the stall, a plastic coffee cup, partly filled, was still on the floor.

Outside, the nurses' lounge was deserted. She went through several open lockers until she found a nurse's cap and a pair of white shoes that fit her. This was not the way I was brought up, she told herself; but it's all in a good cause. A woman has to kiss a lot of toads before one turns into her Prince Charming. Then she'd better not let anything happen to him.

Besides, she'd bring the cap and shoes back.

She knew exactly where she was going when she left the lounge. If Rudy was a prisoner, the off-limits building with all its security precautions was where they would keep him. Her plan was simple: to go there and find him. She was quite aware that her plan was unlikely to work. But there was nothing else to do.

She opened the door and moved out into the corridor. She walked with a jaunty step, humming to herself because she didn't want anyone to guess how frightened she was.

Chapter

19

A sign hung from the door, *Do Not Disturb For Any Reason.*

Inside a small laboratory, Peter Bradford was perched on a high stool beside a long tabletop that held a microscope, a cardboard box of slides, and beakers in stirring plates. Adjoining the table was an ultracentrifuge, and nearby was a refrigerator in which were stored enzymes and reagents and labile chemicals.

He made several entries in his open notebook on the lab bench, then moved back to the apparatus of glass columns with an attached computer that was the amino acids sequencer. Here he had worked out the sequence of amino acids, and subsequently synthesized the hormone he had been trying to isolate.

Isolating the hormone secreted in the female womb that nurtures the human egg to a full-grown fetus was an important step in a new task that preoccupied him. Without an artificial womb, it would be impossible to produce Sendais on a mass scale. The development from óvum to a complete creature required a single fertilized cell to multiply billions of times. A workable habitat was needed for the complex process of cell differentiation.

He checked the printout on the amino acid sequencer to see how far it had gotten. In the final preparation of a work, one must be slow, constantly checking details. The finding of simple solutions is a very complex business. Intent on what he was doing, he was able to forget everything, even grief at his mother's recent death. His faculties were so concentrated that every thought of the outside world was banished.

Very slowly he became aware that someone was knocking at the door to his private laboratory.

He finished checking the printout and looked up irritably. "Who is it?"

"Gaby."

"Not now."

"I must speak to you."

Reluctantly he crossed the room. He had been a day and a night without rest, without food, and fatigue had caused an almost physical alienation. He saw how shocked Gaby was at his appearance.

"What do you want?" he asked impatiently.

"There's been a serious breach of security involving Dr. Hartley. He was apprehended a few hours ago trying to enter Phase Three."

"He has no business being in the off-limits building."

"When he left the building he went to Operating Room K and spent some time there, alone. He returned to his room and we monitored his calls. At shortly past midnight, as soon as the switchboard was closed, he telephoned Dr. Gerson outside the hospital. At that point, Delaney intervened."

"Well?"

"Delaney was bringing him for questioning. Dr. Hartley tried to break away. There was a fight and he gave Delaney a bad time. I'm afraid Delaney lost his temper. He's been under a great deal of strain lately."

He stared at her while what she said swirled around in the great misty cavern of his brain. "What happened?"

"Dr. Hartley is dead. Of a broken neck."

He bridged both temples between his thumb and middle finger. His eyes were burning and felt as if they were full of tiny splinters. He murmured, "There's been too much of that. I hoped we'd have no more." To his own ears he sounded as if he were wringing his hands.

He felt the weight of her gaze upon him.

"That isn't all," she said. "A little while ago we found Dr. Gerson in the nursery above Operating Room K."

He was tired; he couldn't think clearly. He had held off fatigue by an effort of will, and now his body was demanding rest. He squeezed his eyelids tight shut, and then opened them and removed his fingers from his temples.

"This is turning into a horrible mess. Had the Sendais been transferred?"

"No."

"He saw them?"

"Yes."

The problem was more serious with every new disclosure. "I wonder if he has any idea of what he saw. The new batch of Sendais look almost human. How about the new one?"

"It arrived on schedule. A baby girl. Thirteen pounds. Completely normal in appearance."

At least something was going right. They had made a lot of progress since the first Sendais a little over a year ago.

"We have to find out what Dr. Gerson was doing in that nursery," he said, "and how much he knows. And whether anyone else is involved."

"I agree. But he's in no condition to be questioned just now."

"What do you mean?" Sudden fear seized him. "If he's been . . ."

She shook her head. "Delaney was a little rough, that's all. He'll recover."

There was an empty gnawing at his intestines and a dull pain in his head. All he wanted was to find a bed and sink into it and forget. "I don't want Delaney interrogating him. I'll handle that myself. But first I've got to rest."

He could tell she did not approve of delay, but there were situations in which delay had its uses. He needed more time to think about the problem of Charley Gerson's son.

He set the alarm clock for an hour and stretched out on the cot in his room. Almost instantly he was asleep. When he was wakened he called Gaby at once.

"How is he?"

"He's come around."

He felt more rested, and his confidence was returning.

"Good. I want to talk to him."

"Delaney can find out what we want to know. We have to act quickly."

"Delaney can't be trusted any more. He has the instincts of a predator."

"He can be effective in a situation like this."

He said gently, "Believe me, this is something I can handle. I know how to talk to him."

"It's serious, Peter. Hartley and Gerson were in it together. And there may be others."

She believed in quick surgical remedies before a problem metastasized.

"I realize that. That's why I'm sure my approach is better. He's Charley Gerson's son. If he's got any of his father in him, I can make him listen to reason."

The room in Phase Two was in semidarkness. He turned on a switch, and light washed over Rudy Gerson lying on a cot with his legs drawn up. His hands were pinioned behind him, his shirtsleeves rolled to the elbows, and the insides of his forearms pressed together and taped.

A plain wooden chair was the only furniture other than the cot. The room was windowless. In a corner was a sink with two faucets connected to a drainpipe.

Gerson tried to sit up. He got only part way before he toppled back. Bradford went over and helped him to sit erect.

"How are you feeling?" he asked.

"The back of my neck feels like I've been decapitated, and everything in my head feels like loose machinery is tumbling around. Otherwise, I'm just fine."

"I regret that you've been inconvenienced."

"Why am I tied up like this?"

"I'll answer that in a minute. I have to ask you some questions first." He pulled the wooden chair to a position opposite the cot and straddled it. "Did you have a reason for being in that nursery where you were found?"

Gerson licked his teeth with his tongue. "Can I have a glass of water?"

He repeated, as if his question had not been understood: "Did you have a reason for being in that nursery?"

Gerson shook his head tentatively.

"This will become very unpleasant if you refuse to cooperate. I will have to turn the questioning over to Delaney. You've already had one experience with him." He saw Gerson grimace. "I will ask you again just once. Did you have a reason for being in that room?"

The reference to Delaney apparently had an effect.

"Yes."

"Excellent. Now that you've started, let's keep going. What was the reason?"

"I was in the operating room below. And I overheard people coming, so I just got into the conveyor and went up."

A childish evasion.

"Who told you about Operating Room K?"

"I don't remember."

"Was it Dr. Hartley? We know that Dr. Hartley called you."

"Did he?"

"Please don't play games. I am trying to help you."

"All right. Hartley called me."

"Why?"

"He wanted me to see the operating room where all the in vitro babies were delivered."

"Did he say why?"

"He thought I'd be interested."

The lies were so transparent that he couldn't help feeling resentment. But he was determined to be patient.

"Did you come alone?"

"Yes."

"This point I must be absolutely sure of. You will make it so much easier for both of us if you simply tell the truth. Did you tell anyone about your plan to come here?"

"No."

"You just got into your car and came?"

"Yes."

"What kind of car?"

"A Porsche."

"What color?"

"Red. 1979 model."

"License plate number?"

"4888 MD."

"Thank you. You can have the glass of water now."

He got up and drew a cup of water from a faucet in the sink. The ceramic cup was slightly chipped. He brought the cup to Gerson, and held it while he took several small sips.

"Dr. Hartley is dead," he remarked.

When you take someone by surprise, especially when that person is eating or drinking, a constriction in the throat reverses the flow of breath. Air being inhaled is suddenly expelled, and the spluttering is quite involuntary. He withdrew the cup from Gerson's lips.

"I'm sorry it happened," he said. "He was trying to get away, and Delaney tried too hard to restrain him."

Belief kept growing in Gerson's eyes until it became the horror of conviction. "He was murdered."

"I had nothing to do with it."

"Delaney was carrying out your orders. You can't escape responsibility."

He spread his hands in a resigned gesture. "One man's life against the important work we are doing. I would have to call that a fair exchange—even though his death was accidental."

"And Bernie Seligson's?"

"He died of a heart attack, a long-standing condition."

"He was murdered."

"Indeed?"

"Dr. Hartley talked to the doctor who did the autopsy. There was no long-standing heart condition. The autopsy didn't reveal the cause of death. It must have been a poison that was untraceable unless the pathologist was consciously looking for it. My guess is potassium chloride. It kills quickly and leaves nothing in tissue but an ordinary element that's always present in the human body."

A clever young man and probably a very good doctor too, despite his disclaimers about being Gerson the Lesser.

"You must admit that it's a painless way of ending life."

"If you've got any idea of getting rid of me that way, I think you ought to know it won't work. I've told the police how I think Bernie Seligson was murdered. If anything happens to me, that's the first thing a pathologist would look for."

He noted a slight tremor in Gerson's eyelids. There is always a sign of inner stress when a lie is told. Polygraph machines aren't needed in such instances.

"If you had told the police, you would not have come here on your own. You must give up this childish attempt to deceive me. It's unbecoming."

"Even if you try to make my death look like an accident, they'd be suspicious."

"I wouldn't be too sure. It would depend on how well the supporting circumstances are arranged. But why threaten? I came here to offer you a chance, if you cooperate."

"What do you want?"

"Why was it so important to you to visit the operating room where in vitro babies are delivered?"

He saw that Gerson was trying to make up his mind whether he should answer. He waited, confident that Gerson would decide to tell him a part of the truth.

Gerson said, "Something is wrong with your IVF program."

"Please go on."

"There are too many dead and deformed babies being born."

"Did Dr. Hartley tell you this?"

"Dr. Seligson sent me some medical charts."

It was depressing. No one can foresee everything.

"What did you hope to find?"

"A connection with Phase Three of the off-limits building. And I think I did. The babies I saw in that nursery were not ordinary human babies. That's why you told the parents they had died."

Go on, he urged silently. Prove to me that you are Charley Gerson's son and how much better it would be if you were on my side.

"Not ordinary?" he asked.

"There was a slightly odd facial configuration. And they were much larger than they should be at their age. Stronger too, if the Pollard baby was an example."

"Do you believe those infants had anything in common with the Pollard baby?"

"This may be the next generation. Much closer to

human in appearance. You're breeding them to prove
that different subhuman life forms can be created in
the laboratory."

"Created?"

"A matter of definition. Choose your own word."

Gerson had the idea but not all the how-to-do-its
were in place. The temptation to tell him was irresistible.

"I call them Sendais—after the virus that makes the
exchange of genetic material possible."

"You mean they're the offspring of two different
species. Human and—what?"

"Not different species. I merely intervened in the
process of reproduction."

"How?"

There was no need to explain how he had discovered
the way in which genes regulate the production within
the brain of appropriate synapses, the connections of
visual and verbal centers with other higher thinking
centers.

"I treat the cells at an early stage of division, modify-
ing the right chromosomes with laser beams. Then, as
with any in vitro fertilization, the embryo is reinserted
into the womb."

"Do the Sendais have anything else but superhuman
strength?"

"They are subnormally intelligent."

"What's the point of that?"

"So they can perform menial repetitive tasks without becoming restless or bored."

Gerson looked directly into his eyes. His voice was
flat, accusatory: "What you're talking about is the
genetic enslavement of a whole species, a blueprint for

the permanent division of the world into masters and slaves."

Bradford sighed. Nothing is as hard to dislodge as an old prejudice fortified by shibboleths. *Master and slave*.

"You're missing the point. Since the dawn of history men have had to do brutalizing labor. Think of the cost in human development." His voice rose in almost a litany: "How many of those who had to work like beasts in the fields might have become Aristotles or Michelangelos, Shakespeares or Beethovens? But they were never taught more than needed to perform their mindless chores. They had to be kept inferior from economic necessity. Now we will have a species—the Sendai—who are inferior from genetic necessity. They will free mankind to realize its full potential." He stared at the shadowed face of Rudy Gerson. "You see why nothing must interfere with my work."

"I don't see anything of the kind."

"I'm sorry you feel that way." His nerves were still edgy, and he found it hard to conceal his annoyance.

"You want to know what I see?" The hardness had not left Gerson's voice. "Scientific megalomania. Until now I couldn't put together the Dr. Bradford who is so matter-of-factly mixed up in murder and the Dr. Bradford, famous geneticist and head of the Karyll Clinic. Now I see they belong together. Both try to play God."

Anger was coming now, like a motor hooked up to a vitalizing current. "Do you think only God can create life? Only God the creator. If there was no God before God, who created Him? Why should we allow human life to be a purposeless movement, blindly reproducing itself, when we can take control of our biological destiny?"

"The risks may be unacceptable."

"In all great enterprises men take unacceptable risks. To do certain things is dangerous, but not to do them is unthinkable."

"You don't have the right to decide. There are too many other people involved."

He had deceived himself about the potential of this young man.

"I should have remembered that I was speaking to Gerson the Lesser. The ordinary son of a great man." He looked at Gerson, his anger yielding to a feeling of near compassion. "We have no more to say to each other."

He left the room without a backward glance. Delaney, standing a few feet from the door, moved toward him.

Bradford said, "He and Hartley were in this together. He knows about the Sendai. He knows altogether too much."

Delaney said heavily, "There's been a new development." He told him about a woman who had brought the police, claiming she knew about a bomb plot at the hospital. Bradford forced himself to pay attention. Why didn't anyone ever come to him with solutions? Always problems, problems . . .

He asked irritably, "What has she to do with anything?"

"She said that the bomb was planted in Operating Room K."

"That's strange." It could hardly be coincidence.

"And it seems she first went to the police with a missing persons report. Dr. Gerson was the missing person."

He had a feeling that the environment was becoming dangerous, that he was losing control.

"Where is she now?"

Delaney answered heavily, "She's disappeared. But we think she may be somewhere in the hospital. Dr. Harrison thinks he saw her wearing a nurse's uniform."

"Our security system isn't working very well," Bradford said caustically. "Keep looking for her. She has to be found."

Delaney nodded. "And Dr. Gerson?"

The only way to reestablish control was to act promptly and with decision. Delay now would be a form of error. Apprehension gave him a rich new source of energy.

"He must disappear. Completely. Do you understand?"

"Yes, sir."

"There must be no evidence that he was ever here at all." He told Delaney the make and color and license plate number of Gerson's car in the parking lot. "Get rid of it. And find that woman. I don't want any excuses."

Chapter

20

A stiff breeze was blowing as Mary rounded the corner of the Genetics Research building. She found the employees' entrance, and a short foyer led her to a glass-paned door. Inside, a gray-haired man wearing a cardigan sweater was seated near a turnstile. He was reading a newspaper.

As Mary entered, he lowered the newspaper and took his feet down. He looked her over slowly.

"Pretty late, aren't you?"

"I guess I am."

"It's your headache. Go ahead and punch in."

On the left were several parallel rows of file card slots beneath a big round white-faced time clock. Most of the cards had been taken from the rows, but a few were left in their slots. Boldly she chose one, stamped it at the time clock, and passed through the turnstile. She had gone only a few feet beyond when she heard the man's voice.

"Just a minute."

She had no choice but to turn. "Is something the matter?"

"You forgot to stick your card in the file."

She was still holding the stamped card. "Oh, thanks." She saw three parallel rows on the wall on the other side of the turnstile, nearly all with cards in the slots. She slid her card into an empty slot. With a brief apologetic smile, she moved on to join a good-looking middle-aged man waiting for an elevator. As the door opened, he stood aside to let her enter.

"What floor?" he asked.

"Six," she said, choosing a number.

"Reproductive Genetics." He pushed numbers Six and Five. "My name is Sutton. Dr. David Sutton. I work in biochemistry on the fifth floor."

"I'm Mary Dodds. This is my first day, so I'm a little nervous."

"Are you? Why?"

"I've heard stories about the security precautions around here. They say every time you turn around you bump into somebody watching you."

"It isn't that bad. Not here in Phase One anyway. The guards get to know you."

"How about Phase Two?" Mary asked.

"Second and third floors only. They've got to have tighter security there. They do a lot with biological research, microorganisms and stuff. Nobody wants any of those things getting out. If people just came and went, they might pick up some nasty little bug and start an epidemic."

Mary shuddered. "Brr. How about Phase Three?"

"I don't know much about that, but it occupies the whole basement level. The first floor is for administrative offices and conference rooms."

The elevator slowed, stopped.

"Thanks a lot. I think I've got the setup straight now. This is your floor."

"Been nice meeting you," Dr. Sutton said. "Come down and see me sometime."

He got off, and the elevator rose to the sixth floor. As soon as it stopped, Mary pushed the button for the third floor. Might as well begin her search in a place where security was a bit tighter. That's where Rudy was more likely to be.

She got off on the third floor and found herself in a long hallway lined with closed doors. While she hesitated trying to get her bearings, a security guard appeared from the vestibule on her left. He was wearing the familiar dark-gray uniform.

"No nurses allowed on this floor."

"I must have pushed the wrong button."

"Where are you going?"

"The biochemistry lab. Dr. Sutton. Dr. David Sutton."

"May I see your ID?"

"Do I look like I'm some kind of spy?" She gave him a brilliant, reassuring smile.

"I have to check your credentials."

In a vague way she had wondered what she would do if apprehended. Submit weakly, or try to run, or . . .

She kicked him in the shin.

His unbelieving look quickly filmed over with pain. She kicked him hard in the other shin. Then she ran down the hallway.

As she glanced back, the guard was hobbling after her, grimacing. He looked very angry.

At the end of the hallway a smooth-grained door impassively denied her entrance. She pounded on it until the door opened, and she was face to face with a large middle-aged woman in a wrinkled white smock.

Mary sobbed, "He tried to attack me! He's crazy!"

The woman looked at Mary with surprise, then saw the pursuing guard. She stood aside to let Mary go past. Just inside, on a side counter, a coffeepot was percolating on a hotplate. There were long tables and bubbling glass bottles and jars. Each jar and bottle contained silky gray blobs that resembled tiny feature-less embryos. Embryos of what? She had the queasy feeling of looking at things that might be looking back at her.

Behind her the woman was saying, "Now, see here . . ."

As Mary turned, the guard pushed the woman aside. Instantly, Mary picked up the coffeepot from the hotplate. As the guard started toward her, he saw what she was going to do. He flung up his arms to protect his face. Scalding hot coffee poured out of the spout, then the whole top of the pot came off and hot liquid gushed. The guard's choked gargle was not quite a scream. He stumbled, cursing, half blinded.

The woman said to Mary, "Go right to the security office on the first floor. They'll send someone up to take care of him."

Mary thanked her, but when she reached the eleva-tor she pushed the button for the floor below ground level. She was like Eliza crossing the ice floes, jumping from one precarious footing to another. To uncover a clue to Rudy's whereabouts she needed more time to think, to be resourceful. She'd already decided that Phase One wasn't a likely place for Rudy to be. But somehow she had to get into Phase Two or Three without arousing suspicion. It wouldn't be easy. That guard was going to give someone a good description of her.

The elevator stopped on the floor below ground level.

Eliza, here we go.

As the elevator door opened, she was confronted at a distance of about four feet by a gray stone wall. The stone wall was a metaphor for her predicament. There really was nowhere to turn. That thought penetrated her mind and struck a vital place that rejected it with violence. She wasn't about to stop trying. Not yet. Not until they really caught her.

She noticed a little farther along the wall an arrow pointing right and the single word: *Pathology.* She followed the direction of the arrow and came to a locked door. On the wall to the right of the door was a red telephone.

She had absolutely nothing to lose.

"Path Lab," said a pleasant female voice on the telephone.

"I have a pick-up," Mary said.

"A pick-up?"

The best way to cut off questions was to act authoritatively.

"They're expecting me," she said in an annoyed tone. "It's for Dr. Sutton in Biochemistry."

"Oh. Dr. Sutton." The reply sounded hesitant, but there was a clicking sound, and when Mary tried the knob of the door it opened.

She passed through the door, and behind a glass partition a young woman was seated at a typewriter. She smiled uncertainly at Mary, who nodded to her and went on confidently. Fortunately, there was another arrow pointing the way to Pathology.

At last she came to a frosted glass door that was unlocked. She opened it cautiously. Inside was a long black table that occupied most of a rectangular space. On the table were filing boxes, bottles of chemicals, several fat reference books and three piles of microscope slides beside an open slide box. Nearby, a black microscope was fastened with clamps to the table edge.

At the far end, in a space above two swinging doors, she could make out a hooded light with a narrow intense beam. From the room there came a high-pitched whine, a bubbling sucking noise and a nauseating malodor.

She opened the swinging doors a tiny crack to peer through.

In a high-ceilinged room with gray walls, two men in oilcloth aprons and rubber gloves were at work beneath a high intensity light. Both wore eyeshades, and their heads were down as they worked. The high-pitched whine was from an electric saw one man was using. Dust floated upward through the beam of light and floated off as lighter specks in surrounding darkness.

The man using the saw shifted position slightly; the other man got a firmer grip on what he was sawing. It was a repulsive distended mass of inert flesh, greasy, several feet in length and about two feet wide, rising in an irregular lump at least a foot from the level surface of the slanted table top. A stream of liquid ran down the slanted top toward a drain in the tile floor. The bubbling, sucking noise came from the drain sucking up the liquid that splashed on or near it.

The whining of the saw stopped. There was a chopping noise, then a wet flopping as a mulberry-colored object was put onto the scale.

"Believe it or not, the damn thing weighs six point six kilograms. How would you describe the texture and consistency?"

"Mush. A chancrous filet of sole."

"For the record . . ." The other man pushed a foot pedal and spoke into a microphone hanging down from the ceiling. "Very pliant and mushy. Ulcerated surface. Color is a mottled crimson. Gross weight, six point six kilograms."

"What do you say caused death?"

"I don't even know what caused life," the other replied with a sarcastic inflection. "Bradford has really outdone himself with this one."

"What do you think he was trying for?"

"Hard to say—but what he got is like nothing I've ever seen. Lungs and a brain. More than a rudimentary brain."

"Somewhere a mother is pining."

"The only mother this thing had was a petri dish. It's going to end up in a glass jar—on the shelf marked *Medical Records, Indeterminate Species*."

"The hell it is. It's going straight to the Disposal Unit."

In the hallway, Mary leaned against a wall and held her nostrils. The putrescent odor from the room was so powerful she couldn't seem to get enough fresh air.

A man wearing a mask and gown entered behind her. He stopped still when he saw Mary.

"Looking for someone in particular?"

Somehow she regained control of her churning stomach. "I-I'm afraid I took the wrong elevator. I'm looking for—for personnel."

"First floor."

"Thanks. I—I'd better go. This place is a little too much for me."

He sniffed. "I smell what you mean. The pathologist's lot is not a happy one. Well, it's been nice meeting you. And if you ever need to have yourself dissected . . ."

"I'll look for you," Mary promised. She retraced her steps. Just beyond the swinging doors she stopped. She heard the unmistakable whirr of a telephone dial.

"Security, this is Path Lab. We've just had an unusual visitor. Young, pretty, wearing a nurse's uniform . . . She just left. On her way to personnel . . . Listen, if she checks out okay, will you do me a favor? Get her name and telephone number."

Now that Security knew her location, the safest place to be was elsewhere.

Nearing an intersection, she heard a rumbling noise, and flattened herself against the wall. The rumbling noise grew louder, coming her way. Ten feet away, down the intersecting corridor, a guard appeared riding in an electric cart. He was looking straight ahead and speaking into a two-way radio: "Check what? The path lab . . . Okay."

As soon as the cart passed, she went swiftly in the direction from which it had come. It seemed that this entire basement area was broken up into small compartmented spaces like the Pathology Lab. Each was more or less isolated from the other. She tried each door she came to, but none opened.

Finally she came to an open stairwell where a dozen steps led down to a small vestibule and a narrow door with neither knob nor keyhole. Frustrated, she banged her fist against it.

A voice from a speaker over the door said challengingly: "State your business."

She was so startled that for a moment she could think of nothing. Then, reminding herself that a partial truth was better than a lie, she answered, "I'm from the Path Lab."

The door unlatched with a definite click. She pushed it open.

Directly ahead on a stone wall was a large television monitor. She confronted the image of a pink-faced chubby man who was looking at her quizzically.

"I don't know you. Do you have clearance for Phase Three?"

"Would I be here if I didn't?"

"Turn left. Through the archway."

She followed instructions, passing through into a stone arcade. Bright spotlights were set into the ceiling at intervals, and the stone walls appeared wetly coated. The air was humid and cool.

At the end of the arcade was an iron gate anchored in rock walls and secured in its center by a padlock. Beyond the gate was a long narrow stone-walled tunnel.

A man came out of a door thirty feet ahead. He was the man whose image she had just seen on the television console. He wore a flower-print shirt open at the neck, tan slacks, and sandals, and he was holding a bloodhound on a short leash.

He came to the gate. The bloodhound bared its teeth, and she saw that it was not entirely a bloodhound. The head was dark brown and houndlike, but behind it she could discern great powerful feline haunches. The deep eyes were like dark marbles that moved slowly in the head, taking in her presence and the tunnel beyond her. The skin of its body was spotted, and the creature had a long ropelike tail.

"I'm Konrad," the man said. He lifted a circlet of keys from a spike in the wall and opened the padlock.

The bloodhound's head watched her. The jaws opened wider until she could see its white glimmering molars. The long tail swung back and forth with whiplike menace.

"That's an unusual animal," Mary said. "I've never seen anything like it."

Konrad said, "One of a kind."

The houndlike head uttered a low growl. The sight of that head on a feline body was most unsettling.

"I've always been afraid of dogs."

"I'll lock her up while you're here."

He led the creature into his office and closed the door. When he came out he said, "You must see stranger things than that, being from Path Lab."

"The ones I see are dead."

"I suppose that makes a difference."

They started down the tunnel. She heard a confused stridor that became louder and clearer. It sounded like a zoo in full cry.

Konrad said, "They know someone's coming. They're excited."

The stone tunnel emerged into a spacious rock-walled enclosure. Barred cages were set along the walls, some covered with wire mesh. There was a sense of confused motion, of an acrobatic swarming. The cacophony was overwhelming, created by separate distinct sounds of bleating and barking, neighing and whining, a whinny, a squawk, a deep bass resonance.

In the cages nearest to her were a kennel of puppies and a kindle of kittens. They were lumpen and distorted with tumors. Even their heads were misshapen.

In an adjoining larger cage were several rhesus monkeys, their pale, almost human faces marked with distinctive dark eye shadows. One was staring at her through the bars. Its front legs were planted firmly, its long rear legs extended like an athlete at the top of a push-up. From a spot below the deep sloping chest two other legs grew, partly formed natural stumps fully covered with fur. The other monkeys in the cage all had the same extra pair of legs.

In another cage a piebald wolf with short ruffs of brownish red hair put its head back to emit a strange ululation that was more like a whinny. The wolf's feet ended in small ponylike hooves.

She tried not to show revulsion. "I've never seen anything like these either."

Konrad chuckled. "I'd be surprised if you had. Some of 'em has three or more parents. That's how come they grow that way."

In a strongly barred enclosure a gorilla was standing erect. Its powerful long arms dangled to its knees, and the swelling muscular black torso looked about to burst through its skin. The gorilla's head turned to look at her. The skull, narrowing from cheekbones to crown, revealed familiar heavy frontal brows and small, black, staring eyes. But the thickened blue-black lips had an oddly human contour, and the facial skin seemed different in texture and color from an anthropoid ape. The forehead was smooth, and in the cheeks she saw lines that might have appeared in a human face. Wires were taped to the scalp and attached to a monitoring machine outside the cage.

She turned away quickly. "Have you had any visitors here lately?" she asked Konrad in a not quite steady voice.

"Just Dr. Bradford."

If Rudy were in the building, this would be a likely place.

"Could anyone get in here without your knowing?"

"I don't see how."

Neither could she.

Konrad shook his head sadly. "I guess we might as well get what you came for. This way."

He turned right into a narrower passageway, and they followed it until they emerged into a mammoth underground pool area.

"Nessie died an hour ago," Konrad said. "I didn't expect Path Lab to send someone so quickly."

"You caught us at a good time," Mary responded.

"There's Nessie," he said.

In a corner of the pool she saw a creature with a narrow, beaked head and a swollen body that ended in a bulbous bottom. It was floating lightly, despite its apparent grossness.

Konrad said, "I'll get the net."

He returned with a long, round pole attached to a large net with thick cords. "Gotta be quick. The others don't like it when I take one out."

Maneuvering the pole, he worked the net slowly under the floating corpse. The net had just enclosed it when a hissing sound arose. A dark clot sped through the faintly illumined water.

"Get back!" Konrad shouted.

With slithering sliding quickness, something oozed over the side of the pool. A cold substance touched her leg, twined about it. She struck at it with both hands, and the hissing became more strident. A mucous tendril crawled onto her wrist. With the other hand she grasped a softness within which was a stiffness, as though her hand had penetrated dissolving flesh to touch bone.

Suddenly Konrad was beside her. He pushed the end of his pole into the thing clinging to her. A miasmic odor assaulted her nostrils. The hissing became a shrill chirping. She tore frantically at the webbing twined about her, and abruptly it disintegrated into clinging fragments.

Silence.

Her hands were trembling as she brushed off quivering tendrils that crumbled and fell at her touch like loose wet snowflakes.

Konrad said, "Looks like another one for your friends at the Path Lab."

At her feet lay a slender snakelike bone covered in a web of flaky substance. The snakelike head was smashed flat. There was a hollow indentation in the skull the size of the rounded end of Konrad's pole.

She shuddered.

Konrad put the pole down, bent to examine the still, snakelike body. "Two in a single day. Dr. Bradford won't like this."

The pool area reverberated with a loud yet distant-sounding voice: *"Security. A woman wearing a nurse's uniform is in Phase One. She has no identity card. If you see her, report to Security at once. Repeat. Report to Security at once."*

Konrad was crouching near the dead creature.

"You're her," he said. His eyes became razor-thin openings in plump pockets of pink flesh. "You're the one they're lookin' for."

She stooped for the pole a half-second ahead of him. There was no space to wield the pole as a weapon, so she swept it along the ground. That took his legs out from under him. He teetered backward at the edge of the pool, fighting for balance. As he fell in on his back, water geysered.

He came up floundering, swam to the edge of the pool, and tried to clamber out. She pushed him back in with the pole.

As she reached the entrance to the pool, she looked back. Dark shapes were moving through the luminescent water. He began shouting, a high whooping sound. She almost went back to help, but thought better of it.

Konrad had to look after himself. She really hoped that he could.

In the narrow passageway leading from the pool she could still hear him. His voice was strong and infuriated, but there was no fear in it.

She reached the large rock-walled enclosure beyond the passageway. The animals must have heard Konrad. The rhesus monkeys were bounding about their cage, screeching as though a predator had been turned loose among them. Their bodies crashed against the bars in their frenzied movement.

Louder than the howling and shrieking from the other cages was an awe-inspiring, deep-bass frenzy. The gorilla was trying to propel its huge body through the bars of its cage. Its head bellowed, while the eyes turned to glare at Mary with a wild, murderous rage.

She put her hands over her ears to shut out the barbarous yawp. And then she had an auditory hallucination. For the thundering roar took on a kind of meaning.

"KONRA-A-ADDD!"

She backed away from the cage. The gorilla was staring directly at her. He opened his mouth to bellow his reverberating cry again. She didn't think she could stand to hear it.

"KONRA-A-A-ADD!"

With renewed savagery the mighty shoulders hurled themselves against the bars. Any moment she expected the bars to give way before that violent assault. She could not go past the gorilla's cage. There had to be another way. Any other way.

She retreated, found a passageway on the left, and followed it to a small low-ceilinged stone enclave. There was only a single door, closed with a heavy sliding bolt.

"Come in, please."

A high-pitched chirrup. She hesitated, wondering where it came from.

"It's perfectly safe," the chirrup said.

"Who are you?"

"A friend."

The chirrup was coming from inside the bolted door. She lifted the securing bolt and entered.

Absolute darkness.

"Don't be frightened."

"I can't see."

"I'm sorry. I'll fix that."

The darkness showed a faint color, a deep purple glow.

"Can you see now?"

"A little."

"Then please come in."

Ponderously the door closed behind her. She was in what appeared to be a large room with deep heavy carpeting. At the end of the room a black shape was visible, outlined against the murky dimness. It appeared to be a great bulky bird with black folded wings.

Then she heard music, contrapuntal, of a rich complexity.

The music of Johann Sebastian Bach.

The light strengthened to magenta, lavender, violet, orchid. She saw that the music was coming from a stereo on a Lucite table in a corner.

"Welcome. You're the first visitor I've ever had."

The huge bulky bird was an overweight young man in a wheelchair. His large bald head resembled a milk-filled balloon.

"I wish I could offer you a chair, but, as you see, there are no chairs."

The young man wore dark round glasses taped to his temples. A blanket was across his knees, a cloak over his shoulders. The blanket was brown wool, the cloak dark with a scarlet lining—an odd touch of elegance.

"Is there any way out of here except through that door?" Mary asked.

Cupid's bow lips pursed in the moon-shaped face. "None."

It struck Mary that the young man might be in isolation because he had a communicable disease.

"Why do they keep you locked up like this?"

"I can only survive in a highly controlled environment."

"How long have you been here?"

"Seven years, nine months and two days. Ever since I was born."

She peered at him in the dim light coming from luminescent walls. "You can't be seven years old."

"I have Dr. Bradford's word for that."

"You don't speak like a child."

"I know. I am much more intelligent. Not even Dr. Bradford realizes how intelligent I am."

She suddenly felt pity for the boy. The dark glasses were taped to his temples because he had no ears.

"You live here alone?"

"Dr. Bradford comes. So does the caretaker. Dr. Bradford doesn't think anyone else should see me. Apparently, I am some kind of a monster."

"You are not a monster," she said emphatically.

"You're not horrified by what you see?"

"Not at all." She hoped she sounded convincing.

"Perhaps you have not seen enough." With a shrug of his shoulders, the boy made the concealing cloak slide off.

His shoulders ended in tiny vestigial hands, append-ages more suitable to a newborn infant. But the hands were not plump or wrinkled with promise of a filling-out to come; they were tiny and withered, with fingers like little dead branches.

"Does that shock you?" The boy's lips parted in a pink imitation of a smile. At both sides of his mouth the gums grew together, leaving only a small orifice between.

She replied steadily, "No." For a nice young woman from Philadelphia, she had seen a lot of strange things lately. She was having a surreal experience, a Kafka nightmare.

Leaning back, the boy worked the cloak back over his shoulders. "I am the result of one of Dr. Bradford's first genetic experiments. Not an unqualified success. My legs are not of much more use than my arms. And I wear these glasses because they correct a serious problem with my vision. Without them I see everything in multiple images—rather like a housefly. I presume that what I have read about houseflies is true, although I have had no contact with *Musca domestica*, or indeed with any other common dipterous insects. I have only one physical advantage, which hardly compensates for my other deficiencies. I hear in a range above and below human hearing. Otherwise, I am really quite fragile and I shall probably not live very long."

The boy said this without a hint of self-pity, with an air of total detachment. His brain seemed to exist scornfully independent of his body. He added, "In a way, I suppose, I am a victim not only of a misguided experiment but of certain preconceptions. I am told that everyone views with affection a newborn baby. A newborn baby possesses a relatively large head attached to a medium-sized body with diminutive hands and feet, has huge eyes, a small chin, and a bulbous cranium. Viewed from a different perspective, that baby could be regarded as a repulsive little monster. And if the baby were to grow to an adult and not acquire a more slanted lower-browed head, a heavier more pronounced jaw, and eyes relatively small to the face, its appearance would become quite strange to everyone."

"You're probably right." She glanced about the room. "Is there no way out of here?"

"Are you anxious to leave? Now that you're here I would like to talk to you."

"I'm afraid I don't have time. Someone is after me."

"Really? Why?"

"Because I know too much about Dr. Bradford's genetic experiments."

"I never realized that he wished them to be kept secret."

"If anyone knew what he was doing here, he'd go to prison."

"What an astonishing idea. He's always told me his experiments will open a new era in human development. What can possibly be wrong with that?"

"Don't you feel any resentment about what he's done to you?"

"Should I?"

Mary felt the tension in her throat muscles. "Yes," she said finally. "You should."

The balloonlike head bowed a moment, dark spectacles glinting in the luminous violet light.

Suddenly he looked up. "I would like to help you. If we had more time, I'm sure I would think of something. But a person is arriving. He has an animal with him. I believe he is coming for you."

She glanced about, looking for a place to hide. In a corner she saw a grille over an intake opening.

The boy said, "That's the climate control. The air in my room is filtered, sterilized, kept at a constant humidity and temp . . ."

The door burst violently open. Konrad rushed in. His flower-print shirt clung wetly, and his tan slacks were soaked dark brown. The sleeve of his shirt was torn and his arm showed the marks of sharp puncturing nettles. On a short leash he held the strange houndlike creature. The dog's head snarled at her, and ribs heaved within the lean feline body.

Konrad said, "I can turn her loose. Or you can come quietly."

Mary felt drained and empty of any will to resist. All she felt was fear as she looked at the cruel jaws open to show long, pointed fangs, the sleek spotted body quivering.

"I won't make trouble," she said. "Just don't turn that thing loose."

Chapter

21

Delaney removed all identifying marks from the engine and chassis of the red Porsche. He opened the lid of the trunk. From the garage floor he took a five gallon can of gasoline and placed it carefully on the floor of the trunk. He lifted another five gallon can and put that beside the first. Enough for a long trip.

He drove the Porsche carefully to the place he had chosen, a large tract of land above Stony Point on the Hudson. The late Hector Karyll had deeded the tract in his will to become the site for a public park. Matching funds from the state were still not forthcoming, and the land remained undeveloped and unused.

On the way, Delaney encountered little traffic. He turned off 9W onto a road that led only to the unrealized park. In Hector Karyll's lifetime this road had not been open to the public and was not shown on maps of the region.

Nevertheless, Delaney kept well within speed limits in the unlikely event that a state highway patrol was near. He was a cautious man.

He turned on the radio, twisting the dial until he found a station playing disco music. He glanced in the rearview mirror. A quarter mile behind him was a dark green Mercury Monarch sedan.

The odometer in the little Porsche clicked off the miles. 40,987. 40,988. Lots of life left in this buggy. He had a feeling for expensive foreign cars, having worked as a chauffeur for Mr. Karyll, who kept a fleet of BMW's, · Mercedes and Lancias. One evening, while driving Mr. Karyll through the streets of Rome to the Hassler Hotel, he saw a car turned crosswise in the street ahead of him. He reacted swiftly, opening up the powerful Lancia and racing ahead. The gunmen inside the other car barely had time to get off a couple of shots before he was on them. He aimed for a glancing collision near the gas tank. The impact knocked the other car over, and flames shot up in seconds, while the Lancia rolled on and got Mr. Karyll safely back to the hotel. The next day they discovered that the incinerated men in the ambush car had been members of the Red Brigade, intent on kidnapping the notorious rightwing American billionaire.

Not long after the incident, Mr. Karyll had promoted him to bodyguard. Mr. Karyll had a lot of enemies, personal and political, but Delaney had taken good care of him, which was one reason Mr. Karyll died of old age.

The road ended at a chain fence and a padlocked gate. Private Property. No Trespassing. Delaney braked to a stop, got out, opened the padlocked gate with a key and swung the gate open. After he drove through, he got out and locked the gate again.

The green Monarch came to a stop fifty feet short of the gate.

Delaney drove a short distance farther on an unpaved

road. Near the cliff edge there was a warning marker. A faint mist was rolling in. He drove past the warning marker for fifteen yards, then stopped. He shifted the gear into neutral but did not turn off the ignition. He got out, and paced off the distance. Three, possibly four yards ahead, with a space of about eight yards on the left and ten on the right.

He returned to the Porsche and tied down the accelerator. The pitch of the engine rose to a racing level while the car remained stationary, like a runner at the starting blocks with all its speed locked safely inside.

As he stood at the open door, for just an instant his hand rested on the car roof. Then he reached in and flipped the transmission into gear.

Released, the Porsche leapt forward, sped to the edge and went over. The sky lit with a flare as though the mist itself had ignited, and a split second later he heard the explosion. The ground shook under his feet. There was a final crunch as a surviving hunk of metal impacted on the rocks below.

No one would ever identify the red Porsche as a car that had been parked in the Karyll Clinic's hospital lot or connect it with the disappearance of its owner.

The mist reflected intense yellow light for another ten seconds. Delaney could still see a little glow as he reached the gate. A heavy blond man with a moustache was at the wheel of the green Mercury Monarch.

"Shove over," Delaney told him.

The man moved over obediently, and Delaney got behind the wheel.

Delaney didn't like to ride; he liked to drive.

When they arrived at the Karyll Clinic the blond

man, whose name was Sean, got off at the entrance. Delaney drove his car around to the indoor parking lot reserved for hospital employees.

A few minutes later, as he neared the security office on the first floor, Sean was outside waiting for him.

"We got the woman. Konrad picked her up in Phase Three."

"Where is she now?"

"I sent two men for her. She'll be here in a minute."

Delaney flexed his big hands. "I'll tell Dr. Bradford the good news."

When he placed the call, he was told that Dr. Bradford was working in his laboratory and could not be disturbed. All his calls were being routed through Dr. Latolier. She told him to bring the woman to the biological research laboratory where she was working. Apparently she could be disturbed.

As Mary entered, she saw a room covered with shelving from floor to ceiling. The shelves were divided vertically into foot-long segments. Within each segment there was a small dish, shielded by glass that contained protective wire netting.

Gaby Latolier was seated in a chair before a long table with filing boxes and several fat reference books.

Latolier did not address her, however. She said to Delaney just behind her, "I would like to know how she got as far as Phase Three."

"Dumb luck. Konrad let her in, thinking she was from Path Lab."

"It doesn't speak well for our security system." She turned her attention to Mary. "You're Mary Oliver. I remember speaking to you when your sister was in the hospital."

"Giving birth to a dead baby."

"Most unfortunate. Is that why you've been making trouble for us?"

"Was I making trouble?"

"I don't know what else you would call it. Bringing the police here on a ridiculous bomb scare. Stealing that uniform you're wearing. Trying to get into places you don't belong. You might have caused a great deal of mischief, a very great deal, if you'd blundered into a place like this, for example. Those petri dishes behind safety glass contain dangerous bacteria."

Mary glanced at the shelves. It was difficult to see how anything could escape.

The telephone rang, a startling intrusion.

Gaby said on the telephone, "Yes, Delaney is here with me. All right, I'll tell him." She replaced the receiver and said to Delaney, "Dr. Bradford wants you to bring Dr. Gerson to the Disposal Unit at once."

"What about her?"

"She'll go next."

One afternoon, when Mary was eleven years old, the telephone had rung at home and someone told her that Mr. Wendell Oliver had suffered a heart attack. When the person at the other end realized she was talking to a child she would give no further details. Not until Mother came home and they went to the hospital did they learn that Father was dead. That telephone call was the most shocking news Mary had ever received—until now.

She said, "I wouldn't do anything to Dr. Gerson if I were you. You can't get away with another killing."

Gaby Latolier looked at her with a smile. "My dear, what are you talking about?"

"Dr. Seligson. You murdered him, too."

After a moment Gaby Latolier said, "You'd better hurry, Delaney. You don't want to keep Dr. Bradford waiting."

"Shall I post a guard? I can't leave you alone with her."

"It won't be for long. Give me your gun."

Delaney opened his jacket. He wore a gunbelt and a holster. He removed a large silver-colored pistol and handed it to Gaby. Then he guided Mary over to a wooden chair in the room and sat her down. He unbuckled the belt and used that to wrap Mary's hands together behind her back.

"You ever fired a gun?" he asked Gaby.

"No."

He showed her how to release the safety catch. "If you pull the trigger, pull it easy. Don't jerk. Point your hand and arm straight."

"I don't think I'll need to use it."

"I'll be back soon," Delaney said, and hurried out.

Mary's relief at Delaney's leaving didn't last long. Gaby Latolier was holding the gun firmly, aiming it directly at her chest.

Gaby said, "I'll kill you if I have to," and thrust the gun barrel forward a little for emphasis.

Mary said quickly, "All right, I believe you." She looked around at the shelving on the walls. "Is the stuff in there really dangerous?"

"Keep still."

She said, "I have to keep talking when I'm nervous. It must be dangerous. You said you were afraid something might get out, right?" Her finger moved carefully up to where the hook entered a hole in the belt.

"I won't warn you again to be quiet."

"If I don't talk, I'll start to scream. You don't want an hysterical woman on your hands."

She slipped the hook out of the belt hole. Now there were only the twists in the belt to deal with. She sat quietly then, and kept working on the belt. There wasn't much time. Delaney would be back. As she began on the last loop of belt confining her wrists, Gaby Latolier looked at her suspiciously.

"What are you doing?"

She leaned forward to block Gaby's view. The last loop came undone. She gripped one end, moving her fingers up until she had a firmer grip. As Gaby came within range, she whipped the belt around with all the force she could muster. To her surprise, the maneuver worked perfectly. Part of the belt struck Gaby's hand and sent the gun spinning away. Then the heavy buckle struck her full in the face.

By then Mary was out of the chair and lunging foward. She drove hard into Gaby and propelled her back two, three running steps. Gaby crashed into the glass shelving, slowly slid down and sat dazed, with her legs splayed out before her.

Mary stooped to pick up the gun on the floor.

When she turned back, Gaby Latolier was still sitting stunned in the same position, staring in front of her. Liquid was dripping from a shelf where her head smashed in. She had got a nasty crack. Like a child wiping away tears, she wiped her face with the backs of both hands. A few drops of liquid spattered to the floor but more fell on her face. A wet trickle moved down her forehead and along both sides of her nose.

Suddenly she began to make shrill sounds. She wriggled convulsively away from the wall, looking up at a broken petri dish from which the dripping came.

Her eyes turned blank with horror.

Mary said, "It was an accident."

Then she ran out of the room.

She jammed the gun into the pocket of her tunic, holding her hand over it so the butt wouldn't show. Her idea was to reach an elevator and return to the level below the ground floor. In Path Lab someone had mentioned a room where they disposed of what remained after an autopsy. *The Disposal Unit.* Delaney was taking Rudy there.

Before she reached the elevator, she heard a short piping sound. Dr. Latolier's calm voice said, *"Decontamination Squad. Emergency procedures! Report to Room 304 in Phase Two. Stat!"*

Mary jammed the elevator button and kept pushing, the button didn't light up and there was no noise in the elevator shaft. She dashed down a long hallway and tried an exit door that led to the stairs. That too was locked.

A window nearby looked out on the square that connected the off-limits building with the central hospital. The window was a permanent installation. Even if she broke it open, there was no ledge outside. Nothing but a sheer two-story drop.

She heard voices coming. Frantically she looked for a place to conceal herself. A small archway opened into an area with cabinets and a long shelf holding jars with identifying labels. The labels indicated that these were different stages of cell divisions. The largest mass was marked: *Trophoblast ring: extra-embryonic membrane*.

At the far end of the area was a twelve-foot-high behemoth—a freezer. She opened it, and the interior went even deeper than she expected. She stepped inside. On the shelves surrounding her were hundreds of square boxes containing rows of ampules, standing vertically in their individual slots. As soon as she closed the freezer door the lights inside went out. The temperature was no more than thirty degrees.

She moved to a corner where she would be hidden by the door if it opened. Through the thick soundproof walls she could hear nothing, so she was startled when the door swung open and the interior light went on.

"She can't be here," a woman's voice said. "She'd freeze stiff."

"My orders are to search everywhere," a man's voice replied. His hand appeared around the edge of the door. Mary saw the dark gray cuff of a sleeve. A security guard.

"Say, what *is* all that stuff?" the guard asked.

"Sterile capsules ready for testing."

"Of what?"

"Well, if you must know, they're semen ampules. They're gradually cooled here until they can be immersed in liquid nitrogen at minus 321 degrees Fahrenheit. After that, the semen is stored in the tank indefinitely."

"No kidding?" The guard chuckled. "Aren't you afraid you'll get pregnant?"

"When you're through breaking yourself up, would you mind getting out and closing the door?"

They left. A few minutes passed. Mary was becoming uncomfortably chilly when she heard the freezer door unlatch again, and the light came on.

A woman in a white smock entered and began to search the shelves. She chose an ampule from a box, turned, and the ampule shattered on the floor. Her face became a white blur, her mouth a round red O.

Mary pointed the gun at her. "I hope you'll be sensible."

The woman nodded, blinking her eyes.

Mary said, "The exit doors and the elevators aren't working."

"That's emergency procedure. No one can leave Phase Two now until the Decontamination Squad has finished its job."

"Is there another way off this floor?"

The woman shook her head. "I don't know of any."

"Don't leave here for ten minutes. I'll be somewhere nearby and if you come out, I'll have no choice except to shoot you. You understand?"

"Y-yes."

Mary left, closing the freezer door. She was reasonably sure the woman was frightened enough to give her the time she asked for. But what good would it do? If there really was no way off this floor, she would soon be discovered.

She moved out cautiously, and almost immediately saw a guard riding an electric cart down a transverse corridor. She ducked back quickly, hoping he had not spotted her.

The rumbling of the cart continued for about two seconds, stopped, started again, stopped, began again. That sequence of sounds meant only one thing. The guard had turned around and was coming back.

She darted down the hallway. In a connecting passage she glimpsed a door discreetly marked *Ladies*. She raced inside and closed the door. The room was large. There were six booths, and three sinks before a large mirror.

She remembered the intake grille in the room where she had met the strange boy. She had helped to design enough air conditioning systems in large buildings to know that the intake outlets for air conditioning would be quite large, especially in an area where there was a need to carry off odors.

She found the grille at floor level on the far wall beyond the booths. The grille had tubular openings to control air direction, and was held in place by four large screws.

She took the gun out of her pocket, made sure the safety catch was on, and used the butt to knock a screw in the direction she wanted it to go. After striking the screw several sharp blows, she tried to loosen it. There was a little turning movement. She kept pounding until she was able to remove the screw, and pulled at the loose corner until another screw popped out. The top of the grille came away. Grabbing both sides of the top firmly, she wrenched the entire grille from the wall.

She was holding the grille in her hands when the door to the ladies room opened and closed. Footsteps moved in. A woman wearing crepe-soled shoes entered a booth.

Mary remained quite motionless. She heard the slight shift of weight on the toilet seat and then the ratchety spin of the paper roll. The toilet flushed. Crepe soles left the booth. A minute at the sink, then she went to the door and opened it.

The door stayed open.

"Anyone else in there?" a man's voice asked.

"No one."

"Thanks."

The door creaked shut.

She placed the grille carefully against the wall near the outlet. Belly flat on the floor, she pulled herself into the outlet.

Foot by painful foot, she crawled up the duct. She had no fear the shaft would buckle under her weight. The galvanized sheet metal was rigidly attached to the inner structure of the building. She reached an elbow in the shaft and was able to reverse direction and head downward. Light filtered through occasional interstices in the sides. The elbow connected a short distance ahead to the main shaft, inclined at a thirty-degree angle. She followed the main shaft down.

The interior of the shaft was lined with felt, a sound-absorbing material. As she wriggled forward through it, foreign matter crumbled under her fingers—scales, rust, and dirt. Her knees became chafed and sore.

She was lucky that the shaft was not conveying cooled air. There would be a number of central conditioners at strategic points in the building's interior space. During times when the load level was light a condensing unit could be shut off, enabling the plant to run with maximum economy.

She continued her descent until she had gone down one floor. Squinting ahead at the narrow metal corridor, she could see that it was still a long way to below ground level. Too far. At one point her nurse's uniform caught on a projection inside the shaft, and she had to pull it loose, leaving a ragged tear. She was matted with dirt. It was on her face, in her hair, under her nails. Her fingernails were broken and ragged and black.

From a distance she heard a voice that sounded as if it were making some kind of announcement. She stopped to listen. Something about an evacuation for decontamination procedures. Disturbing. She had seen enough and heard enough about the advanced experiments going on in the off-limits building to hope that the announcement really was a drill, not the real thing. There must have been something dangerous in that broken petri dish, or Gaby Latolier would not have reacted in that extreme way.

But she couldn't worry about that now. Her situation was too perilous. She had no illusions about what would happen if she were caught. They had made that plain enough.

The Disposal Unit.

A whiff of cold air reached her as the condensing unit in this area resumed operation. She tried to crawl faster, but it quickly became a very cold journey. She had no idea where she was in the building, but she knew she was headed in the right direction. Down.

Before she went much farther she was chilled through. She had never been so acutely miserable. Her fingers could no longer feel anything as she scrabbled down the shaft. Every second added to her overall sense of helplessness and futility.

She needed to stop and rest. She felt exhausted. But she forced herself to keep going a few feet farther . . . a few seconds more . . .

Help, please. It was a most peculiar sensation to make all the proper movements to utter a sound and to hear nothing. Her vocal cords must be frozen. She cleared her throat to try again.

"Help," she croaked. The froggy rasp startled her.

A dim crack of light through an interstice enabled her to see as far as the next bend in the shaft. She could go that far. Then she would allow herself to rest. She pressed on, listening to the steady panting of her breath.

Her breath?

Suddenly she was tense, sensing danger.

Was someone . . . some *thing*, following her?

Chapter

22

When Peter Bradford heard Gaby's voice on the loud-speaker asking for the Decontamination Squad, he realized the worst had happened. He and Delaney arrived at the biological research laboratory almost at the same moment. Delaney left soon to supervise the hunt for the missing woman. Bradford stayed on.

He gave Gaby a brief examination, and then a seda-tive. There was nothing more he could do. He waited until the Decontamination Squad had finished their work.

He nodded to the men as they left, and returned to where Gaby was sitting quietly on a chair in the room. Her eyes were closed and her auburn hair hung loose-ly. Even in repose the strength of her features was evident: the wide forehead, the slightly projecting bone ridge supporting the finely arched eyebrows.

"Peter?"

"It's me." He sat beside her.

"There's no danger of contagion, is there?"

"I don't think so. The bacteria are engineered so they can't survive long outside the laboratory."

"I'm glad." She opened her eyes. "She had no direct contact. Only I did."

Gaby's concern was for the safety of the others engaged in the work with dangerous microorganisms, using manmade genes to change the bacteria into living factories that could produce virtually any human hormone. Once they had gene material, they cloned it by using the bacteria to produce the hormone. ·

Across the left side of her face the red welt left by the belt buckle was slowly turning into a livid bruise.

"How did it happen?" he asked, aware that she was watching him and hoping to forestall any questions from her.

Listening to her explanation of the accident, he felt locked in with claustrophobic resentment.

She had called the Decontamination Squad even before calling Security. That was quick thinking. With the elevators and doors locked, the woman could not escape.

He had never felt a personal animus toward the other meddling fools, but he would enjoy being present at this woman's death. He would welcome that opportunity. What had happened was so ridiculous, such a waste. The tragedies in life that are hardest to bear are those that should have been avoided. His emotions were in tumult as he reevaluated the meaning of their years together. He had known she was in love with him, but he had not realized how much he cared for her. The unwavering passion and force of his commitment to his work made all his other feelings appear fluctuating, uncertain, vaporous. Now he was aware of how much he had missed. He experienced the sharp poignance of days that would never come back—like unwritten letters time had sealed in unbreakable bonds.

"Isn't it dark in here?" she asked.

The room was bright enough. The significance of that struck him like the recoil of a rifle.

"I'll turn on the lamp."

With the lamp on she smiled. "Yes, that's better," and closed her eyes again. The sedative he had given her was working.

He sat in a chair near her and took her hand. Over the years she had been his emotional shelter. She and his mother. Both provided him with a refuge from the abrasive ignorance of the world. Gaby was not like many attractive women, all artifice and smiles. She was the mature female of the species, vivid and strong and sure. She shared his impatience with those who cling to ideas from the past, borrowing an intelligence they haven't earned. "The Old Guard never dies," she told him, "*and* never surrenders." She lived only in the present, planned only for the future.

Now her future was over. This was no way station on her journey through life, but the last stop. Dead end.

"Do you know what it was?" she asked.

This was the question he had feared. He girded himself; to deal wounds one must don armor.

"Yes."

Her eyes opened wide. They were almost diaphanous, with a faint tracery of veins. Somewhere in her eyes microorganisms were burrowing into living plasma. Ironic, how all living things influence, shape and destroy one another, yet each is created out of the same essence.

"What was it?"

"Naegleria fowleri."

At that moment the very faint scent of her perfume came to him, soft and fragrant, reminding him again that this valiant cowarrior was also an attractive woman.

"Nasty," she said.

The incidence of victims was extremely rare considering the millions of people who went swimming unscathed every year. Not until recently had scientists isolated the tiny vicious strain of free-living amoebas that attacked human beings in fresh water and killed them by devouring their brain cells. There had been 200 cases identified, and only four survivors.

He said, "The petri dish that was broken contained a culture in which Naegleria fowleri was mingled with the Acanthamoeba species. We don't know what the culture may have produced."

"Not much of an alternative, is it?" There was not the slightest tremor in her voice.

The Acanthamoeba species had a particular affinity for the eyes. If its strain predominated in the culture, there was a good chance her brain would not be affected.

But she would be hopelessly blind.

He stayed with her, holding her hand, while she slowly drifted into sleep. Her separate fragile finger bones reminded him of how he had watched her hands in surgery. What marvelous instruments. The thought that he would never see her hands at work again was unbearable.

He did not leave her until he heard a knock at the door.

Delaney was outside. "We haven't found her. She may have got away before the exits were sealed."

"Impossible. Dr. Latolier gave the alarm at once."

"I can put more men into the search."

He thought of Gaby in a world that to her would grow steadily darker.

"Get Konrad."

"Konrad?"

"That animal can track her down. Evacuate everyone first. Tell them it's a precaution for a full decontamination of the area."

"Right."

The beast made a curious snuffling noise.

It was moving with its muzzle near the ground. A leash attached to a brown leather collar was about its neck. Konrad held the other end of the leash. Dr. Bradford and Delaney followed at a prudent distance.

The third floor of the off-limits building was deserted, eerily quiet. The evacuation facilitated the trackdown, and also kept anyone from seeing the hybrid. There was no point in arousing curiosity.

In Bradford's opinion, the beast was a splendid example of the power of recombinant DNA techniques that made possible a transfer of genes from one species to another. Matched talents of canine and feline, tracker and killer, conferred upon it a high capacity for survival. When enough of the hybrid creatures had been bred, he intended to release them in various wilderness areas. That would test their ability to cope against other species in a natural environment. Survival of the fittest.

Meanwhile, there was a job for it to do. They had given it the scent from the belt that had bound the woman's wrists. It had picked up her trail and was now leading them down a corridor, its head buried in shadow and its muzzle scraping the floor.

The pursuit stopped in front of a door. The massive dog head, with its large floppy ears, came up.

"She came in here," Konrad said.

As soon as they entered, Bradford saw that the room was empty. The beast pulled ahead, whimpering eagerly. They passed the last row of booths.

Konrad gave a surprised exclamation. He was looking at a loose covering over an air conditioning outlet.

Delaney stooped, measured the grille opening. "She might have gone in there."

"Where does it go?" Bradford asked.

"Air conditioning ducts run all through the building. If she got into a main shaft, she could go anywhere."

The beast, still whimpering, managed to get its head into the grille opening. Its long, sleek, catlike body was outside, haunches roiling with powerful muscles beneath the spotted skin. Konrad was trying his best to hold it back.

"Can it follow her?" Bradford asked.

Konrad, barely managing to keep the beast out of the opening, said, "It damn well thinks so."

Bradford asked, "Just locate her and keep track of her?"

Konrad shook his head. "If it tracks something, it will kill."

Delaney said gruffly, "That will be a bloody mess."

Bradford stared at the grille opening while he tried to decide what to do. The ducts ran everywhere in the building. There must be a hundred similar outlets. She could come out anywhere, see anything, talk to anyone. A woman in desperate straits might even find someone willing to help. That was far too dangerous.

"Let it go," he said.

Konrad detached the leash from the collar around the beast's powerful neck. The catlike shoulders sloped downward, and the torso thrust forward. A claw caught at the edge of the opening and helped to propel the rest of its body through. The tail gave a final vicious swipe.

The beast was gone.

Mary was cold, so cold. And mortally tired of this long, effortful, tedious journey through twists and bends, curvings, wide and narrow places. She wanted to shriek in protest and beat her fists against galvanized metal sides.

Ahead, the main shaft connected to a more steeply descending duct. Was there no end? Would she make a wrong turn and end up in some kind of cul-de-sac?

All she wanted was to lie still and close her eyes and drift away to a place where she would feel no more cold or pain. But she crawled on, a part of her still listening for a sound that she told herself had to be inside her head, born of fear and fatigue.

She heard it again, distant and faint. Definitely not inside her head. A heavy panting breathing, at the shadowy borders of hearing. She rolled onto her back in the constricted space and stared back into the darkness. She saw nothing.

When she reached the connecting duct she paused, listening intently. The sound had increased slightly. Now it was steady and measured rather than intermittent. She heard a slight rustling, as of movement within the shaft.

Creeping terror invaded her brain. Dear God. Something *must* be behind her.

She decided to turn off into the connecting duct. Crawling along a narrower passageway, she began to hear the noise of thrumming. That meant she was nearing the plenum chamber, from which air passed through the ducts directly to the areas to be conditioned. What she heard was the giant fan motor and the pulsing surge of the compressors. Soon the noise was too loud for her to hear anything else.

She halted, prompted to uneasiness by a signal from another sense.

A cool current of air carried a steaming stench, a pungent smell.

The fear she felt at that moment was not quite rational. She scrambled on in a frenzy. The metal duct no longer had any felt cushioning because near the plenum chamber there was no need for soundproofing. Each time her fingers touched cold metal she felt tiny electric shocks.

As she reached the end of the duct the thunder of the giant motors was deafening. Beyond the grille opening she glimpsed the plenum chamber. She pushed hard at the inside of the grille. It held firm. She cursed and pushed at it, and at last an edge of the grille swung loose. She tore the rest free of its fastenings, and wriggled out into the plenum chamber.

She stood up and looked back.

Within the dark opening behind her two lambent spots suddenly appeared.

Eyes!

She uttered no sound. Even if she screamed, she would not be heard in this chamber of bedlam.

Her hand touched the pistol in the pocket of her nurse's uniform, and with numb fingers she flicked the safety catch.

She backed away toward the giant motors and great coiling pipes. The pounding motors caused a vibration in the floor beneath her feet.

From the dark opening a shape emerged. Dark brown and yellow. Powerful leg muscles and huge, soft pads. Large head with drooping ears. Jaws open to reveal long killing teeth.

She had a confused impression of the glaring eyes coming swiftly at her. A glimmering shape swelled precipitously.

Somehow (not knowing how) she drew the gun and pulled the trigger. A jarring soundless concussion was lost in the roar of the plenum chamber.

The beast was arrested in mid-spring and hurled back, rolling and spitting and clawing at where the bullet had struck in the soft flesh of its jaw and neck.

Cautiously she edged toward the side, intending to retreat behind a large cold-generator for protection. But the catlike body rolled over and with incredible swiftness came for her again.

She aimed, gripping the pistol firmly with both hands, and fired at a spot between the glaring eyes.

She missed.

The bullet struck the beast's shoulder, smashing bone and flinging it sidewise. Its mighty rear legs pistoned, trying to gain purchase. Over the clangorous din in the chamber, she heard its hideous howling fury.

Behind the blower motor a ladder climbed to a trapdoor exit. She moved back toward it. She was in the cramped aisle between the motor casing and the wall when the beast came again. She fired wildly, and a bullet spanged off metal piping with a sound like a faint clash of cymbals. The beast's head entered the aisle, dripping bloody saliva from snarling open jaws.

She fired into a gaping redness.

The bullet penetrated the beast's open jaw and struck the back of its throat. A torrent of dark blood gushed. With a deep, soughing cough the beast rolled onto its back, trying feebly to slap at its wound. Its long, powerful body writhed in death agony.

Mary ran toward the ladder that led up to the trapdoor. She grabbed a rung of the ladder and lifted one foot. Then a strong quivering revulsion came over her. She choked back a sob, leaned her forehead against a metal rung, and her stomach retched.

In a few moments, more in control, she lifted her head.

Her heart almost stopped.

A grotesque terrible shape was crawling toward her, its muzzle all crimson. Its eyes glared with mad malevolence. The sleek cat body had wrinkled in deeper folds of skin. Still it lurched on, dragging its dying body.

She could not move. She was immobilized with horror.

How *could* it still be alive?

She moved back from the ladder into a corner, into the deceiving shelter of converging walls. The beast reached the ladder and went around it in a wavering zigzagging movement, leaving a gruesome trail of crimson.

She lifted the pistol, but could not control or aim it. Her hands jerked uncontrollably.

The beast was so close that she heard its snoring

exhalation of breath. Its long, killing teeth began making a scissorslike movement.

In a moment she would feel the crunching power of those jaws, the savage raking power of those claws. But she could not move even to save her life. The pistol fell from her hands. She had spent her last strength.

The beast raised itself to stand on widely planted legs. She closed her eyes and heard a guttural choking snarl. After a moment she opened her eyes again. The beast was standing still. Its head lowered slowly, then the torso began to settle until it was belly flat. The bloodied head went completely level with the floor. And the glowing stare became fixed on empty space.

The beast died.

Chapter

23

The filament tape that bound Rudy's forearms together was too tough for him to pull apart. After a while he accepted the futility of trying.

He should not have provoked Bradford to anger. That had been foolish, considering his situation. What the devil had possessed him? Moral outrage? An expensive attitude.

He should have played up to Bradford's megalomania. Let him play God. What difference did it make if Bradford intended to repopulate the world's lands and oceans with a diversity of creatures of his own creation? That was far in the future, and Rudy's predicament was in the present. He should have strictly and exclusively worried about that.

He could have treated Bradford as a great scientist who was merely bringing the results of his lifelong study to an extremely difficult and risky experiment, a superior intelligence with an absolute right to be untrammeled by his inferiors. He could have pretended that he wanted to learn, to become involved, and implied that if he could only understand the marvelous implications of Bradford's work he would never oppose it. He might even have reminded Bradford that Charles Gerson was almost as much his father as Rudy's, that they were, in a sense, nearly brothers. All this was painfully clear to him now that it was too late. Too late even for regrets.

Think, damn it! There has to be another way out.

The police.

He had told the police about the driver of the Mercury Monarch who had tried to kill him. Perhaps they would discover who owned the car, and if it was someone at the Karyll Clinic . . .

Just another entry on a police blotter. A report to file and forget. The police chief, Monroe Thorpe, practically told him so.

Wouldn't Mary have become concerned about him by now? Of course. Concerned enough to go to the police? Probably. If they believed her, they would come with her to look for him. . . .

How would they find him? Or even know he was here?

His car.

The Porsche he had left parked at the emergency entrance to the hospital. That would prove he was here. If they found it in time.

That little red Porsche was his last remaining hope.

A door opened and a light went on in the windowless room. Rudy blinked, as if suddenly pinned by a beam that had picked him out of darkness. The figures that entered were foggy, their outlines indistinct. Then he saw Dr. Bradford with Delaney.

"Leave his hands tied," Dr. Bradford said.

Delaney bent down, got a grip on the filament tape binding Rudy's ankles and with a strong yank peeled it back. The only pain was at the end when the tape took hairs with it.

Delaney yanked him to his feet. His knees were so weak they nearly gave way.

"Where are we going?"

There was malice in the reply: "To see a friend."

Suddenly Rudy was afraid. He looked at Bradford, and Bradford turned away very much as a member of a jury returning with a guilty verdict might look away from the man condemned. So that was it.

An emergency exit door opened onto a staircase. Going down the stairs, he stumbled once, but Delaney kept him upright with a grip like a nutcracker's. At last they emerged into a corridor, narrow with black linoleum flooring. Then they entered an L-shaped room.

The moment he turned the corner of the L and saw the plain brick wall and the oven door set into it, he knew what was about to happen.

His breath caught in a ragged gasp.

A cot covered with a sheet was already waiting. A body was outlined beneath the sheet.

Dr. Bradford said, "We call this our Disposal Unit. It's where we dispose of failed experiments—after an autopsy. We always try to learn everything we can first." His voice was perfectly clear and calm.

Rudy never understood why anyone would walk quietly to an execution when there was nothing to lose by fighting for life. Why go like a lamb to the slaughter?

But there was something he had to know.

He nodded toward the sheeted figure on the cot. "Who is that?"

Delaney answered, "I told you were were taking you to see a friend."

He pulled back the sheet, and a pulse began to beat painfully in Rudy's head. He heard Ken's voice saying softly, *I may be in trouble, real trouble.*

Ken Hartley was not in trouble now.

Delaney laughed softly. "We didn't need an autopsy. He died of a broken neck."

Mary stood beside the ladder in the plenum chamber, shuddering, mewing in shock. Blood trickled from beneath the dead beast to gather around the toe of her shoe. The gruesome reality of what had happened in the past few minutes rushed over her and left her rooted, unable to move, in a nervine paralysis.

When she recovered she stooped to retrieve the pistol before resolutely putting her foot on the ladder and climbing to the trapdoor exit. Only one thought was fixed in her mind, a flag planted on a bloody battleground: Get away from this hellish place of noise and death, and find Rudy.

The heavy trapdoor was insulated with felt covering at the bottom. It lifted easily to her touch, activated by a powerful spring. Above was a tiny dark areaway. She climbed up inside and stood with one hand on the raised trapdoor. The area was the shaft enclosing the trapdoor, and its walls were heavily insulated against noise from the plenum chamber below.

The continuing roar of the plenum chamber seemed to exude malignance. She pushed the trapdoor, which closed slowly until level with the floor. The roaring ceased.

A door was outlined in vague light. Go on, she urged

herself; open it. You don't know what's ahead, but you know what's behind. Clutching the pistol in one hand, as though it were a flashlight that could probe ahead for danger, she left the tiny areaway and emerged into a wide corridor with a floor of polished black tile.

She was dirty and bloodstained and haggard. Looking like this, she could hardly afford to encounter anyone. She moved cautiously along the empty corridor. As she passed an open doorway, she could see into a room with a desk, a blackboard, and a half dozen chairs in a semicircle. Farther along the corridor a partly open door revealed a small worktable on which was a dinner plate and a green-colored beer bottle.

She heard footsteps and ducked through the partly open door. She waited a moment, then risked a glance.

At the far end of the corridor, three men were crossing toward an open archway. One was an older man, rather tall, somewhat bulky, wearing a doctor's smock. The other was Delaney, head of hospital security, wearing a dark gray uniform. The third man's hands appeared to be taped behind his back.

A pulse beat painfully in her head.

The third man was Rudy!

Bradford opened a panel on the wall near the oven and pushed a switch down with his thumb. A round staring light appeared over the oven door.

"The Unit will be ready in a minute."

The white light turned pink and began darkening. If I am going to run, this might be the time, Rudy thought, but his legs weren't reliable and he wouldn't get far. Delaney would catch him in a stride or two. He couldn't put up much of a fight against Delaney with his forearms taped together behind his back. Why kid himself? He couldn't put up much of a fight if he had two free hands. Or four. His only chance—as chances go it was remote—was to catch Delaney unawares.

The light turned crimson.

Delaney pulled the sheet over Hartley's face, glancing at Rudy with disappointment. Rudy thought: The sadistic bastard wanted me to run.

Delaney pushed the cot slowly toward the oven door. Bradford opened the door, revealing a fiery glow through the aperture. The cot lifted at Delaney's end, and the body under the sheet slid through. The door clanged shut.

The unmistakable overpowering smell reached them, the nauseating semisweetness of roasting flesh. A human body was being reduced to four quarts of unidentifiable ashes.

Bradford removed a hypodermic and a small bottle from his white smock. He pushed the plunger through the top of the bottle and the tube began to fill.

Now! Rudy thought. He would have to make his move just before Bradford reached him with the hypodermic.

He drew in a breath sharply. His muscles tensed.

Before he could move, his shoulders were pinned back with jolting power. He felt as if the bones were cracking.

He had underestimated Delaney.

Bradford said, "I promise this will be very quick and painless." He moved forward, holding the needle poised, ready to discharge its deadly contents.

"Don't," a woman's voice said.

She was scarcely recognizable, a blood-spattered

ghastly caricature in a soiled, torn nurse's uniform, holding a silver-colored pistol.

"Mary!" Rudy said.

"Step back or I'll shoot," Mary said to Bradford, who remained motionless, holding the hypodermic ready to plunge into Rudy's arm.

She said to Delaney, "Let him go."

The sheer unlikeliness, the stunning coincidence, had loosened Delaney's grip a little. Rudy crouched and made a galvanic effort. He pulled Delaney forward, but the big man's strength was too much. The cruel hold tightened again.

Then the big man gave an odd little grunt, and suddenly, inexplicably, Rudy *was* free.

He whirled, butting hard into Delaney's face. Warm sticky fluid splashed on the back of his neck. He expected battering fists to club him, but nothing happened, so he tried to butt him again. This time he hit empty air.

Then he almost stumbled over Delaney. The big man was down on his hands and knees, making twitching jerking movements. His breath grated, deepened, and he slid forward until his face touched the floor, his knees raised in a ridiculous parody of a Muslim praying. His breathing became stertorous.

A hypodermic needle dangled from his arm.

Bradford was pale, staring down at Delaney, who was not breathing at all now. Mary moved up beside Rudy. Bradford slowly raised shaking hands to his face.

Mary said, "Rudy, take this," and handed him the pistol.

Rudy aimed it carefully. "Dr. Bradford?"

Bradford did not take his hands from his face. He seemed to wait in a dazed silence.

"We'll call the police now," Rudy said.

Chapter

24

Early one evening Rudy returned to his Riverside Drive apartment to find Mary watching television. He sat down to watch with her.

On the small screen the Pollards were telling again the suddenly credible story of how their baby had died. Every news program featured special interviews with parents of Sendai infants or with anyone associated with the Karyll Clinic. Photographs of the exterior of the Genetics Research building were becoming as familiar to television watchers as photographs of nuclear plants at Three Mile Island some years earlier.

Rudy had heard rumors that some of the staff at the hospital were going to leave because of the notoriety. He hoped not. Most people outside a hospital are not aware of what every resident and intern knows: A hospital is a complex entity wholly dependent on the knowledge and competence of the individuals who work there. Quality medical care is hard to come by, and in its field, the Karyll Clinic was the best.

Mary said, "I wish it were all over and Bradford was safely in prison. Or in a mental hospital."

"Do you think he's insane?"

"He must be. Did you read the newspaper this morning? That statement Bradford's attorney released to the press."

"I read it. In fact, I memorized it."

Bradford had said, *I have spent my life in a purposeful effort to make a large scale improvement in the human species. If one is dedicated to improving man, no form of experiment is wrong.*

Mary sniffed. "Pretty high and mighty, considering."

"I think he's perfectly sincere."

"Some of the most dangerous fanatics in the world were sincere."

True, Rudy thought. Fanatics are better at getting things done because they have a singleness of purpose and an indifference to social restraints. Pure ego raised to the nth degree has sustained tyrants, religious prophets, and so-called military geniuses. They set out to remake the world, and become deranged with their dreams of glory.

Peter Bradford would not be punished for his dreams, but for his crimes.

A framed photograph on a nearby table showed a distinguished graying man wearing rimless spectacles. Rudy had taken the photograph from a closet shelf and moved it there that morning.

"Your father?" she asked.

"Charles Gerson himself."

She studied the man whose character and genius had so influenced Rudy's life. "He's a little too determined-looking around the edges."

"He never could see individual people clearly enough to be concerned with their little problems. On the other hand, maybe we don't see the future of mankind as clearly. It's the forest and the trees. I think he'd have sympathized with Peter Bradford."

"That's a terrible thing to say."

Rudy shrugged. "They were both working at the frontiers of science—a lonely outpost. Perhaps the men out there shouldn't be judged by ordinary standards."

"I don't understand how you can make excuses for a man like Bradford!"

He answered softly, "It is necessary to sail the seas, but not to live."

"What's that?"

"An old Norsemen's saying. The Norsemen might have understood Bradford too. Like him, they set sail into unknown waters where dragons dwell."

She replied with exasperation, "I've never seen anyone like you for arguing two sides of a question."

He smiled. As an undergraduate in college, intoxicated by his first introduction to the Ubermensch, he had scrawled on a wall: *God Is Dead—Nietzsche*. Underneath his proclamation, someone else had scrawled: *Nietzsche Is Dead—God*. Looking at that wall, he had agreed that there are two sides to any question. Sometimes more.

They watched the rest of the television news together. An enterprising reporter got through the police escort as Peter Bradford was being taken to the courthouse for arraignment. The reporter asked the question that was on the minds of millions: "Why?" Bradford's reply was muffled, but Rudy did not need to hear it. He knew what Bradford would say.

Later on in the newscast they were told Gaby Latolier was being kept incommunicado in a hospital, undergoing treatment for rapidly failing vision. Dr. Roy Harrison and the others involved in "the greatest medical scandal of the twentieth century" had pleaded guilty. They had been promised lenience in return for their testimony at the trial of Bradford and Latolier.

There was a footnote to the news. The "Dungeon Boy"—an appellation that had replaced earlier attempts to label him as "Insect Boy," "The Hybrid," "Monster Boy," and even "Future Freak"—had signed a multimillion dollar deal for his memoirs, with hardcover book rights, paperback, and a film to follow.

Rudy turned off the television.

Mary said, "I talked to Emily today. She's decided to keep her baby. She doesn't think it will be harder than raising an ordinary child. The baby is really quite good-looking—and so sweet-tempered."

Rudy nodded approvingly. "There are a great many human beings in the world with strong backs, weak minds, and much uglier dispositions."

"What will the next generation of Sendais be like—when they marry and have children of their own?"

"I don't know. What interests me more is the attempt to breed humans of superior intellect. That Dungeon Boy, for example. For all we know, Bradford's experiments might eventually have created a man and woman genetically programmed to exceed us as much as we exceed our Cro-Magnon ancestors. The right mutation in the DNA of a cell could enable mankind to leap ahead a whole era in evolution."

"I don't want to think about that."

But he did. Somewhere in him a wheel had made a quarter turn, and a process had begun whose ending was not predictable. He was aware of it, and afraid, and at the same time tremendously excited. Knowledge seekers are by nature unprincipled meddlers. And he was, after all, Charles Gerson's son.

Later that night, he was particularly tender in lovemaking. Afterward, Mary hid her face against his shoulder and murmured sleepily, "I'm glad it won't happen soon."

"What, darling?"

"That new era. I want a family of nice normal children. And the present method of making them is quite satisfactory, thank you."

He put his arm around her. "It's much more than satisfactory," he said. "For now."

Afterword

What you have just read is *not* fiction.

It is fiction immersed in fact.

Perhaps the best way to introduce you to the reality of the scientific events described in this novel is to check out a few of the fictional "shockers" against the facts.

Do you think that humans mated with mammals of a much lower species is mere speculation?

Fact: Human sperm has already been used to fertilize hamster cells. (In an unrelated experiment, human sperm has also fertilized human egg cells obtained in autopsies.)

Do you doubt that animals are regenerating parts, like a salamander?

Fact: In England (*The New York Times,* November 28, 1978) human infants have regrown severed fingertips, including a knuckle joint. *Human* infants, not animals. In a more recent instance, a child not only regrew a severed fingertip but even the same complex pattern of fingerprints.

Do you think that the description of a creature born of as many as six different parents is a fantasy?

Fact: At Yale University, a normal mouse has already been born that was conceived of three different mothers and three different fathers.

Are the descriptions of hybrid animals a novelist's invention?

Fact: Stanford University's Dr. Paul Berg, a leading biochemist, has already transplanted a functional gene from one mammal (a rabbit) to laboratory-grown cells from an African green monkey. A mouse with the head of a chicken has been produced in a laboratory. And other mice have been born to a normal mouse mother, with no father except the nucleus of a cancer cell. This happened at the laboratory of Dr. Beatrice Mintz at the Institute for Cancer Research, Fox Chase Cancer Center, Philadelphia. The mice are perfectly normal and have no trace of cancer.

Are the Dungeon Boy and the Sendai infants described in the novel mere fabulations, with no basis in science?

Fact: *Time* magazine (July 31, 1978) reports that scientists' control of basic life processes has reached the point where we can have "baby hatcheries" that will produce everything from superbrainy "Alphas" to dronelike "Epsilons."

Genetic engineering has the potential to alter mankind as no other science ever has or likely ever will.

Shall we let our scientists do it? Do we have a right to stop them?

Clearly, this question is beyond the scope of a novel conceived as an entertainment, but I hope the implica-

tions of the question raised here will concern you long
after the book is forgotten.

William Woolfolk
New Canaan, Connecticut